300 TRILLION

MILES FROM HOME

00 Trillion Miles From Home
by Jared McVay
Published by Creative Texts Publishers
PO Box 50
Barto, PA 1950a
www.creativetexts.com

ISBN: 978-1-64738-049-6

300 TRILLION

MILES FROM HOME

Jared McVay

My many thanks to my publisher, Dan Edwards and his belief in me.

And to Jerri Burr, my friend, my lady, and the one who keeps me on the straight and narrow with punctuation and spelling. Thank you... You're the best.

TABLE OF CONTENTS

You cannot be a hero without first being a coward.

-George Bernard Shaw

A hero is a man who lets no obstacle prevent him from pursuing the values he has chosen.

-Andrew Bernstein

A hero is no braver than an ordinary man – he is just braver five minutes longer.

-Ralph Waldo Emmerson

Chapter 1

THE ABDUCTION

On the morning of August 23, 2169, the world woke up to large, shiny, orbs filling the skies. Each one was the size of the Dallas Cowboy's football stadium. They didn't make any noise or fire any weapons; they just hung there in the sky, doing nothing, which put the entire world on nervous alert.

Immediately, every military in the world prepared for war. The leaders of each country tried to communicate with the orbs, but no one got a response. Second, they sent planes to do flybys to investigate, but when the planes got within a quarter of a mile of an orb, the controls of the plane were taken over and the plane was turned back in the direction it came from.

World leaders were in communication with each other, trying to decide what to do…

"What can we do?" the President of the United States said to the Prime Minister of Russia, who had called in a panic.

"We have to do something!" the Russian Prime Minister screamed.

"Whoever or whatever they are, they aren't responding to any of our communication signals, and they haven't done anything aggressive. They just hover out there. At this point, all we can do is hope they communicate with us to let us know why they're here."

The Russian Prime Minister sighed and said, "We have our rockets ready in case they attack and at the first sign of anything happening, we will blast them out of the sky!"

The U.S. President, likewise, sighed and loosened his tie that was suddenly choking him. "As you know, they seem to have a protection shield around them that extends out around a quarter of a mile. How do you plan to penetrate that? Plus, whoever they are, they have the power to take control of our planes. How do we combat that?"

"We have to do something," the Prime Minister said. "If they attack, we have to fight back, don't we?"

President Sterling Collier was in his second term as President of the United States. He was fifty-four years old, and the son of a prominent attorney whose Kansas City law firm was held in high esteem. Sterling was actually born in the small town of El Dorado, Kansas, where at the time his father was the District Attorney. His father was lured away by a large law firm in Kansas City, where, in a few short years, he left and started his own law firm.

Like his father, Sterling had become a lawyer after attending Yale where he was captain of the hockey team. He also ran the decathlon in track and could have gone on to the Olympics but decided his law career was more important since he had become engaged to his high school sweetheart, Ellen McCarthy.

At the age of thirty-six, Sterling entered politics and became the Governor of Kansas, becoming known as a man who thought for himself - unlike many leaders who relied solely on their cabinets and close advisors. He was also known for his loyalty to the American people. As far as he was concerned, he worked for the people, not the government or the politicians. His platform for both the governorship and the U.S. presidency had been run as an independent and he had been successful both times, winning by a wide margin.

He stayed in tip top condition and ran several miles each morning. He even had a gymnasium in the basement of the White House, where, at his insistence, his personal bodyguards worked out with him. Sterling went so far as to practice hand to hand combat with them and was able to hold his own.

Sterling Collier stood five foot ten, with a roguish, handsome face, a fit body, and a strong mind. He was considered by many to be the most eligible bachelor in the country.

His wife, Ellen, died two weeks after Sterling's second inauguration. She had just stepped onto the podium at a Women's League of Nations meeting and before uttering a word, she dropped to the floor. The official diagnosis was a massive heart attack. She was fifty-three. That had been sixteen months ago, and the President still mourned her passing every day. She had been his rock, and confidant. He was seen on several occasions, standing next to her grave, talking to her, asking advice about this or that.

Although several of his acquaintances had tried, unsuccessfully, to pair him up with prominent female companions, he told them, "Sorry, but I'm not ready, yet."

Now, he was facing perhaps the most daunting challenge of his career.

"I agree, we need to be ready to fight back," the President told the Russian Prime Minister. "But I'm not convinced we have the firepower to defeat them. Not from what I've seen. And to be honest, I don't think they're hostile. They could have destroyed our planes, and possibly us, too, but they didn't. They just turned the planes around and sent them back. That doesn't seem like a hostile act, to me."

They hung up, agreeing to keep in contact. It was four o'clock in the afternoon when President Collier leaned back in his chair and let out a gush of air. He had been on the telephone constantly all day with calls from not only Russia, but India, China, Japan, England, France, Germany, Spain, Ireland and several others that he couldn't think of at the moment, along with senators, congressmen and U.S. Generals and Admirals.

Sterling walked over to a cabinet on the far wall of the Oval Office and opened the door to a liquor cabinet. He rarely drank hard liquor, but with everything that was going on, he felt the need for one. His drink of choice in situations like this was Brown Sugar Bourbon over ice. He always limited himself to just one, which seemed to do the trick.

He opened the French doors and walked out on the veranda. As he studied the shiny orbs just sitting there, filling up the sky, he sipped on the bourbon and considered his options. First, he had to try to keep the country from mass panic. Nothing like this had ever happened before and the people were afraid and had every right to be. They knew nothing of who or what controlled these giant orbs, or if there were beings inside - and had they come in peace or seeking to take over the planet?

Second, he, himself needed to keep a level head and not panic. Every leader of every nation he'd spoken with today was ready to rush into war. Being prepared to defend oneself was one thing, but to attack an unknown entity such as these was, in his opinion, just plain suicide. They needed more information. What if whoever was inside those orbs were merely observing them and were peaceful? What if they were trying to make contact? If handled right, this could turn out to be the greatest event in the history of the world. As far as he was concerned, the first move was in their court. If they were intelligent enough to travel through space with that many ships, they would be intelligent enough to make contact.

He took the elevator down to the basement and the communications center where he asked the assembled group of advisers, "Anything?"

The communications center was run by Colonel James Michaels and had been ever since Sterling Collier became President. During his twenty-two years in the Army, James had worn many hats. He was, first and foremost in his mind, an Army Ranger who specialized in code breaking. He was from Montana and had joined the army right out of college. He was bright and had quickly moved up in rank during a highly publicized conflict in Afghanistan. The President knew of him because he had presented him with an award for saving eighteen men and in the process, taking nine bullets to his body.

Colonel Michaels saluted the President, who returned the salute. "Sir, you're just in time. I sent another verbal message out three minutes ago and this just came back.

Colonel Michaels punched a button on a huge control board and the President and everyone in the room, heard, in good English, "We are not here to harm you."

When the President looked at Colonel Michaels, he shrugged his shoulders and said, "That's it. Nothing more."

The President thought for a moment, then looked at the head of his communications department and asked, "Any thoughts or opinions as to why they are here and what they want?"

Colonel Michaels was a man who didn't jump to conclusions. As much as he wanted to tell the President something positive, he was as stumped as everyone else. "I'm sorry, Sir, but I doubt if my thoughts are any better than yours. There could be a hundred reasons, but until they tell us something, or do something, I'm in the dark just as much as everyone else."

The President nodded his head up and down, then looked at Colonel Michaels and said, "Keep me posted."

Colonel Michaels stood up straight and saluted, saying, "You will be the first to know, Sir."

To work off some of his frustration, the President went to his private gym and worked out for an hour, turning down phone calls from the Vice President and the heads of state from a dozen countries, two senators, and three generals. He needed time to think.

After a vigorous workout and turning things over in his mind, the President took a long, hot shower, then switched to cold water, making him shiver - bringing his frustrations under control. After getting dressed and going back to the Oval Office, he called in the head of his security detail, Liam Biggers, a man he'd gone to high school with, who was his best friend.

Liam stood six feet four inches and weighed two hundred and twenty-five pounds. He played first string linebacker on both his El Dorado high school and Kansas State University football teams. Liam majored in construction engineering, then spent a few years with the Navy Sea Bees, and ten years as a Navy Seal.

Technically, he was still in the Navy. The President had requested him as head of his personal bodyguard team, and being the head of the military, the President's request received no opposition. The rest of his team was made up of secret servicemen.

Liam came to attention, but the President waved him down, saying, "Grab a seat, Liam, I need to talk to you. And you don't need to stand on protocol when it's just you and me. You want something to drink?" the President asked, walking over to a refrigerator, and retrieving a bottle of lemon water.

"Yeah. Lemon water for me, too, if you have enough?"

"I've kept the cooler well stocked ever since you introduced me to it," the President said with a grin.

"I'm guessing you want to talk about those orbs out there," Liam said after taking a sip of his water.

"I do. I'd like…"

President Collier stood with his mouth hanging open. The chair where his friend had been sitting was empty. He looked around the room, but Liam was nowhere in sight. In the blink of an eye, he'd simply disappeared.

The President sat down in his chair and swirled around to look out through the windows at the shiny orbs filling the sky.

"No. It couldn't be… Could it?" he said to himself.

"Ahem," came a voice behind him, causing the President to swing his chair back around.

There in front of him, stood the hologram of a man whose pale skin made him look sickly. He stood maybe five feet tall and was very thin. His eyes held an intensity that made Sterling feel helpless to move, which was no easy feat.

"Do not call for help. I am not here to hurt you. I came to explain our presence," the man said.

Released from the mental grip, the President shuttered and shook himself. When he felt able, he observed the man in front of him, and didn't see anything threatening. Except for his being so pale and thin, he looked just like any man off the street.

But now that he was able to take a better look at the man standing in front of him, he realized he was not a real person. It was a hologram – an image of the man he was speaking with. A very realistic image, but none the less, just an image. Taking a deep breath, he asked, "Did you take the man who was here in my office?"

The image smiled and said, in good English, "Yes, we have him."

"Okay," the President said. "I can see that I'm not talking to a real person, but I guess that will have to do. The important thing is, we're communicating." There was a moment of pause before the President continued. "So, I guess the logical question is, who are you? Why are you here? And why did you take my friend?"

"Yes, what you see is a hologram. I did not come down in person because I wasn't sure it would be safe. You see, we are a very passive people who have need of someone with aggression, and, after observing your planet, it seems you have an abundance of men and women who may suit our needs." There was a brief silence, then the image spoke, again. "Don't think just because we do not like to fight or that we can't destroy this planet if we are attacked, because we can. But we don't want to."

"I, I don't understand," the President said.

"Let's start over," the image said with a slight smile. My name is Emmelor. I am from another solar system… a planet called X-162. And, yes, it is a long way from your Earth. We have technology far exceeding yours and can travel at many times the speed of light. Yours is not the first planet with life on it that we've observed, but the only one who could be our sister planet."

President Collier felt a jolt. Other planets with life? He was brought back when the image continued. "Before I reveal anything more to you, as to why we are here, I must have your sworn oath not to repeat what I say - not to anyone."

Sterling looked at the image and said, "You have to understand, I am not the ruler of this planet. I am only the President of these United States of America. There are many countries out there and each one of them has its own leader – and they all want to know who you are and what you want. In all honesty, I don't think I can make that promise."

"Very well," the image said, as it began to fade.

"Wait a minute!" the President called out, but the image faded away, with a voice trailing. "We hear your contact pleas. When you are ready to comply with my demand, send word to me, but don't wait too long. We don't have much time before we continue on with our mission. Just say, Emmelor, I comply."

"Please! Wait! Don't go yet," the President said.

The image resumed its brightness. "Yes?"

"Will I ever be able to explain it to the rest of the world?" the President asked.

"Once we are gone, you can say anything you want," Emmelor told him.

"I'm getting hundreds of calls from leaders all over the world. Can I at least tell them we are in communication?"

Emmelor thought for a moment, then said, "All right. I will allow that, but nothing more. And if you do not keep your word, the consequences will be devastating, I assure you."

"Fair enough," the President said. "You have my word."

"Rest assured; we are not here to harm you. But like I said, any aggression on your part, or from any other leader on this planet, will be considered as an act of war and we will retaliate with a vengeance so strong, this planet will be left in a state of destruction," Emmelor stated in a voice that allowed no rebuttal.

The President, thought for a moment, then asked, "If you're not here to take over this planet, then why are you here?"

"We are in need of someone to represent us at the Council of Battles, and your man may be the one we select," Emmelor responded.

The President was flabbergasted. "But… there are thousands of men on this planet that could fill that bill. Why him?"

Emmelor nodded his head. "We have over a hundred men and beasts aboard our ship from here and other planets. This planet is our final destination. Each one will be put to a test and the final one standing will be given our greatest consideration."

"Consideration for what?" the President asked.

"As I said, we need someone to represent the Council of Battles," Emmelor said, lowering his head.

"If you're so powerful, why do you need a representative to do your fighting for you? Why can't you just annihilate your enemies?"

President Collier watched as the image put his hands together and raised them to just under his chin, as though he were deliberating on his response.

"Yes, we are very powerful, as are the other planets in our solar system. So powerful that we would destroy each other in an all-out war. So... when one planet wants to go to war with another planet, rather than total destruction, which would leave both planets void of life, we have adopted a plan where each planet sends a representative into an arena on a neutral planet. The two representatives fight – and the winner takes control of both planets. In case they kill each other, the war is declared a draw, and everyone goes back to living like nothing has happened, for at least a century... It's all very civilized."

President Collier was having a hard time wrapping his mind around all this. Several planets with life and all communicating with each other – even going to war with each other – in what they called, a civilized manner.

"Okay," the President said. "So... assuming you take one of our men to fight your battle for you, will the people of the planet you're at war with come and also take one of our men?"

Emmelor's image thought for a moment and then said, "It is possible, but highly unlikely since this is the first time any of us has traveled so far to find a representative. It is also the reason for not talking about our visit."

The President nodded his head and said, "Hopefully, if our man is taken, he will win. What then? Will you return him to us?"

Emmelor's image got a questionable look on his face and said, "That is a good question. In the nine-hundred and sixteen million years we've been in existence, this is the first time we've been challenged." He turned his head and said, "Just a moment."

The image was still there, but more like a statue. The President had no choice but to wait.

Five minutes later, Emmelor's image came back to life. "I'm sorry about that, but I had to do a bit of research. It seems in the past, on other planets, the winner, if not from that planet, was given the choice to stay or go back and in one hundred percent of the time, the representative chose to stay, because he was treated like royalty. The new world he'd fought for was his oyster, as they say."

"So, what happens now?"

Emmelor's image thought for a few seconds, then said, "We will be holding tournaments on the ship – which, I believe will take at least ten of your days. At the end of that time, we will make our decision. If your man does not win, and if he is still alive, he will be sent back, as will all the others we've taken. Once we have made our decision, you will wake up one morning and we will be gone."

"So, what you're saying is, we just wait. Is that it?"

"That would be correct. And with that, I bid you *adieu*."

"Wait, one more question, if you will?" the President cried.

"Yes?" Emmelor asked.

"What is so secret about this that I can't tell the rest of the world?" the President asked.

Emmelor smiled and said, "For all we know, our enemy from planet X-160 could have followed us or is in communication with someone on this planet and we cannot take a chance on them finding out what we're doing. If they find out about you, your planet could be in grave danger. So, until we leave, you can say, nothing." And just like that, he was gone.

Sterling Collier, President of the United States of America, swirled his chair around and stared at the giant orbs floating in the sky. There were people and beasts inside at least one of the orbs, and he had just spoken to one of them! He had actually spoken to a man from a distant planet, someone from a different solar system, and he couldn't tell anyone what they'd talked about. He could tell them not to worry but more than likely they wouldn't believe him.

He laughed. Even if he could tell them, why would they believe him? He was having a hard time believing it, himself.

Suddenly, he had a feeling of dread. What if Liam was chosen and taken to the distant planet to fight who knew who or what, and was killed? Would they tell him? And, if they did, what would he tell Liam's people? That he'd been killed on a foreign planet, fighting a single-handed war for people he didn't know?

Sterling Collier the man, not the President, stood up and went to the liquor cabinet and made another drink.

He was standing at the window, staring out at the sky when his desk phone rang and he turned around, reaching for it. When he answered it, his secretary said, "They want you to go to the United Nations Building tomorrow morning and speak to them."

The President didn't need to ask why. He knew. It would be about the spaceships hovering all over the planet, and what he was going to do about it. Being the most powerful country on the planet, he knew they looked to him for advice.

"Tell them I'll be there," he said, and hung up the phone. Yes, he would go and speak to them, *but what he would say?* was still running around inside his head.

He looked at the clock on the wall. 12:03. He headed for the White House kitchen wondering what he would tell the secret servicemen waiting just outside the door when they asked where Liam was.

Walking into the hallway, he saw them looking for Liam and said, "He's on a special mission." And without further explanation, he continued down to the kitchen where he could speak with his friend and chef, Archie, about all this craziness.

Chapter 2

THE FIRST CHALLENGE

Liam Edward Biggers opened his eyes to total darkness. He felt as though he was floating on air. When he reached his arms out, he felt what appeared to be glass. He was in a glass container of some kind, and he couldn't see anything. The only thing he could hear was the sound of air hissing.

He continued to drift in and out of a dreamless sleep, for how long, he had no idea, but when he finally woke up, he was sitting in a chair with his wrists and ankles strapped to the arms and legs.

A small, very thin man with pale skin was staring at him.

"Mister Biggers, I'm glad to see you are finally awake. Did you have a good sleep?"

Liam stared around the room. There was a bed, a dresser, two side tables with lamps sitting on them and over against one wall, a small desk and swivel chair. The last he remembered was being in the White House, the Oval Office to be exact – speaking with the President.

"What have you done with the President?" Liam asked. "And how do you know my name?"

"I see you woke up confused, which is understandable. Maybe some breakfast will put you in a better mood. Steak, medium, eggs over easy, toast, lightly buttered, and coffee, black. Does that sound about right?" the strange little man asked.

Liam's stomach was growling from hunger, but he looked at the man and said, "I'm not hungry. Now, give me some answers or so help me, I'll do things to you that you won't like."

After his talk with the President, Emmelor decided to attend to Liam himself. He was impressed with the man's persistence that he was the one in charge, not the other way around. "Your President and your planet are both, fine. We want to do you no harm. All will be explained shortly. Now, if you're not hungry, maybe we can do something to help you burn off a bit of that built up anger and hostility."

The man spoke into a microphone attached to his left shoulder and the door swished open and two men about the same size as the man in front of him came in and attached a collar around his neck.

Liam tried to pull away and was rewarded with an electrical shock that almost made him pass out.

"As you can now appreciate, it is we who are in control. Do as we ask, and you will save yourself a lot of discomfort. Although, what we have in mind for you next will more than likely not be painless.

The restraints from Liam's wrists and ankles were removed and he was told to come along with them.

"After you prove yourself worthy, we may consider removing the collar and giving you a further explanation.

Not wanting more pain from the collar around his neck, Liam went along with them, biding his time until he could make heads or tails of what was happening and figure out a plan to do something about it. The giant orbs filled his mind.

They stepped inside a module inside a glass tube and was whisked along at high speed to another part of the ship.

When the module came to a hissing stop and they got off, Liam was marched into a large arena where several hundred people sat, staring at two men inside a roped off area. The two men were fighting in what appeared to be mortal combat.

One of the men was a giant of a man, who stood at least six feet nine and weighed close to three hundred pounds. He had what appeared to be a chain and mace in his right hand – and was swinging the mace around and around over his head, waiting for an opening to attack his opponent.

The other man was a couple of inches shorter and had the look of an Asian. He was wielding an axe in his right hand, with a shield in his left.

"What the hell is this?" Liam asked.

For this, Liam got a small shock that he was able to endure without his knees buckling.

Emmelor smiled and said, "I think it speaks for itself. These two men are in mortal combat, such as you will be shortly."

A picture in Liam's head beamed brightly, with him in the ring, fighting an unknown man.

"Please, no shock treatment," Liam said, raising his hands, palms forward. "I only want to find out what's going on and why you are wanting me to do this?"

The man holding the shock control raised it and was about to press the button, but Emmelor raised his hand. "Hold on."

Emmelor looked at Liam and said, "Not that it will make a difference, but I guess you should know why you are here."

Liam looked at his surroundings and didn't like what he saw, as a gnawing feeling began to build in his stomach. Emmelor's next words confirmed the feeling in his gut.

"You are to be a participant in the games. You will face opponents in mortal combat, each time you are called upon. Your first opponent will be from planet, X-159."

"And if I refuse, I'll get more shock treatment?" Liam asked.

Emmelor shook his head back and forth. "No. One way or another, you will be put into the arena. Whether you fight or not is entirely up to you. If you choose not to fight, your opponent will kill you and you will not have to worry about fighting anyone else. Nor will you have to worry about seeing your friend, President Collier, or your family, ever again. The choice will be entirely yours."

Liam was led down to the side of the roped off area and watched as the giant beat his opponent to the floor with his chain-mace.

He too, had a collar around his neck and was led away from a stoic crowd that showed no emotion, one way or the other.

A crew of men took the dead man away, while others cleaned up the blood.

"Choose your weapon," Emmelor said.

Liam looked down at a table filled with several different medieval weapons but didn't see what he would really like to have – a pistol, so he could possibly shoot his way out of this place."

Not knowing who his opponent would be or what his weapon of choice would be, Liam said, "I'll wait and see what my opponent chooses."

He didn't have long to wait. Within a minute, two men came into to the area, leading a creature that reminded him of Big Foot, only several times meaner looking. The creature turned and looked at Liam and gave out with a growl.

Emmelor looked at the creature, then back at Liam. "Well, it seems you won't be needing a weapon. The rules state that if either of the warriors choose not to use a weapon, then neither shall have one and the duel will be hand to hand combat."

Liam gave a grunt as he climbed through the ropes and stood up. Maybe this was for the best; he could move better without a weapon in his hand. And besides, according to the law back on Earth, his hands were registered as lethal weapons, so in essence, he had several weapons.

Liam was pointed to a corner and he went there, looking out across the hundreds of faces. He was puzzled by the fact that none of them showed much interest in the fight. They were merely observing two males fighting each other for their lives, to see which one would move on.

He turned and looked across the area at the creature he was to fight. By now, he realized he'd been abducted and was being tested for his fighting skills – but why? Were they trying to see how tough the men on earth were? There were far more questions than answers.

His thinking was interrupted by a bell clanging. There had been no instructions, which to Liam's reasoning meant there were no rules. It was kill or be killed. He knew he could kill. He'd done so before. But it had been against known enemies of the United States and this was something altogether different.

The hairy, Big Foot creature ran across the ring, growling and spitting phlegm from his mouth.

Liam could see the muscles in his arms and shoulders, bulging like large pieces of rope and his fingernails looked more like claws than fingernails.

Immediately, Liam went into a defensive mode and let his training take over. Knowing he couldn't overpower this monster; his only choice was to outmaneuver him until he could figure out what he was going to do.

When the monster got close, Liam dropped down low and kicked out with his foot, catching the creature in the shin, causing him to lose his balance.

Liam was on his feet and backing away as the creature fell face first down onto the floor.

Snarling and growling, the creature came to his feet and once again, ran toward Liam with those long, muscled arms reaching for him.

This time, Liam took a different approach and slipped just under the outstretched hands and drove his shoulder into the creature's stomach and lifted up - raising the monster off the floor, then shoving him over the ropes and onto the front row of people.

The creature shook it off and climbed to his feet, then climbed back inside the ropes, angry about the way the fight was going.

He was more cautious this time and approached Liam like a mountain lion stalking its prey.

Liam circled, first to his left, then back to his right, sizing up his opponent. The monstrous creature was slow in his reactions and he knew he could kill him easily with moves he'd learned as a Navy Seal. But the truth was, he didn't want to kill him. He didn't even know him and figured he'd been abducted just as he had been.

If he could somehow render him unable to fight back, then he would win without killing him.

Suddenly, the creature rushed him and smashed him along the side of his head, raking his claws down across Liam's face.

Blood was running into Liam's left eye and the pain was excruciating, but he didn't have time to dwell on his pain. He needed his head to be clear while he did some damage of his own, which at this time, wasn't to be. The creature crashed into him and grabbed him in a bear hug.

Liam felt those huge arms wrap around him and begin to squeeze. It was like a giant anaconda had him in his grip and wasn't about to let go.

He could feel the arms tightening around him and knew he didn't have much time before his bones would begin to break.

With what effort he had left, Liam squeezed his arms up through the creature's arms, then reached up and slapped the creature on each ear with the palms of his hands and watched as the creature's eyes grew wide. The creature released Liam and grabbed his head. He was howling in pain. Broken eardrums were something not even the toughest of men or creatures can endure.

Once he was loose, Liam grabbed the hair on the creature's head and jerked down, while at the same time, lifting his knee. Liam heard his nose break. Next, he raised the creature's head and drove his fist into his throat – then smashed him in the jaw, sending him backward. The creature dropped to the floor, and lay there, trying to breathe and stop the pain.

Liam walked back to his corner and stood there as the referee walked over and looked down at the creature, then declared the fight was over.

There was no cheering as two men gave the collar a slight buzz to let Liam know they were once again in control.

Before climbing out through the ropes, Liam had a thought. He'd just done hand to hand combat with a creature from, possibly another planet, and had won!

As Liam was taken back to his room, he looked at one of the men and asked, "Is there any chance I could have that breakfast now?"

"You were right in choosing this one," a man dressed in a general's uniform said to Emmelor. "It will be interesting to see how he handles himself against the giant from the planet, Zora."

Emmelor nodded his head and said, "Yes, indeed it will."

Inside the room that was, for all practical purposes, his prison cell, Liam searched the room from top to bottom for a possible way out, other than the door he'd entered. There were no windows and no secret panels. The entrance to the room was a pocket door that was made of metal and couldn't be pried open. After exhausting all possibilities, he walked over and sat down on the chair in front of the small desk, contemplating the possibility of jumping whoever brought his breakfast, but dismissed the idea. Where could he go, even if he were able to get out? Even if he got out of the ship, there would still a lot of space between him and the earth – and he didn't have wings.

While he was in the bathroom cleaning the blood from his face, he tried to use rational thinking. He was inside one of the orbs floating above the earth. It was the only thing that made sense. For what purpose, he still wasn't sure, but it did have something to do with him being a warrior.

At the hissing of the door, Liam turned and watched as a very petite, but quite attractive woman came in with a tray of food, which included a pot of coffee. She sat the tray and coffee on the desk and turned to go.

"Wait," Liam said, standing up. "Can I ask you a question?"

She stopped and turned back to him, a smile on her lips. "Who are we, and why are we here? Is that the questions you want answered?"

"Yes. That's about it," Liam replied.

"I'm sorry but I'm not at liberty to say. Emmelor is the one to ask those questions."

"And…" was as far as Liam got before the woman raised her hand and said, "Emmelor will be along shortly to answer all your questions. Now, eat, before it gets cold."

And with that, she turned and left, the door swishing closed behind her.

Chapter 3

FACING THE UNITED NATIONS

Colonel James Michaels, head of the Communications Department, looked at the President and started to raise a question but President Collier raised his hand and said, "Colonel Michaels, send the message exactly as I said it, "Emmelor, I comply." And, please, don't ask any questions at this time. Understand?"

Colonel Michaels snapped to attention, saluted, and said, "Yes Sir!"

President Collier stood by and watched until his message was sent, then turned and left the Communications Center, calling for his car to take him to the United Nations building where he was to speak to the world's representatives about how to deal with the crisis facing them, as it had been put to him many times since the arrival of the orbs.

He was taken to a small waiting room, where he was given a cup of coffee. He was only half finished with his coffee when the door opened and a young woman stepped inside and said, "It's time, Mister President." Gabriella Stevens held the door open for him.

The President stood up, nodded and walked past her, saying, "Thank you."

Gabriella Stevens was just twenty-four – fresh out of college and this was her first job. Her job was to make sure speakers got to the podium of the United Nations on time.

"Thank you, Sir. It is my honor," Gabriella said. "If you will follow me, please."

She led the President and his bodyguards down a short hallway that led into the room where Sterling was to speak to the heads of nations from all over the world – along with reporters from across the globe.

As they entered the room, flashbulbs drew his attention, along with lights from the many video cameras that were trained on him.

He raised his hand in front of his eyes so he could see, leaving his bodyguards looking over the crowded room for anything they thought to be a threat.

Sterling sighed. He wished Liam was here.

He stopped and looked out over the massive room, filled to capacity, wondering what he could possibly say that would calm their fears. He had made a promise to the man from outer space that he wouldn't reveal why they were here.

Alfonso Almada, the current Secretary General, banged his gavel on the podium and said, "Please welcome, Sterling Collier, President of the United States of America!"

Sterling stepped up to the podium and raised his hands to quiet the applause. When the crowd quieted down and he was about to speak, a rush of questions came from the reporters. "Can you tell us who is in those orbs?" "Can you tell us why they are here?" "Are we at war with aliens?" "What is the military doing about the intruders?"

There were so many questions, Sterling couldn't keep them straight. He raised his hands and said, "Please. Please, hold your questions until after I'm finished speaking. The people from the many countries assembled here today will be the first allowed to ask questions – then if you have any further questions, I will address them as best I can. Thank you."

Begrudgingly, the press quieted down and waited.

Sterling's speech writer had tried to prepare a speech for him, but he'd rejected it. At this point, he preferred to speak for himself. The speech writer's version was much too complicated and far too convoluted.

Placing a hand on each side of the podium, Sterling began. "I'm not quite sure how to begin. Like all of you, yesterday morning we woke up to giant orbs floating over our countries. And like you, we sent planes that were turned back."

Sterling took a moment to collect his thoughts for his next statement. He wanted to reveal that he was in communication with the aliens, but just how to state it without causing an uproar, or violating his confidentiality, he wasn't quite sure. He could see the concerned looks on their faces as they awaited his next statement.

"And like you, we sent out a communications plea. The only difference is, we received a reply."

A giant gasp came from the crowd and questions in more than twenty languages came at him like a giant roar. Sterling raised his hands and waited.

Once they quieted down, he continued. "Please... Allow me to finish, then if you have questions, I will try to answer them. Now, as I said, we sent out a request to speak with them, but that didn't happen. The answer we received was short and to the point. The answer was in English, and the voice said, "We are not here to harm you." That's all that was said."

There. He'd told them about the communication without saying anything about the man, or, the hologram, or the conversation in his office.

Sterling took another short pause, then before he could continue, Marcy Helens of the New York Times, asked, "Where is your head of security, Liam Biggers?"

Without showing the alarm he felt inside, Sterling said, "He's undertaking a special mission and that's all I can say about it at this time," hoping that would be enough.

"What kind of special mission?" Marcy Helens asked.

"I'm not at liberty to comment at this moment," Sterling told her and then tried to move on, but Asbury Borne, the representative from England stood up and asked, "Mister President. Does his mission have anything to do with those orbs out there – and the people inside them?"

A hush washed over the crowd as they all awaited the President's answer.

So, there it was – one of the many questions he didn't want to be asked. Sterling hesitated for only a moment, then said, "I know you want answers and believe me, I'd like to give them to you, but at the present, I cannot. There is much more to this than I know. But the one thing I do know, and can relate to you is, as long as we are not aggressive, we are in no danger – and I can assure you, they are not here to do us harm."

"Then why are they here?" the representee from France asked.

21

Sterling Collier was a man who believed in being up front about everything - keeping no secrets from the people. If it was bad news, they needed to know – as was the same as good news. But this was something altogether different.

"I'm not at liberty to say," Sterling said with a sigh. "I wish I could tell you more, but I can't, at least not right now. Please," he said, raising his hands, "you've put your trust in me in the past and I'm asking you to do it now. Believe me when I say, as soon as I'm able, I will explain everything."

And with that, Sterling Collier, President of the United States, turned and walked away from a room filled with questions, as the Secretary General banged his gavel on the podium, calling for them to quiet down.

Gabriella smiled as the President passed in front of her. He looked tired and she felt sorry for him. He was carrying so much pressure on his shoulders, she wondered how he could do it. Did he know more about the orbs than he was telling? And if he did, how had that come about?

She wanted to chase after him and tell him she believed in him, then blushed at the thought. What would his bodyguards do if she rushed up to him and put her hands on him? Probably shoot her. She watched as he disappeared down the hallway.

Instead of going to the Oval Office and answering the growing list of phone calls, Sterling went down to the kitchen and greeted the chef, Archie Brooks. "Hello, Arch, you have any coffee left?"

The chef smiled. He was used to the President coming into the kitchen at all hours, looking for a snack. "Just made a fresh pot. Have a seat, I'll get you a cup. Anything else? Maybe a snack?"

Sterling pulled a chair out and sat down at the kitchen counter.

"Maybe a BLT, if you have the makings – and coffee and sandwiches for the boys if they want something – if you have the time, that is?"

"For you, Mister President, I always have the time."

Archie poured coffee all around and began making BLT sandwiches for everyone. He glanced over his shoulder and looked at the President. "Seems like they have you between a rock and a hard place."

Sterling looked up at him.

"I listened to your speech at the UN on the telly," Archie said.

"Ahh, yes… That was less than fun," Sterling said, as he stared at the chef. After graduating high school, Archie joined the Navy, where he went to Cook's School and his skills had not gone unnoticed. He had a natural affinity for cooking and soon moved up to the rank of Chief and held the title of Master Chef. He spent twenty years cooking for high-ranking officers – his last assignment before retiring, was at the Naval Air Station, Corpus Christi, Texas.

Sterling was in his first term as President and happened to be touring the Naval Air Station, in Corpus, where Archie was the chef at the ceremonial dinner. He was so impressed; he went back to the kitchen to meet Archie.

He was due to retire in three weeks and Sterling pressed Archie to be the White House Chef – which he agreed to and had been there ever since. Over the years, Archie and Sterling had become close friends and when the President needed a sounding board, he went to the kitchen and discussed things with Archie.

"Don't let them get to you. They're like everyone else on this planet – they're scared and they think you should have the answers."

Sterling looked at his bodyguards and asked them to have their coffee and sandwiches in the dining room.

When they were gone, Sterling looked at his friend as he sat a BLT sandwich down on the counter in front of him. "And what if I do have some of the answers, but can't say what they are just yet?"

It wasn't that he didn't trust his bodyguards – he did. But in this matter, he didn't feel he could discuss it in front of them, which would have to include information about Liam.

Archie poured a cup of coffee for himself and sat down, opposite of his friend. "Sounds like you made a promise to someone, to not talk about what you'd discussed. At least not now."

Sterling smiled. Talking to Archie was better than talking to a bartender. He always seemed to grasp the situation, immediately – and he was spot on this time, too. "Yes, I have communicated with them, but I promised not to reveal our conversation at this point."

Archie's mind was reeling. They'd had some pretty heavy discussions in the past but talking to someone from another planet was on a whole new level. He wanted to know every word that was said, along with a hundred other questions, but he knew he couldn't ask – not if he wanted to remain the President's confidant. "It has to be tough. I know you've always been open with everyone, but this is a whole different ballgame," he said, pointing to the sky. "You just think things through, then do what your gut tells you to do, and you'll be all right."

Sterling could see it in Archie's eyes. He too, wanted to know what had gone on, but he also knew better than to ask.

Back in the Oval Office, the President stood looking through the French doors at the orbs, still hovering over the planet. Pictures of all sorts of cruel fighting went through Sterling's mind and he said, "Do well, my friend... Do well and come back to us, safe and sound."

He turned back and sat down at his desk and rested his arms on the surface, giving a huge sigh. He knew he had a meeting with the Joint Chiefs of Staff within the hour and he dreaded it. The topic would of course be, the orbs hovering over the planet and what he was going to do about it, as if there was anything he could do.

There was a knock on the door and the President called out, "Come."

The door opened and one of his bodyguards said, "There is a Miss Gabriella Stevens to see you, Sir."

The name sounded familiar but for the life of him he couldn't put a face with the name.

When Gabriella walked in, Sterling stood up. It was the very attractive young woman who had led him to the general assembly room of the UN building.

He walked around and held a chair for her. "It's nice to see you, again. Please. Have a seat and tell me what I can do for you?"

After sitting down, Gabriella looked up at the President. He had very nice, but tired eyes. "I overheard something that I think you need to hear."

Sterling sat down in his chair and looked across his desk at her and asked, "What might that be, and where did you hear it?"

Gabriella thought for a moment, not sure she should have come, but in the end decided she had to tell him what she'd heard.

"Mister President, what I have to say is just hearsay, but from a reliable source."

"Go ahead," Sterling told her, leaning forward.

"Well, sir, I overheard the representatives from England and France speaking and the representative from England told the representative from France that he had been in contact with the Speaker of the House, Thornton Howell, and he was very upset over the way you are handling things. He thinks you are in league with the aliens to overthrow the planet and plans to start impeachment proceedings against you. And I'm sure you are aware of what a rumor like that can do, and how fast it can spread, true or not."

Sterling leaned back in his chair and shook his head from side to side. This was hard to believe Thornton would do such a thing, since he was the one who appointed him. If what Gabriella said was true, it was total betrayal on the Speaker's part. Until this very moment, he'd always thought of Thornton as a supporter of him and his ideas, but now he wasn't so sure.

"And you're sure you heard correctly?" Sterling asked, continuing with, "I don't mean I don't believe you, I do, but Thornton Howell has always portrayed himself as a loyal friend."

"I'm sorry to bring you such bad news, but yes, I'm very sure of what I heard," Gabriella told him. There were also grumblings among some of the other English-speaking representatives at the UN, Sir."

"Like what?" Sterling asked.

Gabriella hung her head for a moment, took a deep breath, then raised her head and said, "They believe you're hiding something from them; something about the aliens that could have an effect on our planet. They want you brought in front of them and made to explain why you are being so secretive."

Sterling stood up and walked around his desk, taking Gabriella's hand as she stood up. "Thank you, Miss Stevens. You were right to bring this information to me."

He walked her to the door and thanked her again, and when she'd gone, Sterling called for his chief advisor, Daniel Glazer, Speaker of the Senate.

Chapter 4

THE SECOND CHALLENGE

Liam was sitting on his bed, reading a book he'd found on the desk. It dealt with the history of the planet, X-162 and he was amazed at what he was reading. In the beginning they were much like the people of Earth, warriors who almost obliterated each other but as the centuries went by, they began to change and after another few hundred years of determination, the Passive Act was enabled. There would be no more wars as there had been in the past, killing hundreds of thousands of men and women on each side. From that time on, wars would be settled by single combat between the two fractions. He thought that to be strange because in other ways, they were still just as primitive as the people back on Earth. At least that's what he gleaned from what he'd read so far

Liam set the book down on the bed and was thinking about how something like that would work on Earth. – but decided they were still a long way off. He also decided that if he could somehow return, he would do his best to start such an idea.

He heard the door swish open and looked in that direction and smiled. The attractive woman he'd seen earlier entered the room as the door closed behind her.

Liam swung his legs over the bed and stood up as she approached him.

"We've not been properly introduced. My name is Lucita. I am the healer for this ship – or as you call them, a doctor. Only my methods are much different than the healers on your planet."

Liam had a chance to get a good look at her and liked what he saw. She was shorter than him, and very attractive. She had the figure of a swimsuit model, with auburn brown hair, large brown eyes and a petite nose. Her mouth looked perfect for kissing and even though she was from another planet, he felt himself stirring.

He gave a sigh and dismissed the idea as foolish.

"Is something wrong?" Lucita asked.

Regaining his composure, Liam grinned a sheepishly and said, "No. Everything is fine. So, what brings you to my humble abode?"

Lucita looked around and smiled. "I'm happy to see your room satisfies you."

"Yeah, right," Liam said, waving his hand around the room.

"Is there something you want that isn't here?" Lucita asked.

"Maybe, cable TV with a sports channel," Liam said with a big grin.

Lucita thought for a moment then took what looked like a communicator from her pocket and punched in a number, then said, "Our warrior, Liam Biggers, needs cable television with a sports channel. Room 134."

After hanging up, she said, "Please take your shirt and pants off so I can examine you. You have a bout in an hour if you are up to it."

"Really?" Liam said, surprised. "Who do I fight this time, Godzilla?"

Lucita looked at him. "I do not know this Godzilla person, but the answer is no. You will be fighting a man from your world. We took him out of a Russian prison. I think he is called, Dima Nikita."

Liam bristled. He knew the name. The man was not only big and mean, he was an international assassin, known for the brutal way he killed people. He was on death row.

"Why do people on your planet have two names?" Lucita asked.

"What? Two names? Oh, because the first name is the name given to us when we're born and the last name is our family name," Liam said,

"Now, about this..." which is as far as he got before Lucita asked, "What do you mean by 'family name', I do not know that word."

"You know, family – your people. Don't you get married and have children up on that planet where you live?"

"Marriage. I do not know that word, either," Lucita said.

Liam shook his head. "On Earth, when two people want to be together, they get married and start a family. The children get a first name when they're born that goes with the father's last name. Understand?"

She smiled and said, "You make things so complicated. On our planet, when two people want to be together, they just do. If a child is born, he or she is given a name, but that is all."

"How do you keep track of who your people are?" Liam asked.

"We judge a person only by what they can do, not by who their mother or father are, and I guess anyone we associate with would be our family, but I don't recall anyone ever using that word," Lucita said, matter of factly.

Before Liam could comment more, Lucita continued. "Now, please remove your shirt and pants so I can examine you.

"When in Rome," Liam said to himself as he pulled off his shirt and stepped out of his pants.

Lucita looked at the man standing in front of her and was impressed. As far as she was concerned, he was beautiful. He was huge, compared to the men of her planet. Also, he was definitely a warrior. She could tell by the scars on his body.

During her examination, she noticed her heart beating faster and the palms of her hands becoming moist. Was she attracted to this alien from Earth? After shaking off the feeling, she found he had two, cracked ribs and some nasty cuts on his face. But other than that, he was in excellent shape. She placed her hand on the ribs and felt them heal. Next, placed her hand against the scratches on his face and waited as they, too, healed.

She stepped back and spoke into the communicator. "Warrior, Liam Biggers. After a thorough examination, I find him acceptable to fight."

While she was talking to her communicator, Liam got dressed, amazed at how easily his wounds had been healed. When she was finished, he asked, "What if I refuse to fight?"

"Why would you do that?" Lucita asked, astounded by the question.

"Because I don't like to fight," Liam said.

"But you are obviously very good at it," Lucita said.

"Yeah, I know. And I've done my fair share of it. But that doesn't mean I like to do it."

Lucita stared at Liam for what seemed to be a long time before saying. "I only know of one man who refused to fight, and he was thrown into the fighting area to face a beastly looking opponent. They hoped he would defend himself, but the man died without ever raising his hands.

Liam looked down at his feet, then back up to Lucita's face. She was beautiful and if the situation was different, she would be a woman worth fighting for. "Instead of kidnapping men, why don't you ask for volunteers?"

She laughed. "You make a joke, yes? We land our ship on your planet and Emmelor walks out and asks the men he meets to volunteer to go to our planet to fight to the death with someone or something he has never seen, in the hopes of saving our planet. Is that what you are suggesting?"

Liam scratched the back of his neck and said, "I see your point."

Lucita's communicator buzzed and she answered it. "Yes. Right away."

"They want me to bring you to the fighting arena," Lucita said.

This time, they rode in a golf cart type of vehicle and as she drove along, Liam asked, "Have you already examined my opponent?"

"I tried," she said, shaking her head. "But he would have none of it and told me he didn't need to be looked at. He said he was ready and eager to destroy whoever we paired him against."

That would be Nikita's MO, Liam thought to himself. It was a known fact that the man liked to get his victim in a bearhug and squeeze the life out of him as he laughed in their face. He would need to stay out of his clutches.

The arena was crowded, and Dima Nikita was already in the fighting area, prancing around, yelling for an opponent.

Emmelor met them and as Liam stepped off the cart. He smiled and said, "You will need all your cunning to beat this one. He will not be easily bested."

Liam had no more than climbed through the roped off fighting area when Dima ran over and smashed him in the back of the head. When Liam went down, he kicked him in the ribs three times before they could get him to back off.

"I'm beaten half to death and the fight hasn't even started, yet," Liam mumbled as he got to his feet and took a deep breath, hoping he didn't have broken ribs, again.

The referee came over to Liam's corner and asked, "Are you able to continue?"

For just a moment, Liam was ready to climb back out of the ring, but something inside him wouldn't let him do it. He now had something to prove. He could breathe so he knew his ribs weren't broken. "I'm ready when you are," Liam told him as he took another deep breath.

As soon as the bell sounded, Dima ran towards Liam, swinging both fists, wanting to end it immediately, but this time Liam was ready and slipped under the windmill punches and drove his fist into Dima's stomach.

His fist and arm felt like he'd just punched a brick wall and the pain radiated all the way up his arm to his shoulder. Before he could respond, Dima backhanded Liam alongside his head, sending him staggering to try and keep from falling. He knew what that would bring.

Regaining his balance, he looked at the big Russian and said, "That it? That all you got?"

Enraged by Liam's comment, Dima once more, charged like a raging bull.

Liam waited for the right moment, then lunged himself against the ropes, and let them throw him toward Dima.

Liam's leg was outstretched, and he drove his foot into Dima's chest, stopping him flat footed in his charge.

Liam landed back on his feet and could see the shocked look on Dima's face and the pain in his eyes. Immediately, Liam kicked out and smashed it against Dima's right knee. The leg was driven backward, and the big Russian was knocked off balance and fell to the floor, his right leg wasn't broken, but it would make it hard to stand on.

Rather than running over and kicking Dima, he stepped back and motioned for his opponent to get to his feet, hoping he was making the right decision.

Dima got slowly to his feet. He was not used to being in this position and would be more cautious from now on. The man was a fool for letting him get to his feet and he would make him pay for his mistake. Limping, he circled the tall American who was called, Liam Biggers. He thought he knew the name, but couldn't place, where?

Liam knew there would be no, saved by the bell, because there was only one round, and it lasted until only one of them was still standing, or both were down.

After nearly twenty minutes of hitting and being hit, Liam's left eye was almost closed from the swelling where Dima had kicked him, after knocking him down. His nose was bleeding, but he didn't think it was broken. Both his fists were bleeding from hitting Dima in the teeth. He was tired clear down to the marrow of his bones, but Dima was in even worse shape. Both his eyes were almost swollen shut, his mouth was bleeding where three of his teeth had been knocked out. And for sure, both his kidney and his ribs were making it hard for him to breathe, along with his right knee swollen and painful to stand.

The two combatants circled each other, each looking for an opening. Dima's right knee was making it hard for him to keep his balance.

Liam took all of this in as he waited his chance to end this battle. It came when he fainted a jab to Dima's jaw, and when Dima tried to step away, Liam leaned over and kicked his right knee, again, hearing it snap, this time.

With Dima off balance, he drove his fist into his throat and heard his larynx break.

On wobbly legs the big Russian stepped back, grabbing his throat with one hand while trying to hit Liam with his other fist.

Liam knew he couldn't breathe, and it wouldn't be right to let him die this way. The man had been a force to reckon with and deserved to die a warrior's death. He followed Dima and when he got close, he drove his right fist into his heart area and saw his eyes go wide. He was dead before he landed, face down on the floor of the ring.

Liam walked to his corner and awaited the referee's call. He hadn't wanted to be the one to kill him, but it was either that or let himself be killed, and that wasn't about to happen if he had anything to say about it. Besides, Dima had been slated for the death penalty in a few months.

Liam had barely entered his room when Lucita came in and walked over to him and said, "You know what to do. I want to heal your wounds."

"Why, so I can go kill someone or something else?" Liam said angrily.

Lucita stared at the man from Earth and wondered about him. He had the instincts of a killer, but the heart of someone gentle who hated fighting. He was a curiosity. She found herself wanting to know more about this man. But for now, she had her duty. "Please, remove your clothes."

Chapter 5

DINNER WITH AN ALIEN

When the examination and healing was finished, Liam had to admit he felt much better.

"I'm sorry for lashing out at you," he told her. He pointed at the book on his bed and said, "I know from reading that book how things work on your planet and in theory I like the idea. It saves a lot of lives. It's the final two warrior's part I'm not too keen on.

She smiled up at him and said, "Even so, it's better than slaughtering hundreds of thousands of men and women."

Liam shrugged his shoulders and stared at her. She was right and he didn't have a comeback rebuttal. For some compulsive reason, other than wanting to learn more about him and his people, Lucita looked up at Liam and asked, "Would you have your evening meal with me?"

For a second or two, Liam wasn't sure how to reply. Beautiful or not, she was an alien – or was it him who was the alien? He was, after all, on her ship. Did she have an ulterior motive? Was this some kind of brainwashing method? "Your room or mine?" he said.

Liam saw her eyes light up, but she said, "Neither. We have several dining areas on the ship, designed for various cultures and we're free to choose whichever one we want. I would like to know more about you. It's as simple as that. What is your favorite kind of meal?"

Liam grinned. "I do like a big steak, but if you don't have that, I guess Chinese would be a close second."

She nodded her head and said, "I have never had a steak, whatever that is. It should be interesting. I will pick you up in an hour. You will find presentable attire in the closet."

And with that, she was gone.

Liam took a leisurely shower and, in the dresser drawer, he found underwear and socks. The closet yielded pants and shirts that fit him perfectly, along with a pair of loafer type shoes that felt very comfortable on his feet.

Liam was sitting at the desk, contemplating the evening when the door whisked open. "Are you ready?" Lucita asked.

She was dressed in a lime green cocktail dress and her hair hung down over her shoulders. The light from the hallway made a halo glow all around her, causing Liam to say, "Wow!"

"I take it you approve?" Lucita said. "My computer said this is what I should wear in a situation like this."

"Your computer did good," Liam said as they got into the small, electric-powered vehicle.

They rode along in silence, allowing Liam time to look around. He was amazed at the enormity of the orb. Of course, it had looked huge from down on the ground, but the inside made it seem even bigger. A large tube ran over head and small containers swished past going to who knew where.

They passed one place that looked like a botanical garden behind a glass wall. Lucita noticed Liam looking at it and said, "That's where we grow all the food plants from the many different planets we've explored. There is also a place where we raise animals that are eaten by people of the various different planets. And yes, since coming to Earth we now have animals you call cows," she said with a grin. "If we like them, we will bring them into our culture.

The trip took close to twenty minutes and during that time, Liam saw things he didn't understand and assumed they came from other planets, which took some getting used to. There were apparently quite a few other planets with life.

Liam looked at Lucita and asked, "Do all the different planets speak English?"

She looked at him and laughed. "Again, you make a joke. Heavens no. For every planet there is a different language."

"Then how is it we can converse in English?" Liam asked.

Lucita reached up and took a small piece of something that resembled a hearing aid, out of her ear, showed it to him, then replaced it. "That is a translator. Our computers are able to read and remember dictionaries from any language and translate your language to ours - then tells me how to respond in your language."

Liam could only shake his head in amazement. They were far more advanced than Earth, which took some thinking to wrap his mind around it.

"Here we are," Lucita said, pulling up in front of a walled off section that had a sign over the door that read - Billy Bob's Steakhouse.

"This was created just for you," Lucita said as she stepped out of the cart and motioned for him to follow her.

The interior looked like it had been transplanted from Texas, with all the western look to it.

There was even a Hank Williams song playing through the wall mounted speakers.

"Do you approve?" she asked.

"You couldn't have done any better," Liam replied as they sat down.

Liam turned and looked at the box on the wall next to them when a man's voice asked, "Would you care for a drink before dinner?"

Liam grinned and said, "I'll have a scotch and water," then looked over at Lucita who said, "And I'll have a glass of Jala."

When Liam looked at her, she said, "It's like your wine, but tastier and stronger."

When their order came, Liam ordered the Porterhouse steak with a twice baked potato and a garden salad with ranch dressing. When he looked across the table, Lucita said, "Since I've never eaten a steak, I'll have the same as you."

While they waited for their meals, they sipped their drinks and talked. "Why did you pick me as one of the warriors?" Liam asked.

"I think you should ask Emmelor about that, but I do have a theory if you're interested," Lucita said.

"I'm all ears, as the expression goes," Liam told her.

Lucita chewed her piece of steak, swallowed, took a sip of Jala, then said, "Our two planets, even though they are in different solar systems could almost be sister planets, except for a few things – which are a great interest to us.

You and your people are still in an aggressive state that bodes war and warriors. We have monitored your planet for years. UFOs, I believe you called us. We have wanted to make contact, but you weren't ready yet. But now, with our need for a warrior to fight in the Battle Game, Emmelor and the council hope you will fit the bill, which, hopefully will lead to other things, like a better understanding for your people regarding how to live at peace."

They talked for the better part of two hours, each revealing much about themselves and their country. And when she dropped him off at his room, she touched his hand and said, "Thank you. I have learned much this evening."

"It's a two-way street," Liam told her as he raised her hand and kissed it gently.

As she drove away, Liam could see her staring down at her hand.

He entered his room and when the door hissed closed, Liam sat down on his bed and allowed one major thing she'd said to come to the forefront of his mind. They didn't have separate countries with different governments and leaders. On X-162, there was only one ruling entity – a council – twelve men and women who controlled the entire planet. Oh, they had oceans between the continents, but the council lived on a neutral island, called The Isle of Morupeia and ruled from there. As far as Liam was concerned, it was a very interesting concept.

Liam was roused from his sleep by a man, instructing him to get up and get dressed, and come with him.

"Why?" Liam queried.

"I do not know. I was sent to get you and bring you to the meeting room," the man said.

Liam was taken to a room and met by Emmelor, who told him, "There is trouble. We have to return. You will be one of the few going with us. To travel as far as we have to, at the speed we must travel, you will be placed in a sleep tube. It will automatically awaken you when we reach our destination."

Emmelor walked Liam over to a bank of tubes that was comprised of more tubes than he could count. Most of them were full, already with people from the ship. He turned and looked at Emmelor, who motioned with his hand and said, "Please."

Liam was hesitant, but ultimately knew he didn't have a choice. He stepped inside and as the door closed, a lemony smell engulfed his nostrils and his eyes closed. He felt like he was floating on air and everything was peaceful.

When all the people aboard the ship were in their tubes, Emmelor, checked the control board, then touched a button that read Autopilot before getting into a tube himself.

Chapter 6

RUMOR PROBLEMS

It had been less than an hour when the President's phone started ringing. He knew whoever was calling would be wanting to know how he was going to handle the possible upcoming impeachment and probably also whether he was going in front of the UN general assembly, again, to explain the charges against him.

Deciding to not answer the phone, Sterling called in his secretary, Irene Harper. "Hold all my calls until I tell you different."

"Should I take messages?" she asked, already knowing what the calls would be about. She too, had heard the rumor and what the Speaker of the House was planning on doing to the President.

Sterling waved his hand at her and said, "Yes. Of course – take messages."

As Mrs. Harper left his office, his chief adviser, Daniel Glazer entered the Oval Office and headed straight for the liquor cabinet and poured himself a glass of whiskey.

After dropping into the chair in front of the President's desk and taking a long pull of his drink, he said, "Well, this is another fine mess you've gotten us into," using the term from the old Laurel and Hardy films. They had been friends since high school and had pulled a prank or two together.

"What the hell is he thinking?" Sterling asked as he, too, poured himself a drink.

"If you'll recall, I tried to convince you not to give the position to him, but no, you never listen to me once you made up your mind," Daniel told his longtime friend.

"It was strictly a political move, and you know it," Sterling said, sitting down in the chair next to the one Daniel was sitting in.

"One that's come back to bite you in the butt," Daniel told him, raising his glass as if in a toast. "How much can you talk about?"

Sterling took a good pull at his brown sugar bourbon, swallowed and said, "Not much. At least for the time being. I gave my word."

Daniel sat up and leaned a little closer to the President. "Then you have spoken with them?"

Sterling nodded his head. "Yes. Here in the Oval Office."

"There was an alien from another planet, here in this office?" Daniel asked, excitedly.

"It was just a hologram of the man I was speaking to, but his image was very real," Sterling said, remembering the hologram.

"This is incredible! I hope you realize you are the only person on this planet to actually speak to someone from another planet. You'll be in the history books! Was he short and green, with big eyes?" Daniel was overwhelmed.

Sterling grinned for the first time in days. "He was short and small in structure, but no, he wasn't green, nor did he have big eyes. He basically looked just like you and me. He spoke in English – through a translator, I presume."

"But you can't say what you talked about?" Daniel asked.

"Not now. But I *can* reveal our conversation at some point down the line," Sterling said, standing up and walking around behind his desk and staring out through the French doors.

"Did he give you any indication of when that might be?" Daniel asked.

Sterling turned and looked at his friend and said, "Not a date and time. He said, soon, maybe ten days to two weeks of our time. Maybe shorter – maybe longer."

Daniel stood up, downed the last of his drink and said, "Problem solved. Stall. Don't worry about Thornton, it will take him, months to make it official and in the meantime, go in front of the UN and tell them just enough to appease them. You don't have to lie, but dance around the subject just enough to make them think they have all the facts."

Sterling grinned. He could always count on his friend to see the right path to take. "Thank you, I think I know what to do," he said, walking around his desk to shake his friend's hand.

-

Thornton Howell stood behind his chair and stared down the long table at his cronies, most of which were representatives in the House of Representatives. "We finally have him. He knows more than he's telling and all we have to do is promote the idea that he is a traitor to this country and that he is in league with people from another planet to overthrow our planet. We can even suggest he will be given riches, power, or whatever, when their takeover is complete."

"But we don't know that for sure," Bazile Hawthorn, one of the senior representatives with more than thirty years in office, said.

"Doesn't matter," Thornton told them. "All we have to do is leak the rumor to the news reporters and every newspaper in the entire country with have headlines that read, PRESIDENT COLLIER IN LEAGUE WITH ALIENS TO OVERTHROW THE PLANET! Television news reporters will spread the word faster than a wildfire!

"We plant the seed and keep telling the American people over and over that the President is a traitor and very quickly, in their minds, it will become the truth and we will have our impeachment."

Rodney Warren spoke up. "But then the Vice President, Jules Pepperdine, will become the new President, and we'll be no better off. The man is an idiot!"

Thornton Howell made a slight smile and said, "Let me worry about Pepperdine. He won't hold the position long."

Bazile Hawthorn grinned and said, "I see. If the Vice President somehow can't hold the position, then you are next in line. You want to be President!"

Thornton looked at the men sitting around the table and asked, "Who better for the job? Now who's with me?"

To the man, every hand was raised.

Chapter 7

PLANET X-162

Liam felt like he was waking up from a dream he couldn't remember and when he opened his eyes, he found himself looking into the smiling face of Lucita. There was a hissing sound and a part of the tube he was in slid open and when he stepped out, his legs were a bit wobbly.

Lucita took his hand and said, "Hang on, sleepy head. Just stand there for a moment or two and everything will be fine."

"Where are we and how long have I been asleep?" Liam asked as he felt his strength returning.

"You've been in what we call suspended animation for thirty-one days. That's how long it has taken us to get back to our universe."

Liam shook his head to clear the last of the cobwebs from his brain and said, "Thirty-one days. So, I'm guessing I can't see Earth from here."

Lucita gave a throaty laugh and said, "Our solar system is three-hundred and sixty trillion miles from your solar system, so, no, you can't see Earth from here.

Three-hundred and sixty trillion miles? Liam was having a hard time judging that much distance in his mind. What kind of speed did they have to travel at to go that far in thirty-one days?

Seeing the look on Liam's face, Lucita said, "We travel at hyper-speed. We can do that by using something akin to your nuclear power, only a hundred times more powerful. We retrieve it from sunspots of any of our three suns."

"You have three suns?" Liam asked.

Lucita took his arm and said, "Come, you must be starving. We can talk more while you renourish your body."

Even as hungry as he felt, thirty-one days without food had shrunk his stomach so much he could eat only half of what he ordered.

While Liam ate, or tried to eat, Lucita explained that their solar system had a hundred and sixty-five planets, with twelve of them having life on them of one type or another.

"In our earlier, more primitive years, we fought almost continuously, but as time went by, we adapted the system we have now - although, in a rare case one of the rulers reverts to our former way of fighting – which is what happened this time, and why we had to return."

Liam sipped on something dark and brown, that tasted very much like coffee, but not quite, then asked, "Are you telling me this person you're at war with, broke the rules and attacked you?"

"That is the communication we received, yes. And that's why we had to rush back, in the hopes we're not too late to save our planet from a complete takeover."

"So, how long before we reach your planet?" Liam asked.

"Four of your days," Lucita told him. "That is why I asked permission to awaken you early. I want to show you our solar system – or, at least, part of it."

From the dining area, they got into a cube in the travel tube and were whisked along to the Pilot Room.

Liam was astounded at the giant window in the ship and the many planets and moons he could see.

Lucita spoke to a man sitting at a control board and he punched some buttons and a huge planet loomed up on a giant screen. "This is X-159. Because of its year-round cold temperature, it is inhabited by hairy, manlike creatures. They are intelligent, but still light years behind us."

An image filled a smaller screen. "Sounds kind of like our Big Foot creatures back on Earth," Liam said.

"As I recall, one of their best was your first opponent," Lucita told him.

Liam recalled his first fight, and it was with someone who looked exactly like the image on the screen. He was about to say something when he was thrown off his feet by the sudden movement of the ship.

"Raising shields! Three incoming attack modules approaching! Alert! Alert!" a voice yelled through the wall mounted speakers.

As Liam got to his feet, Emmelor came rushing into the room. "Take evasive moves at will!" he shouted to the man sitting at the control board.

"What's going on?" Liam asked as the ship moved sideways, again, just as a laser light beam rushed past, barely missing the orb.

Bracing himself so he could absorb the moves the ship was making and stay balanced, Emmelor said, "We are being attacked by fighter ships from planet X-165. Their head speaker, Moller, is the head of their council and the one who declared war against us. By the looks of things, he apparently is not a man of honor. He has broken the code by attacking our planet and is now attacking us."

Liam looked through the giant window and saw the three fighter modules, as they were called. They were triangle shaped and looked very menacing – black - just like the black fighter planes back on Earth.

He turned back to Emmelor with a puzzled look on his face and asked, "What happened to all the other ships that were hovering over my planet? Can't they help?"

Emmelor sighed. "Sadly, there was only one ship. The ones your people saw were holograms. If we arrive like a giant invading army, we're less apt to be attacked, so that is what I did."

Liam had to admit, the effect was awesome. He looked around as the fighter modules made another pass and this time, the fighter ship moved up and to the right as two of the three laser lights went off into the night sky.

The third laser light barely grazed the ship, but even so, the effect was brutal as it was knocked sideways, rolling over and over and the people inside were tossed around like a jar of beans being violently shaken – smashing into each other and bouncing off any stationary object they came in contact with, plus, it weakened the shield.

Liam grabbed onto an upright post and hung onto it. "Why aren't we shooting back? Don't you have any guns on this ship?"

Lucita, who was also holding onto a post, yelled, "We have weapons, but no one to shoot them! We never expected to be attacked!"

"Can you get me to one of them?" Liam yelled.

When the ship stabilized, Emmelor called out, "Follow me!"

Liam stared down at a panel board and shook his head. It was like no gun control he'd ever seen. "Where's the gun?"

Emmelor realized their weaponry was completely new to the earthling and was a little bit reluctant to hand the weapon over to him. But at this point, he had no choice. There was no one else who might possibly be able to handle the shooting. "Here, allow me," Emmelor said as he pressed several buttons, then stepped back as a portion of the wall opened and Liam could see the handles and trigger for the weapon, along with a window with a target painted on it, showing him when to pull the trigger. After another sideways jerk, Liam ran to the seat and took control of the weapon, which reminded him of a mounted machine gun a tail gunner in a bomber plane might have. A panel on the exterior of the orb opened and Liam could see the outside.

The seat, the gun barrel and the window moved to Liam's left and he could see the three fighter modules lining up for another run at them. He couldn't believe this was happening. He was aboard an alien ship; about to do battle with alien fighter planes or whatever they were called where he now was.

Taking the handles of the weapon, Liam swung the barrel so that it pointed at the lead module and squeezed the trigger. A streak of red light raced across the night sky and slammed into the lead module. The explosion that followed was a thousand times bigger than the biggest fireworks show he'd ever seen. The concussion knocked the other two modules off to the side, tumbling them over and over. Once the pilots were able to get their ships back under control, they had to circle around to get back on track.

"Well done!" Emmelor yelled.

"Don't get too excited," Liam said. "Now that they know we can fight back, they won't be so easy to hit."

For the next hour, Liam battled with the two remaining fighter modules. His biggest problem to overcome was the sudden maneuvering of the ship, suddenly moving sideways or up or down to escape the enemies fire power. Each time he would have to reposition his weapon to train it on the enemy, which was no easy feat because they kept changing their locations.

The first time that happened and the enemy modules moved behind the ship. To Liam's great surprise, he and the weapon went sliding across the wall of the orb, finally stopping several feet away. "The weapon is locked onto the enemy and is somehow able to follow them wherever they go!" Liam muttered to himself.

With a new wrinkle to the fight, the two fighter modules split apart and came at the ship from two directions. Liam allowed the weapon to choose its target, and when it was lined up. He squeezed the trigger, and again, the explosion was devastating.

Liam could envision that someday – if there was to be a someday – the weapon would no longer need a man. It would lock onto a target, then fire itself. Just the thought of that happening made Liam shudder. Soon, man would have no say in anything because by then, the computers would have taken over whatever planet they were on.

The last of the fighter modules moved farther away and was flying erratically and hard to track.

"Are you going to be able to get him?" Emmelor asked, coming up behind Liam.

"That will be up to the gun's tracking device. He's being very evasive. All we can do is wait for him to settle down and hope I can get him in my sights."

"You've done very well, so far, but we need to eliminate him before he decides to go back to his base. If he does that, he will come back with a whole squad of fighter modules, and you can't be everywhere at once."

"I'll do my best," Liam said, knowing that's all he could do.

-

Inside the fighter module, the pilot stared at the giant orb that he was told was his enemy and was told to destroy. He and his fellow pilots had also been told there would be little or no resistance, but that had proved to be incorrect. Whoever was manning the ship's weapon, was very good, and if he didn't want to return to base like a whipped dog, he had to figure a way to outmaneuver his enemy. He had his orders.

-

Lucita brought Liam another cup of the brown liquid that tasted mostly like coffee, only it wasn't. As he sipped the brew, Liam knew it would help renew strength to his body and brain.

"I thought you might be needing this," Lucita said with a smile. "It helps me when I'm in a stressful situation."

Liam took the cup and put it to his lips, allowing the brown liquid to do its work. He took a quick glance at Lucita, and he could see the worry lines around the corners of her eyes and thought to himself, *This is a very strong woman. I know she's scared, but yet, she says nothing and lends her strength to me by bringing the strong brew so that I might be alert enough to fight.*

"Thank you," Liam said. "This is exactly what I need, right now."

A movement outside the orb caused Liam to hand the cup back to Lucita and turn his attention to the movement. The enemy fighter had started to move slowly toward them, then rolled over on its side, then completed the roll, and continued on this way as the module picked up speed – rolling over and over, making it hard to lock onto.

Then, each time it was upright, it fired a bolt of laser light, which caused the pilot of the orb to react, and the orb began evasive maneuvers, making it even more difficult to line up a shot.

Liam held his finger against the trigger and waited.

The enemy fighter module flew past them so close; Liam could see the image of the pilot through the shield of the cockpit. He could not actually see the pilot but from what Liam could tell, the man was large, and his helmeted head turned and stared at the orb as he flew past.

"He's just a man," Liam said as the module flew off to the side with the ship's muzzle turning to follow him, and when he was on target, Liam squeezed the trigger.

At just the right moment, the enemy fighter rolled over on its side, allowing the red beam of light disappear off into the night sky.

"He's good," Liam said, almost in a whisper.

"What?" Emmelor and Lucita both said at the same time.

"The pilot," Liam said. "The pilot is very good, but he's just a man."

What does that mean?" Lucita asked.

"It means I need to get inside his head to figure out how he thinks," Liam said, shaking his head.

Just then, the pilot circled around, and came to a stop, a good distance away – hovering there as though it was thinking – which of course, is exactly what he was doing.

Several, very long minutes dragged on as Liam stared back at the enemy plane, his nerves ready for action.

"What is he doing?" Emmelor asked.

Suddenly, the answer came to Liam, and he didn't like it. "He's building up courage," Liam said. "He's going to blast his way through the shield and ram us."

"But that would mean his death, too!" Lucita said in a panicked voice.

"Yes, it will," Liam told her. "But he will have accomplished his mission and die a hero."

Chapter 8

DISPELLING THE RUMOR

Gabriella Stevens led Sterling Collier into the General Assembly room of the United Nations building and stepped aside as he walked toward the raised platform and the podium. Asbury Borne saw him coming and pointed at him, saying, "The President of the United States!"

The filled house, as one, stood up, but there was no applause.

This was not unexpected by Sterling as he mounted the platform and shook hands with Borne. "Thank you," Sterling said with a broad smile.

"I don't envy you," Borne whispered, then turned and went to sit down on a chair at the back of the podium.

Sterling turned and looked out over the filled to capacity Assembly Room.

The General Assembly Room was gigantic, as rooms go. It was 165 feet long, 115 feet wide and had a ceiling height of 75 feet – three stories high. There were 193 delegates, with six seats per delegate. Right in front of the podium were tables for six people, who in this instance, were empty. That area was replaced with at least 50 chairs for the press – and each one of them was filled.

The silence that hung over the room was like a graveyard at midnight. They were there to see him try and worm his way out of being impeached.

A small smile creased his lips, and he cleared his throat. "I didn't come here today because I feel threatened by you or the trumped-up charges that fill the newspapers and television news stations. I came here today for one reason and one reason only - to clear the air and be done with the rumors. As I told you, earlier, I am not at this time, at liberty to reveal the conversation I had with the alien."

A giant grumble vibrated throughout the room. Marcy Helens of the New York Times called out, "That sounds like an admission of guilt in itself. Come on, Mister President, the people have a right to know what was said."

Sterling ignored her and continued on. "I will, however, tell you this, I have changed my mind and will tell you what little I know, which is, they are not here to invade us, nor do they want to do us any harm."

"Then what are they doing here, hovering over our planet with all those spaceships? If they're not here to do us harm, why did they bring so many ships?"

Sterling stood there, staring out over the faces staring back at him and said, "Why they travel with so many ships, I don't know, but I can tell you this – Earth is not the only planet they have visited."

There was a giant buzz of voices echoing throughout the room. A reporter from the Kansas City Star spoke up. "Are you telling us there is other life out there?"

"That's exactly what I'm saying," Sterling said, knowing this would be the new headline news. "I don't know how many other planets out there have life but I believe it must be quite a few. I believe, among the many universes, we are a young planet and still far behind in learning and technology.

"Are they then, here to protect us from another planet invading us?" another voice called out.

"That was not part of the conversation I had, which I should add, was short and to the point. To the best of what I understand, they are searching for other planets with which to share alliances with. But first, they must feel we can be trusted with the vast amount of information they can give us. And I was told they're just here to observe us."

"What if they don't like what they see?" the delegate from Spain asked.

Sterling knew he had led them in a new direction – away from the actuations about him being in cahoots with the aliens and the overthrow of the planet. "From my short-lived conversation, the hologram of the alien said that once they get their information, we'll wake up one morning and they'll be gone."

Sterling knew this was a stretch and totally different than the real conversation, but he felt he had no other choice. He was not ready for an impeachment battle right now and giving them a new direction for them to follow, allowed him to stay within his promise to Emmelor. Besides - life on other planets was something scientists could talk about for generations to come.

"Are you saying we're at the mercy of whatever they think of us?" another reporter asked.

Sterling thought for a moment and said, "My honest opinion is, they are a peaceful people who want to unite with other planets who are on the same plane as they are. And being truthful, I believe we are still too hostile and not nearly advanced enough, technology wise."

"We're a peaceful country!" a young, female reporter yelled.

Sterling looked down at her and her youthful ignorance. "Then why do we continue to have wars that kill thousands upon thousands of our people, along with the same amount of the enemy's? And if we're so peaceful, why do we have enemies in the first place? How many people get killed every day, right here in the city? Think about it."

There was dead silence in the room and Sterling continued. "I expect we will wake up one day soon and see a sky empty of spaceships. I'm sorry to say, I believe it will be a while before they are ready for an alliance with us. And just for the record, I am not in alliance with anyone, anywhere, to overthrow this country, or this planet. And that's all I have to say on the matter. Thank you for coming and I hope someday, we can be called a planet of peaceful people."

As the President and his secret servicemen walked past her, Gabriella smiled and said, "Well done, Mister President."

Sterling stopped and looked down at her, saying, "Come by my office tomorrow. I would like to talk to you about working for me."

Gabriella was having a hard time breathing. "Yes Sir," she managed to whisper.

Sterling headed straight for the White House kitchen, where his friend and chef, was waiting for him with a large bowl of Dutch Apple pie, topped with a large scoop of vanilla ice cream.

"So, how did it go?" Archie Brooks asked, knowing by the smile on the President's face, that it had gone over well. Plus, he'd watched the speech on the television.

"Just like you said it would," Sterling told his friend as he climbed onto the stool in front of the bowl of pie and ice cream. "The idea of life on other planets made them forget about the possibility of me collaborating with aliens to overthrow this planet – which I will say, is totally preposterous."

"And it should shut down the impeachment proceedings," Archie said, sitting down across from the President, with his own bowl of pie and ice cream.

-

Thornton Howell turned off the television on his desk and leaned back in his chair. He was furious. He got to his feet and went to the bar on one wall of his office and was pouring a tall glass of bourbon when Representative Bazile Hawthorne came rushing into his office. "Did you watch Sterling's speech to the UN?"

Thornton picked up a second glass and poured a good measure of bourbon in it, then topped Bazile's glass off with ice cubes and seven up. His got only ice cubes.

"I did, but it doesn't change a thing," Thornton said, handing Bazile his drink.

"But how can that be? He came clean about his conversation with the alien. We no longer have anything to impeach him on," Bazile said, taking a long pull on his drink.

Thornton downed almost half of his glass of bourbon before looking at Bazile. "And like the rest of them, you swallowed his load of crap, hook, line, and sinker. You're pathetic."

Bazile got a surprised look on his face and asked, "Are you saying he was lying?"

"I have no idea one way or another," Thornton said, "But what I believe doesn't mean anything. It's what we make the public believe that counts, and

I will be calling him a liar, publicly – through the newspapers and television news. I've already called for a news conference, later this afternoon.

Bazile dropped down in an overstuffed chair sitting in front of Thornton's desk and smiled. "You, my friend, are truly something else. As always, you're one step ahead of the game."

Thornton liked having Bazile around. He knew a lot of influential people and he was easy to manipulate. "By stating publicly that he is covering up the truth with lies, we can continue with the impeachment, and as each day goes by, we add more fuel to the fire."

"Make up new stories to keep the public angry and the President under the bus, so to speak. Like a giant bombing raid on a defenseless city," Bazile said, beginning to see the genius of Thornton's plan.

"If we spread enough rumors, right or wrong, after a while even his faithful followers will begin to have doubts, and from there, it's all downhill for him. He'll be so busy trying to keep up with defending himself he won't be able to stop us," Thornton said with a great deal of confidence.

Chapter 9

GENERAL MOLLER

Liam's only chance at keeping the ship from being blown to pieces was to fire at each of the enemy's laser shots and intercept them, which is what he did.

As each laser light rushed toward the orb, Liam swung the barrel of his weapon in that direction and fired. His shot collided with the incoming laser beam and the explosion was so large it caused the orb to be knocked around, but never hit.

Because of the number of shots coming from the enemy ship, one explosion seemed to overlap into the previous explosion, forming one enormous explosion that tossed the orb around like a single seed in a gourd being shaken by an angry monkey. It was all Liam could do to stay in his seat and keep firing at the oncoming beams of destruction, hoping and praying he didn't miss one.

Then it happened, the pilot of the enemy ship was so intent on firing at the orb and not expecting what Liam was doing that when the explosions began, he was too late to pull up and wound up flying directly into the exploding beams instead of the orb. In less than a heartbeat, his ship was disintegrated into nothing but dust and, in the blink of an eye, the fight was over.

Once the explosions ended and the sky was once again clear, the orb settled back down. Before lowering the shields, the pilot checked to make sure no more enemy ships were anywhere in sight.

Emmelor took Liam by the shoulders and said, "You are truly, the one. I was right to choose you. You've saved us!"

Liam appreciated the latitude but said, "Thank you, but most of it was nothing more than plain ole Irish luck - with a big bunch of your technology thrown in."

"Even as that may be," Emmelor said, "it was you pulling the trigger. Now that we're safe again, I'm buying you a drink. Whatever your tastebuds crave."

Several hundred thousand miles away, on the planet, X-162 where the orb was headed, General Moller paced the floor of the communications room on the Island of Morupeia, that had been the headquarters for Emmelor and his fellow leaders before his takeover. The island and the planet were now in the hands of General Moller.

At the desk of one of his soldiers he asked, "Any word, yet?"

Lieutenant Akees looked at the computer screen for the hundredth time and said, "Nothing yet, Sir."

General Moller walked over to another desk in front of a large wall screen and spoke to the sergeant sitting at the computer. "Sergeant Tolls, what does the surrounding area look like?"

The sergeant touched some keys and turned some dials – fine tuning the picture. What they saw was peace and tranquility – nothing that indicated a small war had just been fought.

"How far out can we see?" the general asked.

Sergeant Tolls looked at the corner of the screen and said, "What we're seeing only goes out about a hundred and fifty thousand miles."

"Can we see farther?" the general asked.

"Sorry, Sir. But when we took the island, the long-range camera was knocked out by one of our fighter modules."

General Moller looked back at the screen, trying to see something in the far distance to give him a clue as to what was happening. Three of his fighter modules had been on their way back from their mother planet, X-165 when they reported seeing an orb from X-162 headed toward its home planet. It had to be Emmelor. To the best of his knowledge, he'd destroyed or grounded all of planet-162's orbs.

He'd ordered the ship destroyed, and that was the last he'd heard from any of the fighter modules.

The general continued to study the picture on the screen, hoping to see his three fighters come into range, but after what seemed an eternity, there was nothing.

By the standards on planet X-162, General Moller was a feared and powerful warrior. When he walked into the assembly room on the Island of Morupeia, there was an audible gasp. At six feet six inches tall, and weighing two-hundred and sixty pounds, he was a giant on a planet where the average height was five-feet-five inches and around a hundred and twenty pounds.

When the general found out what Emmelor was up to, searching beyond their universe for a warrior, he made a decision that would change everything.

For all purposes, General Moller had taken the planet X-162, without much fuss. They had been expecting to fight the war according to the rules – two men in an area on the neutral planet of Zelenos – a small island in the middle Zellernos's huge ocean. So, when the war modules filled the sky and soldiers from the planet X-165 swarmed down and began bombing cities, along with bombing strategic points, the people were not prepared and gave up easily.

General Moller wanted X-162 under his control for several reasons. First and foremost, they were on the same orbit around their sun, so the climates were identical. Second and a primary reason – planet X-162 was rich with ores and an abundance of products to sell. Their technology was somewhat beyond that of planet X-165 and would be useful.

General Moller cared nothing about rules and had only agreed to them to bide his time until he could storm the planet and take control. Except for Emmelor and his bunch, it had been a complete takeover.

That had been, according to Earth's time, thirty-two days ago. Now, he stood with a bottle of Jala in his hand, drinking straight from the bottle, wondering if his three fighter modules had been successful. Surely, they had, he thought. Emmelor would not be expecting to do combat, so they should have been easy prey. Where were his fighters?

-

Emmelor, Lucita and Liam were seated at the bar, talking and enjoying their drinks when a young man in his twenties came in and stopped next to Emmelor. "Sir?"

"Speak up, young man. There are no secrets here," Emmelor told him.

The young man handed Emmelor a small electronic pad, and said, "I hate to disturb you, Sir, but this was taken a few minutes ago by our long-range camera. I thought you needed to see it right away."

He stepped back and waited for Emmelor to study the picture.

Liam watched Emmelor's face go from happy to grim.

Emmelor handed the picture to Lucita, who looked at it and exclaimed, "Damn!"

"What's wrong?" Liam asked.

Emmelor pointed at the picture and said, "This is a picture of the island where we are headed but now cannot go. That flag you see, flying from the flagpole, is not our flag. It is the flag of the planet, X-165."

Liam gave a whistle and said, "Somebody is definitely not playing by the rules."

"That is an understatement," Emmelor said with a sigh. "It's just like General Moller to wait until I was gone to pull something like this."

With a trembling in her voice, Lucita asked, "Do you think he has taken the planet?"

"That, my dear, is exactly what he did. He broke all the rules made by the Council of Battles and invaded our planet, catching them unprepared."

There was a moment of silence before Emmelor continued. "It all makes sense, now. Those fighter modules were not an accidental happening. They were sent by the general to intercept us and destroy us, making his takeover complete."

"But he didn't know about Liam," Lucita said, touching Liam's arm.

"No. Lucky for us," Emmelor said.

"So, what do we do now?" Liam asked.

"I have a hide-a-way, deep in the jungle on the southern hemisphere of our planet. If we can get there, undetected, we can make plans to get our planet back."

Chapter 10

MISSING PEOPLE PROBLEM

Sterling Collier did not get to where he was by being stupid or easily frightened. He was at heart a lawyer and a fighter. The only thing Thornton's trumped-up charges did was to allow him to see the man's true colors. Ultimately, Thornton wanted his job. It was the only thing that made sense. He wanted to be the President.

It was six o'clock in the morning and Sterling hadn't slept all night. He wasn't about to let Thornton get away with this and had been thinking of a plan. Sterling was headed to the kitchen to talk his idea over with his friend, Archie, when one of the cleaning women approached him and said, "Mister President, Sir?"

Sterling Collier was not one of those Presidents who held himself aloof. He was a man of the people and often walked down the sidewalk, talking to this person or that. "Yes, what is it, Karla?" he asked, reading her nametag.

"Have you looked out the window this morning?" she asked.

His senses went immediately on alert, and he said, "No, what's going on outside?"

"Maybe it would be best if you looked out for yourself, Sir," Karla responded.

Sterling made a quick detour and headed for the closest window. He pulled back the curtain and looked out - at first, not seeing anything out of order. Then it hit him. The sky was empty. The orbs that had been hovering above were gone!

He reached for his phone and called Liam's number, hoping they had returned him, but the phone went straight to voicemail.

Sterling turned and hurried down to the communication room and when they all stood up and came to attention when he entered the room, he waved them down and asked, "Did they leave any communication before they left?"

"Before who left?" Colonel Michaels asked.

"You don't know?" Sterling asked.

"Know what? Sir," Colonel Michaels asked, shrugging his shoulders.

"They're gone. The alien ships are gone. The sky is clear and bright" Sterling said.

Being several floors below ground level, there were no windows in the communication room.

A young lieutenant in her mid-twenties stood up and said, "Sir. I came to work no more than half an hour ago, and they were still there when I entered the building."

Sterling looked at her and said, "Thank you. I guess they must have just left because I can assure you, they are gone now."

He looked at Colonel Michaels and said, "Keep the communications open for…"

Computer screens began lighting up and phones began ringing.

Sterling sighed and said, "I guess the whole world knows."

Not wanting to face the astronomical amount of phone calls, Sterling went to the kitchen to eat his breakfast and talk to Archie about the situation. "So, now that the aliens are gone, we have another day of reprieve. I wonder what Thornton Howell is thinking right now?"

"I'd like to be a fly on his wall," Archie said with a grin.

-

Indeed, Thornton Howell was awake and fuming over this new situation as he looked at the newspapers spread across his dining room table. The front pages were covered with the news of the aliens suddenly leaving. His article about the President being a liar and covering up his involvement with the aliens had been moved to page five in some of the papers and even as far back as pages seven and eight in others.

"Calm down," he told himself. "This is just a minor setback. You are still in charge and Sterling Collier will still be impeached." He threw the paper down on the bed and headed for a long, hot shower.

Somewhere along the curbs, men selling newspapers were calling out, "Read all about it!"

Within five minutes of entering the Oval Office, both his cell phone and his house phone began ringing at the same time.

By noon, Sterling had spoken to more than fifty heads of state from around the world, and they all had the same complaint. They were missing well known men – mostly athletes or men of great military importance – like Captains of their Special Forces and such.

Sterling assured them that the United States also had men missing. He had just hung up from a long conversation with the leader of Russia, who insisted the men had been taken by the aliens to be brainwashed and would be sent back to destroy the world.

Unsuccessfully, Sterling tried to convince him that was not what was going on but the Russian screamed at him and hung up on him.

He looked at his watch and decided to go down to the kitchen for lunch but before he could leave the Oval Office, his secretary, Irene Harper, told him there were fifteen congressmen and eight senators sitting in the waiting room, wanting to see him.

Sterling thought for only a moment and said, "Send them to the dining room, then call Archie and have him prepare sandwiches and whatever it is he has to drink – coffee, tea… whatever."

"Good plan," Irene said, realizing what he was up to. As she turned to go, she ran into the Vice President, Jules Pepperdine, as he walked into the Oval Office.

"Excuse me!" he said, grabbing her by the shoulders so she wouldn't fall down.

"I'm fine," Irene said, excusing herself and hurrying out of the office. She didn't care much for the vice President. He always ogled her and at one point had tried to put his hands on her, where they didn't belong.

"What are you going to do about all of this?" the vice President shouted. "Aliens coming and going. Thornton Howell filing an impeachment against you. The polls are going crazy. How can you stand there all cool, calm and collected?"

Sterling was anything but cool or calm. But running around like a firecracker had just gone off in his pants pocket was not the answer. "Have you had lunch?" he asked his vice President, guiding him toward the door.

"Lunch? How can you think about eating at a time like this?" Jules asked, his eyes wide like a scared child.

"Because I'm hungry," Sterling told him as he ushered him into the private elevator that would take them down to the dining room.

The men in the dining room stood up when Sterling and Jules entered but Sterling waved them down. "Sit down. Sit down. You're making my vice President nervous."

There were several chuckles as they sat down. Men and women in white attire were already serving coffee and tea. There would be no alcohol at this meeting.

Once he was seated, he took a sip of his iced, sweet tea, then looked down the table and said, "I know why you're here and I think I can pretty much guess what your questions are. So, with that in mind, let me cover that ground and when I'm finished, if there are still questions, I will deal with them, one at a time."

Just then, the waiters came in with trays of sandwiches. There were ham and cheese sandwiches, deviled egg sandwiches, roast beef sandwiches, corned beef sandwiches and bacon, lettuce, and tomato sandwiches, along with potato salad, chips of various kinds, celery sticks, carrot sticks and several kinds of dips.

"Eat up," Sterling told them. "I'm starving and I can talk while we eat."

During their luncheon, Sterling tried his best to put their minds to rest about an upcoming impeachment. "He's just blowing smoke and doesn't have a shred of evidence to substantiate his claims."

"But what about public opinion?" the senator from California asked.

Knowing that calls from certain influential civilians could sway a representatives or congressman's vote, Sterling said, "I will be making a public address to the people, which I hope will defuse any and all false accusations Thornton and his team puts out."

The discussion switched to the disappearance of the alien ships and the claims that certain athletes and men with military training from around the world had gone missing.

"Do you think the aliens took them? And if they did, for what purpose?" the congressman from Montana, asked.

Sterling was trying to come up with an answer when his secretary came into the room and leaned down next to his ear and whispered something. The men around the table sat, waiting to hear if it was something important.

When she'd gone, Sterling looked down the table and said, "To answer your question, Congressman, No, they were not taken by the aliens to some far-off planet to be brain- washed. As of a few minutes ago, those men were found, walking down the streets of their various towns and cities."

Immediately, this information created more questions. "Do you think they were taken to those ships and brainwashed, then returned?" Several of the men said all at once.

Sterling waited for the questions to calm down before saying, "Gentlemen. To the best of my knowledge, each and every man is being picked up and taken to a hospital where they will not only get checked over, but also studied by military psychiatrists."

"Does that include, Liam Biggers?" one of the men asked.

"I can't answer that until someone calls me or I have time to make inquiries of my own," Sterling said.

As other questions came down the table at him, Sterling stood up and said, "I've told you everything I know at this time. Thank you for coming today, but now, I have a great many things to attend to."

And with that, he left the room.

In the hallway, he saw Irene Harper waiting for him. "Any word about Liam?" he asked.

"I'm afraid not, Sir. He seems to be the only one not accounted for," Irene told him.

"Well... keep me posted," he said as he headed for his office.

-

Thornton Howell's phone rang. He looked at the caller ID and shook his head. He picked up the receiver and heard Rodney Warren's excited voice. "Have you heard?" The missing men have been found. Is that good or bad for us?"

"That depends," Thornton said. "If they are found to be hostile, it bodes well for our cause. If not, we can create the rumor that the aliens conditioned them to react as they did, so as to not reveal their true intentions. So, I guess you could say it will work in our favor whichever way it turns out. Now, leave me alone for a while. I have planning to do."

"But…" Rodney said to the sound of Thornton hanging up.

Chapter 11

A NEW GENERAL IS BORN

Emmelor walked into the navigation room of the ship and spoke to the pilot. "Change our course to a heading of…" He looked at the map on the screen and said, "Change the heading to longitude 70 degrees west and latitude 34 degrees south. When you're done, turn on the cloaking device."

The pilot looked at the map and said, "But, Sir, that will put us right in the middle…"

"I know where it will put us, Captain," Emmelor said, interrupting the pilot. "Just do as I say, or I will do it myself."

"Yes-sir," the pilot said, making the correction to the new course, and then turning on the cloaking device as the giant orb raced toward its new destination.

Emmelor turned and looked at Liam and said, "If he uses the long-range cameras, he won't be able to see us and if he sends out more fighters, hopefully they won't be able to detect us."

"I could, maybe, eliminate them if they show up," Liam said.

Emmelor shook his head. "No. That would let Mellor know we survived his earlier attempt. I want him to think we were destroyed."

"How long before we get to this hiding place of yours?" Liam asked.

Emmelor walked over to the console and studied it for a few seconds, then turned to the pilot and said, "Set the speed to ten thousand miles per hour, and let me know when we are within a thousand miles from our destination."

"Yes-sir," the pilot said as he adjusted the speed dial.

"We should reach our destination sometime tomorrow evening – just after sundown if my calculations are correct," Emmelor said with a sigh. "And hopefully, undetected."

"Knock on wood," Liam said, tapping his head.

"What in the world does that mean?" Lucita asked with a grin.

Liam grinned back at her and said, "It's an old Irish saying that means, good luck."

"What an odd custom. Let's hope it works," Emmelor said.

"You wouldn't happen to have a place where I can take a swim, would you?" Liam asked. "I feel the need to swim a few laps and then take a good, cleansing steam bath."

"We do. Our people love to swim and we also like taking a steam bath." She looked at Emmelor and asked, "May I steal him for an hour or so?"

"Of course," Emmelor said. "And when you're finished, I hope you'll join me for the evening meal. I'd like to introduce Liam to some of our fine dishes."

"Looking forward to it," Liam said as he turned and followed Lucita to a go-cart type of vehicle.

The room she took him to was much larger than he'd expected. There were two pools – one was quite large and filled with people splashing around, while the second one was long and narrow – a lap pool. Lucita pointed to a room where he found lockers and a table where swimming trunks were stacked.

After selecting a pair, he dawned them and went back to the pool area. Lucita was standing next to the lap pool, dressed in a two-piece bathing suit and Liam whistled. She looked stunning.

Lucita blushed and said, "Thank you. If you don't mind, I would like to swim laps with you."

"Sure. I would like that," Liam said, noticing everyone in the room had stopped what they were doing and were staring at him. "Why are they staring at me?" he asked in a hushed tone.

"The men are envious of your height and the women are enthralled with your muscular build."

It was Liam's turn to blush as he waded into the pool and began his routine of swimming laps, with Lucita swimming along beside him. She was a strong swimmer, which surprised Liam and when they had completed twenty laps, she was still right next to him.

"That felt really good," she said when they stepped out of the pool and headed for the showers.

The evening meal was a seafood platter of at least six different kinds of fish that Liam had never heard of, but mentally associated them with fish on Earth. "These taste and look like what we call trout back on Earth," Liam told them as he spooned a different kind of fish onto his platter. "And this tastes like catfish."

"I'm sure there are many similarities between your planet and ours. In fact," Emmelor said, "when I studied your planet, Earth, I was astonished with the number of similarities. It's like we are sister planets, except for the fact that you're a millennium of years behind us in technology and ways of thinking. Although, we too still have many primitive people on our planet that live in the jungles like their forefathers. I doubt they'll ever change."

"And thank goodness they are, or we wouldn't have a warrior like Liam to save our planet for us," Lucita said with a broad smile.

When the meal was over, Emmelor stood up and said, "We'd all best get some rest. We have a big day tomorrow."

He looked at Liam and said, "Try and be on the bridge no later than 0-seven hundred hours in the morning. There will be much for you to see and learn.

Mellor stood looking at the monitor, gritting his teeth. "Where are they?" he asked no one in particular.

One of the technicians stood up and said, "Sir. If they are out there, they haven't yet come within the reach of our telescopes. We have telescopes looking in every direction and overlapping each other. They cannot get within our hemisphere without us seeing them."

Disgruntled that Emmelor's ship, if it was still active, hadn't been detected yet. "Very well. But I want to know as soon as they come within our detection!" he said as he headed for his quarters for some much-needed rest. He would need his wits about him when and if they were detected.

At 06:45, Lucita and Liam stepped onto the bridge and found Emmelor already there, giving the pilot new coordinates. When he saw them enter the bridge, he walked over to Liam and said, "Come and look at my world, the one we will be on in a short while. At least, I hope we will"

Liam walked over and looked through the viewing panel and was amazed at the number of planets he could see.

"There, the one straight ahead," Emmelor told him, pointing at a planet that looked almost exactly like Earth – the oceans and land masses were so similar he could almost believe they were back on his planet.

"Your planet looks like a twin sister to Earth," Liam said, in awe.

"That was my reaction, too, when we saw your planet," Emmelor said.

"We're coming in range in ten minutes," the captain said. "What are your orders?"

Emmelor looked at Liam and said, "Now comes the tricky part – sneaking back onto the planet without Mellor detecting us."

And just how do we go about that?" Liam asked.

"Something new I invented and installed on the ship before we left. I just hope it works," Emmelor said.

He turned to the pilot and said, "On my command, go to the new heading, keeping us invisible, then throw up the fire ring over the outer exterior to make us look like a meteor entering the atmosphere, with as long a trail of fire as you can make."

"Aye, aye, Sir," came the reply as the captain and other technicians hovered over their controls.

Emmelor looked at one of the panels for some time, then yelled, "Now!"

All exterior windows were covered and the lights inside the orb were adjusted as the now, fire covered orb raced forward breaking from outer space into X-162's atmosphere.

-

"Sir," a sergeant said from Mellor's doorway.

Mellor sat up, instantly awake. "Have we spotted him?"

"I don't know, Sir. I was just instructed to bring you to the communications room, Sir."

Mellor hadn't undressed when he laid down, wanting to be ready at a moment's notice. When he rushed into the communications room, he saw something on the view screen and asked, "Is that him?"

The man stood up and said, "I don't think so, Sir. When I saw a blip on the screen, I sent the sergeant for you, in the hopes it might be Emmelor, but as it turns out, it's only a meteor entering our air, Sir."

"Are you sure?" Mellor asked.

"See for yourself, Sir," the man told him as he enlarged the image.

Mellor studied the image, and it did look like a meteor blazing a path down toward the ocean, but something in his stomach told him something was amiss. Yes, he knew meteors crashed into the planet – and had, off and on for centuries. He didn't know why, but this one didn't feel right. Call it intuition, or whatever, but he needed to be sure.

"Track it and have spy units fly over the crash site. I want to make sure it is what it appears to be, and nothing else." he told the lieutenant sitting next to him.

"I'll be in the officers dining room. Keep me posted," Mellor said, turning and leaving the room.

-

Everyone on the bridge of Emmelor's orb was strapped into special built chairs to absorb the shock of crashing into the ocean. But even with the special chairs, Liam felt the shock as the straps strained to keep him in his seat. Liam felt the orb bump against the ocean floor as the straps loosened and he was able to stand up.

Emmelor was already standing next to the captain, and both were looking at a panel of gauges. As Liam and Lucita approached, Emmelor turned his head and said, "We're sitting on the ocean floor at a depth of twelve thousand feet, but we won't be here long."

Emmelor nodded to the captain, who began pressing buttons.

"We'll be rising to ten thousand feet, then moving out of the area. If I know Mellor, and I believe I do, he will be sending spy units to search the area. Spy units can see up to twenty thousand feet beneath the surface of the water."

"So, what happens when he sees nothing. Won't he wonder about that?" Liam asked.

"More than likely. I know I would. That is why, as we speak, the technicians are creating what we hope will look like the remains of a burned-out meteor," Emmelor said, pointing at the now open window.

Liam walked over and stared at the ocean floor. He shook his head as he looked at what appeared to be smoldering rocks, which indeed could be the remains of a burned-out meteor. "You think of everything, don't you?" Liam said, coming back to stand next to Emmelor.

"I try, my young friend. I try," Emmelor said with just a hint of modesty.

Just then, the orb began moving along under water like a giant, round, submarine.

"It appears you anticipated all of this and created a false trail for this Mellor fella to follow while we sneak away, Liam said with a hint of amusement in his voice.

"We have never trusted Mellor," Lucita said. "When he came into power, many years ago, it was by dubious measures. He has never played by the rules and that's why, when Emmelor told me of his plan, we consorted to come up with every possible thing that could come up in our absence. And I have to admit, most of the good ideas came from Emmelor."

"As to where we are going?" Emmelor said, "it's to that secret hide-away I mentioned earlier.

Chapter 12

NOT FOOLED

When the images of the smoldering rocks were sent back to the communication room, Mellor studied them with great intensity, then turned to one of his officers and said, "I want a team to find out the density of those rocks. I want to know if they came from outer space or not! And I want to know, now!"

It took the better part of five hours before the report came back to the communication room and by then, Mellor was pacing the floor, muttering to himself.

"The reports are in, Sir," a young, lieutenant said, bringing the information to the giant screen.

Mellor sat down at a nearby table and studied the massive screen, grinding his teeth. They were geological reports that he mostly didn't understand. But what he did understand was the typed comment at the bottom of the screen. These rocks did not come from outer space. They were infused with a chemical that made the rocks appear to be smoldering.

"I knew it!" Mellor yelled, causing everyone in the room to hunker down a little farther in their chairs. When Mellor was on a rampage, no one was safe.

"I want a meeting of my staff officers in the situation room in five!" Mellor yelled as he stormed out of the communication room and headed for the lounge. When he returned a few minutes later, with a cup of soothing black liquid in his hand, the long table was filled with high-ranking officers standing behind their chairs. "Be seated," Mellor told them as he took a seat at the end of the table.

In a much calmer voice, Mellor said, "Emmelor has returned…"

He let this information sink in, then continued. "I won't go into the particulars, but trust me, he is back on X-162 and I want him found."

"Do we have any information on his whereabouts?" one of the officers ventured.

"Therein lies the problem," Mellor said, pointing a remote at the wall screen and pressing it.

They were looking at the images of the crash site.

Mellor said, "He entered our atmosphere disguised as a meteor and the picture you see is where he crashed into the ocean. At that point he should have been easy to capture, but when I sent spy units to investigate, he was gone."

"From that part of the ocean, he could have gone in any direction," another officer said.

"Did he surface to travel? If he did, we should be able to spot him easily," a different officer said with confidence.

Mellor stared at the officer and said, "Since I already considered that, I know for sure he did not surface to travel. Which leaves only one conclusion. He's traveling underwater."

"Then how are we to track him?" a different officer asked.

Disgusted with his officer's lack of imagination, Mellor took a sip of the soothing liquid and continued, trying to hold his temper in check. "The ship he is traveling in is very large, and round. With the spy units, we should be able to find him without much trouble."

"Sir," one of the officers said. "Are you suggesting we send out spy units to search all of the oceans on this planet?"

Mellor was feeling somewhat calmer now, and said, "No. I am not suggesting. I am ordering you to do exactly that - and I want spy units scrambling within thirty minutes. Do I make myself clear?"

The officers, as one, leaped to their feet and headed for the door, pressing the communicators attached to the breast of their shirts - shouting orders.

Chapter 13

UNDAUNTED

President Collier was standing in the hallway of the White House, discussing with the delegate from France, the return of their man who had gone missing, then suddenly showed up right where he'd disappeared from. "How could that happen?"

"He is unresponsive as to where he has been," Pierre Boulanger, the French delegate said, shaking his head. When asked, his response is that all he can remember is sitting by himself at an outdoor café in Paris, having lunch, and then, floating in a fog. When the fog lifted, he was sitting in the same chair at the same cafe, only days later. Is that not the strangest thing you've ever heard?"

Not wanting to commit to anything, Sterling said nothing but allowed the delegate to continue his questioning.

"Do you think it possible that he may have somehow been transported to one of those giant spaceships, interrogated, then sent back with his mind blanked of whatever transpired?" Pierre Boulanger asked in a voice that pleaded for agreement.

Seeing the confused look on the man's face, Sterling did the only thing he could do, considering. "If you're asking my opinion, I have to say that is one explanation – and a highly probable one, I might add. "But for what purpose?"

"You have been in contact with them, not I," Pierre said, straightening up a little. "You tell me, why they would do such a thing, if not for information so they can invade us?"

"Yes, I have been in contact with them, and I can assure you, they are not here to invade us." Sterling said for the thousandth time.

"Then why, if not for information on how to take over our planet, what other reason could there be?" Pierre asked indignantly.

Sterling looked around as if he was making sure they were alone, then said, "If I say anything, it has to be in the strictest confidence."

The Frenchman's eyes went wide, and he said, "You have my word, Mister President."

Sterling leaned down and whispered, "They are here for breeding purposes. Their men can no longer produce babies and the men of Earth are larger, stronger copies of the men on their planet. They did what they needed to do, then left. It's that simple. But it must be kept a secret. That was what they asked me to promise."

"And of course, that is why they chose a Frenchman!" Pierre almost shouted. "But why keep it a secret?"

Sterling sighed and said, "If the people of Earth knew they had relatives on another planet they would do everything in their power to go visit them, and I'm sure they would not want us invading their planet looking for their long-lost relatives."

The French delegate shook his head in understanding. "Yes, that would be a problem, wouldn't it? Their secret is safe with me."

Just then, one of Sterling's bodyguards stepped forward and spoke into the President's ear. "You need to go to your office and turn on the television, Sir."

"If you'll excuse me. I have business to attend to," Sterling told Pierre. "It has been a pleasure talking to you, but remember…"

"But, of course," Pierre said. "My lips are sealed."

Back in the Oval Office, the television had already been turned on and Sterling watched as Thornton Howell stepped to the microphone in front of his desk and said, "I come to you today because I believe you need to know the truth."

He stood for a moment to let his words have the effect he wanted.

"And the truth is, Sterling Collier is in league with the aliens to overthrow our planet."

Again, there was a pause for effect.

"I do not know what he has been promised, but rest assured America, it is not in our favor, yours or mine. President Collier is not only a threat, but a traitor to the entire planet and we must get him out of office before he can do more damage than he has already done! Yes, our men have been returned, but with their minds in a fog. They have no memories as to what happened to them. If these beings are here on a friendly venture, then why did they communicate with only Sterling Collier? And why can't our men remember what happened to them? Because they've been brainwashed! That's why! At some point down the road, they will turn on us. What they will do, I do not know, but have no doubt, it will not be good.

"As a person who is afraid for my life and the lives of everyone on this planet, I implore you to stand with me in impeaching Sterling Collier! And, along with impeaching Sterling Collier, he must be locked away as a traitor! I also believe that every man taken by the aliens should be gathered together and put someplace they can be watched. We cannot leave them to run free to do who knows what, that will render us helpless when the aliens return… And return they will, to take over this planet. We must unite and make ready for war!"

Sterling turned the television off, then walked over and sat down in his chair. The man was nuts and on a mission to take over the presidency, no matter the cost.

The Vice President, Jules Pepperdine came bursting into the Oval Office, his eyes wide with terror. "Have you seen the television? Thornton Howell was just…"

"Yes, Jules. I saw him and heard every word he said. So, go over to the bar and have a drink to help calm yourself down."

As Jules took a long pull on his drink, he said, "My God, man, he is openly vying for your job! And turning you into a traitor in the process."

"It does appear to be that way, doesn't it?" Sterling said, trying to keep his temper in check.

"I know you," the Vice President said, shaking his finger at Sterling. "You're not going to let him get away with this. You've got something up your sleeve. I just can't figure out what it is."

'*And you never will,*' Sterling thought to himself. If he said anything, it would be in all the newspapers and on every television news cast within the hour. The man he thought would be a good Vice President had turned into a coward when the chips were down and as leaky as a bucket with holes in it when it came to information.

When the Vice President went to the liquor cabinet for a second drink of rum, which was his drink of choice, the President was tempted to join him, but held back. He had a major crisis to deal with.

Chapter 14

ENEMY INSECTS

The ship was sitting a little over nine thousand feet below the surface of the ocean, tucked under the tip of a large land mass in the southern hemisphere of planet X-162.

On the screen, they watched as spy units flew overhead with long probes from the bottom as they searched everything beneath the surface of the water. They were followed by fighter modules with rockets hanging from their wings.

"And they can't detect us, here?" Liam whispered.

"No. The land mass is too thick for their probes detection to penetrate,"

"Why don't you just contact him and insist on the fight between me and whoever he has on his side?"

"Because, as soon as he finds out where we are, he will attack us with everything he has in his arsenal. And, if my guess is correct, he not only has his military forces here, he is also in control of all our weapons, as well. We wouldn't stand a chance."

When the spy units had passed, Emmelor gave the order to continue on, but keeping a lookout for any enemy ships approaching in the close proximity.

"I don't know about the two of you, but I'm hungry," Emmelor said, rubbing his stomach.

Over lunch, Emmelor explained the rest of the routine. "From here, we'll go around the tip of the continent and up along the coast to the mouth of a large river we call, 'The Belgor'. Just a few miles inside the river, I have a shelter that looks like part of the mountain leading down to the water. We can hide our ship there, and unless he looks very closely at a map of that area, we should be safe."

Emmelor took a bite of his lunch and when he'd swallowed, he continued. "From there, we go to my secret place. It is hidden deep in the jungles of the continent, and large enough to hide everyone, including my crew. We will travel by night, with infrared lights.

By the time they'd finished eating, the ship was already underway, still traveling beneath the surface of the ocean. It was slower going, but it couldn't be helped. They needed as much cover as they could until they reached the shelter area.

It was early morning when Liam felt the ship making a right turn and he got out of bed and went to the bridge. Again, Emmelor was already there. "Do you sleep here?" Liam asked with a chuckle. It was strange. By now, Liam felt very comfortable around both Lucita and Emmelor, even though they were from a completely different solar system.

"It seems like it, lately," Emmelor answered. "We've entered the river," he said, pointing to the screen.

The first thing Liam saw, caused him to take in a breath. On the exterior of the ship, a giant snake of some kind was trying to wrap itself around the ship.

"Watch this," Emmelor said as he leaned over and flipped a switch.

Liam could see the electricity striking the large snake and holding it against the ship until Emmelor again, flipped the switch, turning off the electricity. The snake, stunned, shook itself and finally swam away, disappearing into the darkness of the river.

"That's the biggest snake I've ever seen," Liam said, shaking his head.

"Yes, the Loso snake does get quite large." Emmelor said as Lucita came strolling in.

She looked at Liam and said, "You look pale. Are you all right?"

"He just saw his first Loso," Emmelor said with a grin.

"What happens if you're out on the river and one of them shows up?" Liam asked, wanting to know all there was to know about a snake that size.

Lucita looked down at her feet and said, "If it doesn't beat you to death with its tail, it will probably eat you, then throw you up because Loso snakes don't like the taste of humans."

"Oh great. By then you're nothing more than chunks of bait for whatever other flesh eaters there are in the river," Liam said with a groan.

Lucita grinned and said, "Or we could hope that one of our primitive native tribes sees us and comes and kills the snake… Yes, just like you, with all our technology, we still have people who live like wild animals. And yes, they eat the snake."

"Our river craft can stab them with jolts of electricity. We've never lost anyone yet,"

"There's always a first time," Liam mumbled to himself.

"What was that?" Lucita asked.

Thinking quickly, Liam said, "I said, always a good time."

Once the ship was hidden inside what looked to be part of the mountain, Emmelor came over to Liam and Lucita and said, "Best get some rest, we'll be pulling out in about five hours and it's a good six or seven hours to where I hope we'll be safe.

Lucita came to pick up Liam and by the time they got to the hatch where they would board the smaller watercraft, called a Dhoni, which was a lot like a small ferry back on Earth. There was already a long line of people.

"We'll ride in the lead Dhoni with Emmelor," she told him as she guided him to the front of the line.

"Welcome aboard," Emmelor told them when they stepped aboard.

"Thank you," Liam said, looking around. It looked to be around twenty-six feet long and twelve feet wide and could easily hold forty people. The interior was sparsely furnished with very few amenities. This craft was meant for short trips, only.

When the Dhonis were loaded and the orb locked up tight, they put covers over the top to make it look like one of the giant Loso snakes.

There was a half-moon of one of the moons, a three-quarter moon on the middle one and the closest one to them was full and bright.

They hadn't gone more than two miles up the river when the man running the lead Dhoni said, "Incoming spy craft."

"Hang on," Emmelor yelled!

A cover of some kind slid down to enclose the Dhoni, as did every Dhoni behind them. Liam felt the one he was on, begin to dive beneath the water, followed by the others.

"Another safety measure," Lucita said, touching Liam on his arm.

The phony snake had barely gotten under the water when there was an explosion which caused the Dhonis to rock, violently. Then came another explosion, followed by a third one. The entire line of Dhonis were rocking back and forth so hard it was all anyone could do to keep from being thrown to the floor.

Then, as quickly as it began, it ended. Emmelor was on his communicator, asking, "Anyone hurt? Any damages?"

Each pilot responded with such things as, "All clear, number two." "No injuries, no damage, Dhoni three." And so, on down the line until all the pilots had cleared.

Emmelor released the button on his communicator and gave a sigh. "I can't believe it. Those idiots were trying to kill a snake instead of tending to their business."

He sat down on one of the empty seats and said, "That was the one thing I didn't think about. We got lucky."

"How much longer until we turn off into one of those tributaries you talked about?" Liam asked

Emmelor looked at the pilot, who looked at a map on a screen just above the control switches and said, "Forty to forty-five minutes."

Emmelor patted him on the shoulder and said, "Without causing any problems, take us to the fastest speed possible. We don't want another episode like we just had."

Liam felt the increase in speed and when they came back to the surface and opened the shields, he could see the dark outline of the jungle on both sides of the Dhoni.

Thirty-six minutes later, the snake-like chain of Dhonis turned off the river and entered a small tributary. The jungle was so thick it was like traveling down a long, dark tunnel. There was no moon or sky to be seen.

A short time later, when they turned off into another tributary, Liam nudged Lucita and asked, "How does the pilot know where to go in all of this?"

Lucita giggled and said, "He's not actually running the Dhoni. It is set to coordinates that the computer follows. Only those primitive people I told you about know their way around in this."

Before Liam could ask any more questions, they heard a loud buzzing as a swarm of biting insects swarmed the interior of the Dhoni.

The pilot flipped a switch and fans began blowing the insects back out into the jungle with a repellent that killed them. Then the shields once more sealed them from anything outside.

Even so, Liam felt several bites on his neck and when he touched them, his fingers came away bloody. "Little suckers are vampires," he said, wiping the blood on his pants leg.

"Let me see that," Lucita said with a worried look on her face.

"It's just a couple of…." Liam said before the world turned black.

After several more turns, going deeper into the jungle, and close to an hour later, the Dhoni began to slow down.

Lucita walked up and looked through the windshield and muttered, "Come on, come on."

Emmelor also had a worried look on his face. The biting insects carried several kinds of disease that could be fatal to people not immune to the bites or had the shot to make them immune. Most of the natives were born with the immunity but not all, and many of them died at a young age.

"We've given him the shot, and that's all we can do," Emmelor told a sad looking Lucita.

"But we don't know what a human's reaction will be. Maybe the bites have already taken over his body. Or, what if his body rejects the shot? We've never been in a situation like this before. And my healing powers are no good against the bites."

"I don't like it any more than you do, but there's nothing more we can do," Emmelor told her.

"We're here," the captain of the Dhoni said, as the jungle began to open up. And, as the last Dhoni entered the jungle, it closed behind them.

Chapter 15

PRESIDENTAL PROBLEMS

The newscaster stared at the teleprompter and read the words on the screen. "Speaker of the House of Representatives, Thornton Howell, has, as of just an hour ago, filed papers of impeachment against standing President, Sterling Collier, charging him with collaboration with aliens to overthrow our world and treason against the people of this planet. So far, there has been no word from the White House or the President."

President Collier pressed the button on the remote and watched as the screen went black. The President's chief advisor, Daniel Glazer, along with the White House chef, Archie Brooks, sat in silence until the President asked, "So, gentlemen, what am I supposed to do? Do I fight, or just wait this thing out? The man has nothing to go on but his own, twisted accusations against me."

Daniel Glazer had been in politics for nearly two-thirds of his life, and he thought he'd seen it all, but collusion with aliens to overthrow the planet? That was far out in left field as far as he was concerned.

"The man can't have even the slightest piece of evidence. He's blowing smoke and it's hard to believe the senators, congress and other representatives could fall for his line of hogwash. And as far as the people go – Sterling, you're the most popular President since... since Reagan."

"Tell a lie over and over enough times and little by little, the lie becomes the truth in people's minds," Archie said, nodding his head. "It's sad, but nonetheless, it's true."

The President swiveled around in his chair and stared out through the French doors where the sky no longer held the giant orbs. "Thank you, Emmelor. Without you, I wouldn't be in this mess," he whispered to himself.

It was Archie who interrupted the President's thoughts. "You were in contact with the alien, right?"

Sterling swiveled back around and looked at his friend, wondering where this was going? "Yes, he came to this office in the form of a hologram, and we spoke. What about it?"

"Before breaking off the conversation, did he happen to tell you how to reach him if you needed to?"

Sterling thought for a moment, then said, "Yes, but they were still here, hovering up there in the sky. Since they've gone to who knows where, I don't know if a signal will reach them and if it does, how long it would take."

"But it can't hurt to try," Archie said with a grin.

"What are you getting at?" Sterling asked, his interest piqued.

"Yes, how can sending a signal to the aliens possibly help our situation?" Daniel Glazer asked, sitting up straighter in his chair.

"If they are friendly as Sterling said, and I believe they are – if they're not too far away, maybe they could come back and explain everything in front of the national news broadcasters. That would solve everything."

Daniel looked at Sterling, who shrugged his shoulders and said, "Can't hurt to try."

Chapter 16

AN OLD LAW

Liam was standing stark naked in a pool of stagnant water that was swirling around and around, trying to pull him down. The upper part of his body was covered with biting insects and he was trying to fight them off, but they kept stinging him and blood was streaming from a hundred different places. "No!" he yelled as he tried to fight them off.

Emmelor, Lucita and the doctor were standing next to the bed Liam was lying on and thrashing around like he was fighting something.

"Can't you do something, doctor?" Lucita pleaded. Even though she was a healer, there were things she couldn't cure and times when a doctor was needed.

"I'm not sure what to do. He's not from this planet, although all the tests show that we are compatible in every way. I've given him a second dose of the serum. Now, it's up to him. He is a healthy specimen if ever I saw one. We have none on this planet like him."

Lucita stepped closer to Liam's thrashing body and took his left hand, then said, "Liam, this is Lucita; We need you to come back to us. We need you…" And with that, she tugged on his hand.

In his delirium, Liam felt someone take his hand and tug on it. He could also hear a voice talking to him, but it was too far away to understand what they were saying. But it sounded like Lucita's voice, and he reacted to that by stepping out of the swirling pool and stood on dry ground. He swatted at the insects, and they disappeared. He opened his eyes and saw the smiling face of Lucita staring back at him. "Hello," she said. "Welcome back to the world of the living."

"Did I die?" Liam asked.

Emmelor stepped up to the opposite side of the bed and said, "No, but you gave us a scare. You had a very bad reaction from those insect bites. For just a while there, we thought we might lose you."

"I heard Lucita's voice. I couldn't understand what she was saying, but figured I should go see what she wanted," Liam said with a sheepish grin which got a squeeze on his hand.

The doctor stepped in and began checking Liam's vitals, and when he finished, he looked at Emmelor and Lucita, shaking his head. "It's like he's never been bitten. The numbers are perfect."

Both Emmelor and Lucita had broad smiles on their faces when Lucita said, "Did you hear that? You're completely well."

Liam's body and sheets were completely wet with perspiration from where he had been struggling to get out of his dream state. He swung his legs over the side of the bed and sat up. "Other than sweating like I've just run twenty miles in one-hundred-and-ten-degree weather, I feel fine. Is there somewhere I can take a shower and get into some dry clothes?"

After a good shower and getting into clean clothes, Emmelor and Lucita gave Liam a tour of the secret hiding place.

"The place is two miles square and took me nine years to build. Everything had to be done hush, hush."

Liam whistled. The place had everything, dwellings, a warehouse store, medical facilities, science labs, a school, and much more. "Wow. This place has everything," Liam said. "What gave you the idea to build such a place?"

Emmelor studied the ceiling for a moment, then said, "For some years now, several of the planets have been trying to break away from the coalition and form their own group, which would have been all right, except for the man who was behind it all."

Liam nodded his head and said, "Let me venture a guess. The man who has taken over your planet. That Mellor, guy."

"Yes," Lucita chimed in. "He is a very evil man who thinks nothing of murdering people to get what he wants, and everyone is afraid of him. And because of that fear, he has an army of well over half a million soldiers."

Liam gave a long whistle this time and asked, "What if we take him out of the equation?"

"Then I think his armies would collapse. They only do his bidding because they are afraid of him," Emmelor said with a hint of confidence.

Liam shook his head and asked, "What is this guy? Is he ten feet tall and five hundred pounds? Does he have magic powers? Does he shoot bullets from his fingers? What?"

"No, nothing like that," Emmelor said. "He has a certain following. Men who do his bidding for certain rewards, like money and protection from prosecution... Anyone who disobeys his orders, find themselves dead, with their body parts scattered around in public places for the people to see – along with posters that read – THIS COULD BE YOU, along with other threatening sayings."

Liam got the message, loud and clear. "There has to be some way to take this dude down. He can't be that well protected. He does go out in public, doesn't he?"

"Oh yes, he goes out in public, Emmelor said. "It's almost like he's daring someone to try and kill him. But the few who have tried were publicly dismembered and Mellor shouting, "Who's next to try and kill me? Step forward if you dare!"

"Of course, at this point, no one does," Lucita said.

"Well, there has to be a way, somehow. We just need to find it," Liam said. "Is there any chance he will abide by this, two warriors battling it out thing?"

Suddenly, Emmelor's eyes lit up and he said, "No. As soon as he eliminates me, he will be in complete control, but thank you, my boy, you just may have come up with the answer we've been searching for."

Liam looked at Lucita, who shrugged her shoulders, then he looked at Emmelor and said, "I did?"

"Maybe. Just maybe," Emmelor told him. "You two go along and continue your tour of our little hideout. I will meet you in the dining area for our evening meal, and hopefully I will have news. I need some time to do a little research."

And with that, Emmelor strode off, leaving Liam and Lucita to stare after him, wondering what he was up to.

Chapter 17

MELLOR'S RAGE

Mellor paced back and forth in front of the pilots he'd sent out to find Emmelor and his ship. He stopped in front of one of the pilots and leaned in close to him and said, "I believe I told you to find that ship, didn't I?"

The young pilot swallowed and said, "Yes-sir, but..." His eyes went wide as he felt the sharp pain of a knife entering his stomach. As he dropped to the floor, he heard Mellor say, "But you didn't do as you were told, did you?"

Mellor looked down at the dead man lying on the floor, then turned to the next pilot in the line and asked, "What about you? Did you find the ship you were sent to find?"

As one, the entire group of pilots began to step backwards as Mellor yelled, "Not even one of you could complete a simple request! You're all failures! All of you! And I will not abide failure!"

As the group of pilots turned to run down the hallway, they came face to face with a group of Mellor's enforcers. They had weapons in their hands and when one of them looked in Mellor's direction, he nodded his head, then turned and walked away, to the sound of the weapons being discharged.

At the end of the hallway, he turned and yelled, "I want the rest of the pilots assembled in hangar number six, in two hours."

After a thorough rubdown by a beautiful young woman, then bathed by three very pretty young ladies, he was ready to face the pilots.

When he entered the vehicle that looked a lot like an armored tank, he told the driver "hangar six," then sat down in the back seat, next to his right-hand man, Wolfen, and asked, "Will I ever find a pilot who can do my bidding or will I have to kill them all, then go do the job, myself?"

Wolfen thought about his answer. He had not become Mellor's right-hand man by giving the wrong answers. "My Lord, I seriously doubt that other than myself, you're going to find anyone who sees the whole picture as you see it and has the desire to see it come to fruition. If I knew how to fly, I would be the first to volunteer, because I know how much finding Emmelor and his group means to you."

Mellor glanced at Wolfen, then turned his head and looked out of the window. The man would say whatever it took to stay in his good graces. He was a nobody – but a nobody who would do his beckoning without once questioning why he was asked to do it. "I'm sure you would, my friend. I'm sure you would."

The hangar was just up ahead, and Mellor felt a tension begin to engulf his body. Would he actually kill all of his pilots? He thought not. He needed them for combat. It was just that sometimes he got so enraged when his orders weren't followed as he instructed.

When his armored vehicle pulled to a stop in front of the hangar, twenty, armed soldiers ran out and formed two lines, allowing Mellor to walk into the hangar, safely between them, with Wolfen tagging along behind him like a loyal dog.

As he approached the large crowd of pilots, he could see the fear in their eyes - a condition he had promoted from day one. Fear was what kept him in power. The only person he knew of who was not afraid of him was Emmelor.

He stopped in front of the pilots and looked at them, wondering if it was their fault that they couldn't find Emmelor or his ship. After all, they had the best equipped spy units in the universe.

Suddenly, it came to him. It was Emmelor! He had somehow devised a superior cloaking device! That had to be it! Maybe he found it on one of the planets he'd visited.

Was his ship sitting somewhere right out in the open, hidden by this new cloaking device? Was it so sophisticated that even radar couldn't penetrate it?

These questions brought up new problems. If the cloaking device is that good, how do I go about finding him? What other way was there?

The pilots were surprised when Mellor spoke to them in a normal tone of voice, instead of his, screaming, threatening, tone.

"Gentlemen, I brought you here today because I need your help."

There was an audible gasp that didn't go unnoticed by Mellor. "We have an enemy among us that needs to be found. He is out there, hiding in plain sight – under a strong cloaking device. This device is so strong, even our radar cannot penetrate it. But we need to find this ship and the man who controls it. He is an enemy to the state and if we are to control this planet, he needs to be found and destroyed."

One of the pilots took a step forward and waited to be recognized.

"You have something to say, Captain?" Mellor asked, surprised at the man to have enough gumption to speak up – but glad that he had. Maybe this new technique would work out better than screaming threats at them.

"Sir, first, we tried the old-style radar, which accomplished nothing. Next, we tried lidar, which you know is better, but again, it failed to get results because of prevailing weather and the possibility that they are sitting on the bottom of the ocean. What I'm proposing is, old style aircraft, equipped with pulsar. If they are in fact, resting on the bottom of the ocean, or traveling under water, pulsar will find them."

"Are our spy units rigged with this, pulsar?" Mellor asked.

The captain, feeling a little better, said, "No – Sir, and I don't believe they can be – nor our fighters. Even at low speed, they would be moving too fast for pulsar to be effective. I believe they should be smaller, low speed old style airplanes, like the ones owned by civilians. Once they find the ship, they could radio the coordinates to our fighters who could swoop down on them and destroy them, Sir. We don't necessarily need to see them. We just need to know where to drop our explosives."

Mellor stared at the man for what seemed to be a long time, then he asked, "What is your name, Captain?"

"Airibus, Sir. Captain Airibus, Sir."

Mellor walked down and stopped in front of the captain and said, "You are now, General Airibus. And you are in charge of this operation. You have my authority to get the aircraft you need by whatever means you feel it necessary. Then arm them with this pulsar - then find Emmelor and his ship and destroy them!"

His voice was beginning to rise with the excitement of finding Emmelor and destroying him.

He looked at his newest general and said, "You do this and if you are successful, you will be able to retire, anywhere on this planet, with full benefits."

"*And if I fail, it will be the last breath I ever take*," Airibus thought to himself,

Before leaving the hangar, Mellor told General Airibus, "Keep me up to date on your progress. When you find him, I want to be contacted immediately so I can fly my hover craft to the sight. I want to watch as you blow him out of the water."

General Airibus gave a sigh and said, "If we, I mean, *when* we find him, if he is sitting on the bottom of the ocean, our best bet would be to send a nuclear-powered submarine."

"Do whatever you think best. Just find him and let's be done with this. I have other matters to worry about."

Back in his armored vehicle, Mellor nibbled on the snacks that were always there for him to nibble on while he was thinking. Submarines and nuclear power weapons... Why didn't I think of that? he wondered to himself...

Back in his office, Mellor pondered over a map of the ocean where Emmelor's ship had entered the water, trying to read the man's mind in calculating what he would do and which direction he would go?

He was about to give up when he noticed the river flowing into the jungle area of the large land mass to the northwest of the landing sight. From the river, there were endless tributaries where a man might hide.

"Yes," he said out loud. "That's it! That's where he's hiding!"

Wolfen looked at Mellor, wondering what he'd found, but kept his mouth shut.

Chapter 18

A SURPRISE CHALLENGE

Thornton Howell refilled his glass of bourbon again, for the fifth time in the last two hours. It was finally allowing him to feel a slight buzz. He needed something to allow him to relax and bourbon was the only thing that helped. At least that was what he'd convinced himself of. But as the years rolled by, it was taking more and more before it worked. It didn't really matter. By now he was addicted to the stuff and drank it on a regular basis. He convinced himself he really didn't need it, but conceded it allowed him to think more clearly.

The television was on in his bedroom, where he sat on the bed, sipping his bourbon. The newsman was saying something about waiting for a response from the White House about the impending impeachment, but as of this newscast, there had been no word.

"And there won't be because he knows I've got him between a rock and a hard spot. The aliens are gone, and he has no one to dispute my accusations," he said to the television. "And when I become President…"

His head slowly leaned forward as the glass slipped from his fingers and fell onto the floor, spilling the remains of the bourbon on the carpet. The weatherman was now on the television, proclaiming a rainstorm coming in off the coast, which would bring some much-needed precipitation, but Thornton heard none of it.

Even though it was ten-thirty at night, Sterling Collier wasn't in his bed. Instead, he was sitting in the kitchen with his friend, Archie Brooks. They were eating chicken fried steak sandwiches and drinking beer, while watching the ninth inning of a local high school baseball game.

"So, what are you going to do about the impeachment?" Archie asked.

"I said my piece earlier this evening," Sterling said after taking a swig of beer. "Now it's up to whoever they believe. In the meantime, I'm sure I will have a whole passel of other things to worry about – like the world trade center and the stock market, along with several countries siding with Thornton Howell."

"You don't think he can actually pull this off, do you? I mean, it's preposterous," Archie said, just as the young batter at home plate sent the ball over center field fence and trotted around the bases to the roar of the crowd. The home run had clenched a win. The DC Tigers had just won the city title.

Archie switched off the television and asked, "Where are you going?" as Sterling stood up and grabbed his jacket.

"Down to the baseball field to congratulate the team for winning the city championship."

The following morning President Collier was all over the news with pictures of him shaking the hand of each player on the winning team – along with the long table filled with hamburgers, French-fries, and milkshakes for all.

He was sitting in the kitchen eating his breakfast when the vice President came in and poured himself a cup of coffee. "Have you seen the news?" he asked, sitting down across the table from the President.

"If you're talking about my going down to see the boys who won the city championship, then, yes. It's all over every channel."

"No, no, no. Not that! I'm talking about the important news. The ratings! Since that little coup you pulled last night, your ratings have gone up three points! Considering all that is going on right now, that is huge."

"That's fine," Sterling told him. "But this is Washington DC and in politics, the numbers can change faster than a blinking railroad sign."

"You sure know how to burst a person's balloon," the vice President said, standing up and leaving the room.

As the President watched him leave, he heard Archie's voice. "Don't worry about him, he's a worry-wart. Always has been. I'm still not clear on why you chose him as your running mate and vice President."

"Because he has a lot of followers, political clout, and he is loyal to me," Sterling said.

Just then, his secretary, Irene Harper came in with two aides who began filling carafes with coffee and trays with pastry on them.

Irene stopped next to Sterling and looked at her watch. "You have a meeting with several senators and representatives in… twenty minutes, in the meeting room."

"Let me guess," Sterling said. "They want to know what I'm going to do about the alien situation and the upcoming impeachment."

"Along with the declining stock market caused by the impending impeachment," Irene said with a mocking grin.

Sterling pushed his plate away and stood up. "I just need to get dressed properly," he said as he headed for the door.

"I'll tell them you're on your way," Irene said, following him out of the kitchen.

Dressed in a black suit, white shirt, with a black, silk tie, Sterling marched into the meeting room like George S. Patton after taking a major German stronghold. "Good morning, gentlemen. I'm guessing we have a few things to discuss."

In a show of power, he stood behind his chair at the end of the table. When he saw Senator Glen Taylor from Colorado, he said, "Senator Taylor, you're up. What's on your mind?"

Senator Taylor cleared his throat and asked, "Mister President, the people of Colorado want to know if you are planning on resigning rather than being impeached and go down dishonorably."

"Well now, Senator Taylor, how long have we known one another?"

"A long time," the senator said. "What does that have to do with what we're talking about?"

"From my standpoint, a lot. As I recall, you were one of the people who pushed me into politics in the first place. Right?"

Senator Taylor harrumphed and said, "Well, I guess I may have had a little to do with it, but again, I must ask, what has that to do with anything?"

"And if you will," Sterling said, "tell us why you were hellbent on me entering politics?"

The senator looked around the table at the other men, then took a sip of coffee before clearing his throat and saying, "I watched you in a courtroom battle against a man with far more experience than you. You were as tenacious as an ole mama bear defending her cubs. You didn't give a whit that your opponent had more experience than you. You went for the throat and gave him a thrashing he wasn't used to. You felt you had right on your side and wouldn't back down. And in the end, you won the case. I felt you were perfect for public office – maybe governor or one day. Even President of the United States – of which I was right."

Sterling smiled and said, "Senator Taylor, I think you just answered your own question."

House Representative Howard Lawrence, from Iowa, and one of Sterling's strong followers, raised his hand and when Sterling acknowledged him, he said, "Of course you're going to fight. That stands without reason because we all know Thornton doesn't have a leg to stand on – not one shred of evidence. But here's what I believe the big question is. How are you going to deal with the foreign countries that are siding with him, causing the stock market to plunge into depths like we haven't seen since the great depression?"

Every man was staring at the President, and he stared right back at them as his mind strived to come up with an answer. Finally, he decided the truth was the best policy. "To be perfectly frank with you, I'm still trying to put all the pieces of the puzzle together, myself. And I want to say this, here and now, I could use some suggestions."

Every hand went into the air, but Sterling waved them down. "This is not the time for me to try and absorb all your suggestions. So, here's what I want you to do. Put your suggestions down on paper and have them delivered to me here at the White House so I can read them without interruption, and I promise to give each suggestion my full attention. Fair enough?"

There were ayes and other comments all around the table and with that, Sterling left the room to the sound of everyone trying to talk at once.

"Well done, Mister President," Irene Harper said as he walked past her, giving her a wink.

Irene hurried down the hall just behind Sterling, saying. "Thornton Howell wants a televised face to face debate on the issue of the aliens and why you should resign."

Sterling stopped and turned back to look at his secretary, saying, "You're joking. Right?"

"Sorry, Sir. But he's as serious as a snakebite."

Sterling placed the tips of his fingers against each side of his nose and said, "The man has lost his mind."

"So, what shall I tell him?" Irene asked, looking Sterling in the eyes, where she could read the tiredness.

"Let him squirm for a while. I'll give you my answer after lunch. Right now, I'm headed for the gym and then the pool for a few laps," Sterling told her, then turned and headed toward the elevator.

Chapter 19

A REQUEST FROM EARTH

General Airibus went to see a friend of his, Wakil, who was a top executive for a large corporation that supplied the energy for most of the manufacturing companies throughout the planet. He and Wakil had gone to upper school together and had made quite a splash when it came to partying.

He was greeted like an old friend and when Wakil found out his friend had been promoted to general, he insisted they go to a nearby club and celebrate.

During their drinking, General Airibus brought up the subject of his friend's private airplane.

"Ho, you didn't hear did you – you being so busy playing soldier and all. I just got a new one, a twin engine. She's fifty years old and seats four and as sweet a ride as a man could ever ask for."

"No, I hadn't heard," the general said. "I'd love to see her – maybe even take her on a trip I need to make."

"Sure, sure," Wakil said in his drunken stupor. "I'd love to go with you but work keeps me pretty busy. You know how it is."

"The thing is, I might be gone a week or so. Is that still all right?" the general asked, waving the bartender over and ordering another round.

"Take as long as you want. I won't need it for at least a month."

The following morning, General Airibus flew the little twin-engine airplane over to the nearby military base where mechanics were waiting to install the pulsar unit.

"Make sure when this operation is over, you can remove the pulsar and put it back in the same condition as before. I don't want my friend to suspect a thing. Do I make myself clear?"

The technicians came to attention and saluted, saying, "Yes-Sir."

The general was studying the map and instructions that had come from Mellor when the call came in, telling him the pulsar had been installed and was ready to use.

Still, he lingered over the map. According to recent information from Mellor, Emmelor was hiding somewhere in the southern jungle – not at the bottom of the ocean. How he came to that conclusion he had no idea, but if that was where he was instructed to search, that's where he would search. That way, if he found nothing, it wouldn't be his fault. He could remind Mellor that he was just following orders.

When Airibus arrived at the air base, he was amused to find the pulsar unit strapped to the wheel strut, not inside the airplane as he thought it would be.

The technician explained, "you said you wanted to be able to remove it without anyone knowing it had been attached, and this was the simplest way. As you can see, there is a cord that goes inside and is attached to a screen that is sitting on the dashboard and is being held there by removeable tape."

"Well done," Airibus told him, then climbed inside the small, twin-engine airplane and started the engines.

His destination was several thousand miles away and there was no way the small craft could fly that far without refueling several times, so in preparation for this mission he had ordered an aircraft carrier to be loaded with fighter units and wait for his arrival. The aircraft carrier was sitting just three miles off the coast, which made his flight barely four miles.

He set the small airplane down on the deck of the aircraft carrier and climbed down onto the deck of the carrier as men were tying it to the deck.

The Admiral was there to greet him and chuckled. "Looks mighty small sitting there next to the fighters."

Over drinks in the admiral's wardroom the Admiral asked, "Why can't we use the pulsar aboard our ship? It's the latest model available."

"Because where we're going, this ship won't be able to go." He pulled the map from his briefcase and laid it out on the table. "This is the area I need to search," he told him, pointing at the X on the map.

The Admiral studied the map for a few moments then called the bridge and gave the helmsman the coordinates.

When he sat back down at the table, the admiral looked at Airibus and said, "It will take us three days to get to the mouth of the river, and that's at top speed."

"Do the best you can," Airibus told him. "Now, you wouldn't mind, I'd like a tour of your ship. How many people does it take to run something this big?"

The admiral called for the Chief Bosun's mate to come to his cabin and show the General around.

"There are two thousand, five hundred crewmen aboard to run the ship, with a hundred-and-fifty officers to oversee them. We have three doctors and a small hospital aboard. We can carry one-hundred and fifty fighters and fifty spy units, along with five-thousand troops," the captain said, proudly.

"My gawd, man, this is a floating city!" General Airibus exclaimed.

"We like to think of it as a 'floating, ready for war, military base'," the captain told him.

Just then, the chief petty officer arrived and after introductions, the chief said, "Let's start down in the engine room and work our way topside."

While Airibus was taking his tour of the aircraft carrier, Emmelor called Lucita and asked her to meet him in the lounge. When she got there, she saw Emmelor sitting at a table with a worried look on his face.

"You look like you've just been caught doing something wrong," Lucita said, stopping next to him.

He motioned for her to sit down and when she did, Emmelor asked, "Do you remember those signal responders we left along the way to help speed up the process in case we needed to be in contact with the man from earth?"

"Yes," she said, remembering thinking they were a waste of time. The two planets were too far apart.

"Well, we heard from him, and it isn't good."

"You did?" Lucita said. 'So soon? Is something wrong?"

Emmelor took a sip of his drink and said, "I took the liberty," pointing at a glass near her. "It seems we caused quite a stir – taking and leaving the men we used for testing their combat abilities. Plus, it somehow got out that I spoke with the man in charge of the country called The United States – Sterling Collier. And now they think he is in league with us, and we are planning to take over the planet."

"That's absurd!" Lucita said. "Why would we want to do that. We have troubles of our own right here on X-162."

"Exactly," Emmelor said, nodding his head. "But the communication that came in less than an hour ago is a request for us to return and explain to the various heads of their countries, what we were doing there."

"Well, now, that's just crazy!" Lucita said. "Didn't this Sterling Collier explain to them why we were there and that we're not hostile?"

"Apparently, he tried, but they don't believe him and now they're trying to throw him out of office," Emmelor said.

"Have you informed Liam about the communication, yet?" Lucita asked.

"Not yet. That's why I called you here – to discuss whether or not we should inform him. Since there's nothing we can do about it at this time, I see no reason to tell him. It will only upset him and take his mind off of our problem," Emmelor told her.

"I see your point," Lucita said. "And I agree. We need him to be ready when the fight comes here on our planet."

So, the communication from earth never reached the ears of Liam, who was in the workout room, trying to get his body into condition in case he had to fight someone else, or something.

Chapter 20

AN ANGRY REPORTER

Blurry-eyed and hung-over, which he seemed to be a lot these days, Thornton Howell sat down behind his desk and opened the bottom, left-hand drawer. Under a stack of papers, was a bottle of bourbon.

After looking through the window of his office, carefully, to see that no one was nearby, he lifted the bottle to his lips and took a good measure, swirled it around in his mouth, and swallowed. He could feel the burning clear down into his stomach and waited.

Within a minute of returning the bottle to its hiding place, he felt his nerves begin to relax. He punched a button on his call box and when his secretary responded, Thornton asked, "How much time until the reporters get here?"

"Thirty minutes. Would you like some coffee or a donut?" his secretary asked, knowing her boss was, more than likely, hung over, or still in his cups.

What Thornton really wanted was another drink but he said, "Yes, a small pot of coffee and a maple bar would be nice. And call me before you let them into my office."

"Yes-sir," was the reply and the connection went dead.

The coffee was hot, but to Thornton it tasted like muddy water. He could eat only half of the maple bar. He was about to reach for the bottle of bourbon again when his secretary's voice came over the call box, "They're in the elevator. They'll be here in three or four minutes."

"I've decided to see them in the meeting room. Take them there and I'll be along shortly," Thornton told her.

His secretary said, "Yes-sir," and clicked off.

Thornton reached in the drawer and lifted the bottle of bourbon to his lips. "One small drink to help my nerves stay calm," he told himself.

Before heading for the meeting room, Thornton put a piece of mint in his mouth and a couple of others in his jacket pocket. He didn't think they would be able to smell the liquor, but in his position, a little insurance couldn't hurt.

When he entered the meeting room, they were already there. The cameraman had his camera set up and pointed at where he would be sitting. The lighting man had the light stands in place, ready to be turned on. The man who would be holding the long boom microphone was eating a donut, the boom microphone laying on the table next to him.

Debra Boxlighter was a young, aggressive news reporter who was trying to get a story that would make her boss look at her and the lush she was about to interview, who was trying to take down the President of the United States, was her ticket to the front line.

She didn't like Thornton or what he stood for. The man was trying to take down one of the best Presidents this country had seen in many years. At least, that's how she saw it. But, if she could get Thornton to say something he shouldn't, like admitting he was just out for the President's job, well, that would certainly get the attention of her boss.

She stood up and walked over, with her hand out. "It's a pleasure to meet you, Sir. Thank you for agreeing to this interview."

"Whatever," Thornton said, brushing past her and sitting down in his chair. "Let's get on with it. I have important things to do."

The snubbing didn't go unnoticed as Debra took her seat, motioning to her people.

The lights came on, shining on Thornton's face. "Shut those damn things off! They're blinding me!"

"Sorry, about that," the cameraman said, hiding a grin, as he refocused the lights, so they didn't shine directly in the man's face.

The man with the boom held the microphone just far enough above Thornton's head so it couldn't be seen in the picture, and the camera man adjusted the lens so that just Thornton's upper half showed in the picture. "In, five, four, three two, one – rolling camera... and... action."

"Mister Howell, as Speaker of the House, why do you think it is your responsibility to bring these charges against the President?" Debra asked, smiling her best smile.

Thornton Howell was not new to this kind of interview and said, "When you see a wrong, it is everyone's duty to fight for justice."

"And you truly believe the President is collaborating with an alien power to help them take over this entire planet?" Debra asked.

Thornton's stomach began to grumble. He should have eaten something instead of taking the two drinks of bourbon. "I do." He would keep his answers short, and to the point. That way it would be hard to challenge his answers.

"And you have evidence to back up your claim?" Debra asked, watching Thornton's eyes for a tell-tale of nervousness.

Thorntons's brain was suddenly on alert. The woman was trying to push him into a corner, and he wasn't about to let her do that. "I'm not at liberty to say at this time, but everything will be disclosed at the impeachment trial."

"Did you hear the President's denial on his television speech?" Debra asked, waiting for the right moment to pounce.

"I did," Thornton answered as if he was bored with the conversation.

"And what did you think of it?" Debra asked.

Thornton made a harrumph sound and said, "As usual, he is covering up his real intentions. The man is a hopeless liar."

"Mister Howell, isn't it true that you're the one who is making things up so you can eventually wind up as President of these United States? Isn't that the truth of the matter?"

Thornton's face went from pasty to blood red, and instead of answering the question, he jumped to his feet and yelled, "I won't be talked to in this manner. This interview is over!"

And with that, Thornton Howell stormed from the room on wobbly legs. He needed a drink, in the worst way.

Debra turned to the camera and said, "Well, there you have it. Speaker of the House of Representatives, Thornton Howell did not deny his main goal in this impeachment is to wind up with the presidency."

Later that evening, Debra's video interview with Thornton was not shown on the news as she expected. In fact, she was called into the producer's office, dressed down and fired. The man delivering the evening news looked at the teleprompter and read, "Tonight's news was supposed to highlight an interview with Speaker of the House, Thornton Howell, but will not be shown because the reporter tried to slander this man who has done nothing short of trying to save this entire planet from being overrun by people or creatures from another planet. This channel sends its most humble apology to Mister Howell and wants him to know that the reporter in question is no longer with us."

Sterling happened to be in the kitchen of the White House, snacking on leftovers from the refrigerator with his friend and chef, Archie Brooks, when the news came over the television. When it was over, Sterling stood up and walked over to the wall phone and called his chief advisor, Daniel Glazer. When he answered, the President said, "I presume you saw the news?"

"I did and as far as I'm concerned, that young lady got a raw deal. I know her father. He's a big supporter of ours," Daniel said.

"I'm calling for two reasons," Sterling said. "First, I want a copy of that tape, and second, I want that young lady in my office, no, make it in the kitchen, asap."

"I'll do my best," Daniel said, and hung up.

Forty-five minutes later, Daniel led Debra Boxlighter into the White House kitchen and introduced her to the President of the United States where she explained that she was told the tape had been destroyed.

Sterling wasn't sure he believed that, but for now he had no other choice but to go along with it. "Have you eaten," he asked the pretty young woman standing in front of him.

Still dumbstruck to be standing in the kitchen of the White House with the President of the United States of America, all she could do was nod her head no.

Sterling looked over at his chef and said, "Archie, would you be so kind as to fix Miss Boxlighter anything she desires."

He then turned back to Debra and asked, "Would you like some coffee?"

"I would prefer tea, if that's all right?" she stammered.

"Tea it is," he told her, then looked toward Archie who nodded his head and said, "Coming up. Cream and sugar?"

"Just sugar," Debra said, still wondering if she was in trouble over the interview."

Chapter 21

BOMBING THE JUNGLE HIDEOUT

They had been in the jungle hideout for a week now, and all Liam had done was eat, sleep, go to the workout room, swim laps in the pool, and run around the indoor track – and he was getting bored.

He was headed to see Emmelor and find out what the delay was when the first bomb rocked the hideout.

"What the...?" Liam yelled as he was thrown to the floor.

Then, like a mighty aftershock, the hiding place was shaking like they'd just had an earthquake. And, they might have believed it was an earthquake, if not for the sound of the explosion when the bombs went off.

-

Two days prior, the aircraft carrier had dropped anchor just a couple of miles off the coast to the entrance of the big river. Mellor was called and within an hour, he arrived on his private hover plane.

The following morning, General Airibus began sweeping the jungle with his pulsar beams but it wasn't until the morning of the second day that he hit pay dirt, so to speak.

He marked the spot on his map and flew back to the carrier. "Are you sure?" Mellor asked excitedly.

"As you can see," the general said, pointing to the picture, "there is no doubt there is activity going on down there and it isn't animals."

Mellor turned and looked at the Admiral and asked, "How soon can we have the fighters in the air?"

"Within fifteen minutes," the admiral said.

"Make it thirty. I want time to get my hover plane in position," Mellor said, anxious for the raid to begin.

As he lifted the hover plane off the deck of the carrier, he said to himself, "And now, my dear Emmelor, I will finally be rid of you and all your pandering ways. I will be rid of you, once and for all, and this planet will be mine."

As Liam climbed to his feet, he heard the overhead speakers come to life as the voice of Emmelor came roaring out. "We are under attack! Evacuate! Evacuate!"

Liam looked around, confused. "Evacuate to where?" he asked no one. During his short time there, there had been no talk of being attacked or evacuation because Emmelor believed the place to be beyond detection.

Women were screaming. Light fixtures were being torn from the ceiling and crashing to the floor, scattering glass everywhere. Furniture was being tossed around like being thrown by an unruly child. Through all the panic, Liam saw people running toward the rear of the compound and fell in behind them.

He'd been running for no more than a minute when he heard Lucita's voice, "Going my way?" she asked as she ran up alongside of him.

"Are we being attacked?" Liam asked, just as a rocket slammed through the ceiling of the compound a good distance behind them. But even so, the blast picked Liam and Lucita, along with a dozen others, into the air and flung them down the pathway.

Climbing to their feet, Liam looked at the destruction and said, "Well, at least it wasn't a nuclear bomb or we'd all be dead."

"No," Lucita said. "I think Mellor wants as many of us alive as he can to make examples out of us. Plus, I also believe he hopes to take Emmelor alive and make him watch the death of the rest of us."

"You really think he hates Emmelor that much?" Liam asked as they turned and continued running toward wherever the evacuation place was.

Just ahead of them, people were pouring through a set of double doors, and as they followed, Lucita said, "Mellor has hated Emmelor since their days at university together. Emmelor bested Mellor in grades, sports, popularity and in a national championship of strength and endurance that took three days around the clock for them to complete, Emmelor won by a landslide.

As they passed through the doors, Liam hauled up and his eyes went wide. The orb was sitting there with its doors open and people were entering as quickly as they could.

Emmelor eased up behind Liam and Lucita and said, "We'd best get aboard. I'd hate for them to leave without us."

Once they were inside, Emmelor looked at Liam and said, "Follow me."

Liam found himself standing, once more, in front of the big gun, its seat beckoning him.

"I'm afraid we're going to need your skills, once again, my friend," Emmelor said with a sheepish grin.

Mellor jumped back in his seat when the orb rose into the sky no more than three-hundred feet to his left.

He watched in horror as the giant orb moved around like a frightened deer, positioning itself so that whoever was in control of the big gun could easily dispel of any and all of the aircraft as they tried to lift off the deck of the aircraft carrier.

Nothing they tried was fast enough to get away from the orb's gun.

Mellor found himself screaming into his shoulder mounted communicator, ordering the pilots to continue trying.

Again, he watched in horror as the orb positioned itself in front of the aircraft carrier and as each fighter tried to lift off, it was shot, and disappeared beneath the waves.

The aircraft carrier was at the orb's mercy and was receiving heavy damage.

Mellor cursed himself for not bringing along a warship or two.

Liam had decided not to sink the big aircraft carrier, but he did put the deck out of commission. No aircraft would be able to land or take off from her deck anytime soon.

When all was secure, Emmelor turned the orb back in the direction of the little hover craft but found the sky empty. Mellor had fled.

"Where could he have gone?" Lucita asked. "There's nothing but jungle down there."

"I don't know," Emmelor said as he ordered the orb to begin searching the small towns along the coast. "His hover craft doesn't have enough fuel for him to go too far. He has to be along the coast here, somewhere."

One would think that would be the case. It was rational thinking, but Mellor was anything but rational. During his escape, he'd gone deeper into the jungle and just before running out of fuel, he saw a small, open area and set his hover craft down.

Once on the ground, he looked around and saw nothing but dense jungle.

"Another endurance test," he said to himself, hoping he could remember the things he'd been taught back when he'd gone through the military academy.

After thinking about it, he climbed back into the hover craft and tried to call for help. He clicked the microphone on and said, "This is General Mellor, I am out of fuel and have landed in the jungle. Use the tracking device to find me."

He clicked off and waited for an answer and when he didn't get one, he clicked on the microphone and repeated the message – but still got no answer. Disgusted, he once again climbed out of the hover craft and this time he stared at the sky, looking for someone to bring him fuel. After nearly half an hour, he turned and stared at the forbidding jungle.

He turned around and around, searching for a road, a path, anything that might allow him to get out of this godforsaken place, but found nothing but dense jungle.

Chapter 22

THORNTON'S FOLLOWERS

Sterling was due to visit the children's hospital and do storytelling, which he was advised not to do. There had been multiple threats come in the mail, telling him his traitorous days were numbered, and the number one threat, of which he'd received several, read, RETIRE TRAITOR OR DIE!!!!

Of course, Sterling told his advisors, "They're nothing more than threats, and I will not let them scare me into hiding behind locked doors like a coward. That would play right into Thornton's hands. No, I will go about my business as planned."

Before allowing Sterling to go down to the garage to get into his limo, the passageway was patrolled. While the garage was searched for anyone not allowed to be there, the limo was scanned top to bottom for any bombs or other type of threats.

On the way to his car, security was so tight Sterling felt like he was in a cocoon. Two security guards were already inside the car when he climbed in.

As the President's car left the White House, there was a car in front and in back of it. Even with so much security, three blocks from the White House, someone atop of a three-story business building sighted down along the barrel of a shoulder mounted rocket launcher, took a deep breath, and squeezed the trigger.

The shooter didn't wait to see if he scored a hit or not. Instead, he turned and ran for the exterior fire escape and made his way down to a waiting car.

Fortunately for the President, the rocket hit the street in front of his car. The car was tossed into the air by the concussion, then dropped back down onto the street, just in front of the gigantic hole made by the rocket.

One of the security men in the car in front of the President, jumped out of his car and looked at the tops of the buildings, trying to spot the shooter, but he saw no one. He pulled out a receiver, pushed the button and asked, "Hello, helicopter one. Where are you?"

After a short pause and no answer, the security man pushed the button again, and said, "Come in, helicopter one."

There was still no answer because the helicopter had never taken off. The pilot sat slumped in his seat with a bullet hole in his temple.

"Sir," the security guard said, "we're taking you back to the White House where you'll be safe."

"Like hell you are," Sterling said. "I have a date with some sick children to do some storytelling and I'm not about to break my word. Now, move out! I'll be going to the children's hospital!"

"But, Mister President…"

"Are you deaf? Do I need to repeat myself?" Sterling asked with a determined look on his face. He looked at his driver and said, "Sam, take me to the children's hospital, now!"

The limo swung out around the hole made by the rocket and continued on down the street with the security men scrambling to catch up.

At the hospital, Sterling didn't wait for his security team. As soon as the car came to a halt, he opened the door himself, and ran into the hospital.

The woman at the desk looked up and her eyes went wide and she swallowed.

Sterling grinned and said, "I'm here to do storytelling to the children. Can you direct me in the right direction?"

"Right this way, Mister President," she said, jumping to her feet and heading down the hallway to the play room.

When they entered the room, not waiting for a formal introduction, Sterling ran up onto the small stage and yelled, "Hello. My name is Sterling! Who wants to hear a funny story?"

The room was filled with shouts of, "Me." "I do!" "Yes." "I love funny stories," along with several other commits.

"So, do I. Who's going to tell one?"

There was a moment of silence, then the room erupted with laughter. "You are silly," a little girl in a wheelchair shouted.

"Oh, that's right. That's why I'm here today. I'm the storyteller. Well then, let's get right to it. This is a story about a little boy named Randal Owen Hudstedler. Once upon a time..."

The security guards arrived just as Sterling began his story and when he saw them, he motioned for them to stay just outside the room.

For the next hour, the President of the United States of America kept the sick and lame children of the hospital, laughing, giggling and shouting, "Tell us another story!"

And when it was time for him to leave, the children did not address him by his title, but, yelled, in unison, "Goodbye, Sterling."

As they left the hospital, the President was once again surrounded by the security guards.

Everything went fine until the back door of his car was opened and, as he bent down to get into the car, a shot rang out and slammed into the President's back, driving him head-first into the back seat.

Immediately, the security team honed in on the rooftop where the shot had been fired from, and pistols were blazing.

"Take him to the nearest hospital!" one of the security team yelled at Sam, who already had the car in drive and was pushing down on the accelerator.

As the car sped away, one of the security team saw a man running across the roof of the laboratory building next to the hospital. He sighted down the pistol and squeezed the trigger.

The man surged forward and went flying over the side, falling four stories to his death. The shooter had been taken down, but now that he was dead, it would be hard to find out why he did the shooting, or who he was collaborating with, if anyone?

Television news broadcasters were already broadcasting the firing of the rocket from coast to coast, when the local television announcer said, "This just in. We've just received word that the President has been shot by a sniper from a nearby rooftop. The shooter was shot by one of the President's security team and he fell to his death. At this point, we don't know if the shot to the

President was fatal or not. Our roving reporter, Connie Stableman is in route to the hospital right behind the President's car."

At that point, the screen changed to the President's car driving at high speed down the street, it's horn blaring loudly.

The announcer's voice continued. "We will keep you updated as soon as we know anything."

Thornton Howell switched off the television and refilled his glass with bourbon, added two ice cubes and took a drink. "Well, that's another one I won't have to pay any money to," he said to his private secretary and most devout supporter, Luella Barnes.

"Let's just hope our second shooter's aim was better than the first one," Luella said.

"And we're sure shooter number two, took care of shooter number one?" Thornton asked.

"Just minutes after his rocket missed the President's car, I received a message on my phone that read, "'Dinner is on you tonight', which means he was successful in getting rid of shooter number one. And, now that he, too, is dead, he is no longer a liability," Thornton said, taking another sip of his drink.

"I have a bit of a headache. I'm going to take a nap. Wake me up as soon as you have word about Sterling. And I hope the news will be that he's dead," Thornton said as he left the room.

Chapter 23

THE CHALLENGE

Mellor was standing next to his hover craft, staring off into the dense jungle when he heard a sound. He turned to see where the sound was coming from just as something hard slammed into his forehead, rendering him unconscious.

Mellor woke up to the sound of drums beating and several men's voices chanting a song in a language he couldn't understand. He was hanging upside down from the limb of a large tree. He could see a large fire in the center of a cleared-out space, and small huts surrounding the cleared area. There was a large pot hanging over the fire and several women were putting what looked like herbs into the pot.

He tried to move his hands but his arms were strapped to his sides – bound by vines.

"Hey! Get me down from here!" he yelled at the top of his lungs.

Mellor's yelling stopped the drums, the chanting, and dancing. Forty some faces turned to look at the man hanging from the tree – the one who had fallen from the sky.

At first, they thought him to be a God, but when he climbed out of his flying machine, they saw he was only a man, and took appropriate measures. One of the men in the tribe put a rock in his slingshot and let it fly.

Slowly, the people of the tribe inched their way over to stand in front of Mellor. One of the women reached out and poked him in the eye with her finger.

"Ouch! Stop that!" he yelled.

Another woman pulled his lip back and looked at his teeth, then stepped back, nodding her head.

"Let me down from here! Do you know who I am?" Mellor said in a harsh voice that normally made men quiver.

One of the men stepped up and slapped Mellor across the face and pointed his finger at him and said something Mellor couldn't understand.

The man then turned and said something to one of the women, who turned and rushed off.

"I am General Mellor, soon to be the ruler of this planet, and I demand you let me down, now!" he yelled.

This brought a round of laughter.

Mellor was quite angry by now and yelled, again, "If you do not let me down this instant, when my soldiers arrive, I will have them burn this village to the ground, with you in it!"

As they stared at him, not understanding a word, the woman returned, carrying a good size pot, and when the man nodded his head up and down, she walked over and held it just beneath Mellor's head.

Mellor's eyes went wide when he saw the man remove a very sharp looking knife form his waist and walk up to him. "What are you planning on doing?" Mellor screamed as he felt the edge of the knife, slice across his throat.

-

Emmelor was looking at one of the droid scanners when the call came in. It was from one of his pilots that had been sent to try and find Mellor. "Found his hover craft, Sir."

He then went on to give the longitude and latitude, and when Emmelor looked them up on the map screen, he gave a sigh and touched a button and said, "All craft, return home. I repeat, all craft return home."

When he stepped back, Emmelor looked at Liam and said, "The hunt is over. He landed in a very bad part of the jungle."

"Lots of snakes and bad animals?" Liam asked.

"Worse than that," Emmelor said, giving a big sigh. "He landed right in the heart of LiLi country."

"And I'm assuming that is bad?" Liam asked.

"The LiLi are a small group of natives who practice the art of turning large heads into small ones, and then eating their prey," Emmelor informed him.

Liam thought for a moment, then said, "But you don't know for sure they got him, do you?"

"No, not for sure. But I will go and find out. I have to be sure," Emmelor said, nodding his head.

"If they're so dangerous, how are you going to get in there to find out?" Liam quired.

Emmelor grinned and said, "Several years ago, I happened to be in the right place at the right time. I and a crew of men were going up the tributary in our boat when a young girl was rafting her way across the water from one shore to the other. She was poling along when a Himus, what you call a crocodile, only several times larger than the ones on your planet, upended the raft, throwing her into the water.

"There was a lot of yelling coming from the far shore and when I looked, I could see a large group of natives jumping up and down. They were yelling and throwing spears and shooting arrows at the Himus, but he was too far away for them to do any harm. The girl was thrashing around in the water and I grabbed my laser pistol and shot the Himus, then dove into the water and swam over and took the girl in my arms – then swam to the shore and gave her to one of the male natives. It just so happened she was the daughter of the medicine man, and he declared me to be good medicine. Over the years, I've spent some time with them, taking things to them, and learned their language and a lot about them. They're still primitive, but I will be safe going in."

Without hesitating, Liam asked, "Do you think I could go with you?"

There was a long pause as Emmelor thought it over, and finally, he said, "Why not. I think it will be a good experience for you. Although, I think you'll be safe with me, I cannot, in all honesty, guarantee that."

Liam grinned and said, "I'm ready when you are."

The pod landed next to where the abandoned hover craft was sitting. The two men got out and Emmelor put his hands together over his mouth and blew into them, making a high-sounding whistle.

Within minutes, the area was filled with natives carrying several kinds of weapons. There were spears, slingshots, bow and arrow and even a couple of rifles.

Emmelor looked at Liam and said, "They more than likely got the rifles from some of their victims."

The chief came walking toward Emmelor, smiling broadly, with his arms outstretched in welcome, chattering off with a bunch of grunts and groans Liam didn't understand. After the two men greeted each other, the chief eyed Liam suspiciously. He looked Liam up and down like a butcher looking at a side of beef.

Emmelor turned to Liam and said, "Liam, I would like to present Chief Wy, of the LiLi tribe. Nod your head down like a bow."

Liam did as he was instructed and saw the smile on the chief's face.

Emmelor chuckled and said, "The chief wants to know if I brought food for him and his tribe."

"I hope you told him, no," Liam said, shaking his head.

"I did, but he said for you to be welcome to the people of the tribe, you must first earn the right to be welcomed. I'm sorry, my friend, but I do recall telling you there were no guarantees."

"So, what do I have to do to earn the right to be here? Not some fight to the death, I hope?"

Emmelor grinned and said, "They pride themselves as great hand to hand warriors. To win your fight, you must go against their best warrior and win, or at least make a good showing of it. If you win, you will be received with much honor and praise. If you lose, you will be supper tonight."

"But what if he wins, but I've made a good showing?" Liam queried.

Emmelor thought for a moment, then said, "That depends on how good a showing you make. If it's close to a tie, you will be accepted and honored as a good fighting man. But if you are only mildly successful in staying on your feet, they will vote on whether to let you go, or keep you as a slave until sometime down the road you become their next meal. My advice is to let him win, but barely."

119

Emmelor and Liam were surrounded by the natives as they made their way through the jungle to the village. During the trip, Emmelor and the chief chatted like nothing was amiss.

At the village, Emmelor was treated like royalty, while Liam was pushed into a large, open space, and surrounded by the men of the tribe.

Liam stood there, wondering which one of the men would be his opponent, when the men parted and his opponent arrived and Liam sucked in a gulp of air.

It wasn't that the man was tall. In fact, he was only maybe four inches taller than Liam. It was the rest of him that made Liam swallow a large gulp of air. He looked like a large Oak tree. His arms were as large as Liam's legs and he had the largest chest Liam had ever seen.

The muscles in his arms and shoulders rippled as he walked into the center of the space and stared at Liam – a sneering grin on his lips. He said something that got a huge laughter from the rest of the tribe.

By now, Liam could see a large number of women had mixed in with the men and were chanting something Liam couldn't understand, but realized they were there to cheer their warrior on.

Liam's opponent made a motion with his hands and arms, indicating the fight should begin.

Liam began to circle around the man, looking for an opening to do what? Hitting him with his fist would be like punching a solid wall. It would only gain him a broken fist.

The man stopped turning around and said something, again, while motioning for Liam to come to him and fight.

He knew he couldn't keep on circling. At some point he had to defend himself. Liam took a deep breath and feinted to his left, then ran toward the man, jumping into the air and kicking him in the stomach with both feet.

Liam landed on the ground, and got quickly to his feet, expecting to see the man on the ground. Instead, the man had only stepped back a couple of steps, then came running at him. Right at the last moment, Liam ducked down and drove his fist into the man's stomach as he stepped to the side. It was like driving his fist into a brick wall and the pain radiated up his arm all the way to his shoulder.

For his size, the man was quick and he reached out and grabbed Liam's wrist and jerked him up close to him. The crowd of people began to shout encouragement to their warrior, as he grabbed Liam around the upper part of his body and began to squeeze.

The man's arms were like a giant vise that was steadily getting tighter, and tighter. Liam knew he had to do something or he was done for.

Liam leaned into the squeezing arms and dropped his feet to the ground, then, kicked upward, throwing his feet high over his head, then letting his legs come down behind the big man, throwing him over backward.

Liam landed on his feet and jerked free of the man's grip, then stepped back.

Suddenly, the crowd of people went silent. This was something they hadn't planned on and they weren't sure how to react.

The man rolled over onto his stomach and got slowly to his feet. The fall had knocked the wind out of him and he was trying to get his wind back.

Seeing an opportunity, Liam ran toward the man with his shoulder lowered and drove it into the man like tackling a fullback.

The man let out a gush of air as he was driven backward and once again, landed on his back. Only this time, he grabbed onto Liam's shirt and held him close.

When they landed on the ground, the man smashed his fist against the side of Liam's head and knocked him to the side.

Lights were flashing off and on in Liam's head as he rolled over, trying to make the bright lights go away. He'd just climbed to his hands and knees when he felt himself being jerked in the air.

Liam shook his head and looked down. The man had him in his hands and held high over his head. He lowered his arms, just a little then threw Liam into the air. Liam landed on his side and rolled over just in time to feel the toes of the big man's foot kick him in the stomach, driving the wind out of him.

The big man stepped back, motioning for Liam to get up.

The chief poked Emmelor in the arm and laughed. Emmelor tried to smile but he felt bad for Liam. The odds were stacked against him in this fight. But, to be honest, if he was to fight for him in a contest for the entire planet, the odds against him just might be as bad – and it looked like Liam wouldn't have been up to the task, like he'd hoped.

Liam was now on his knees, motioning for the big man to come to him, and was obliged by the man running toward him with the intention of kicking him, again.

Liam waited until the last moment and when the man's foot was thrust out, Liam caught it in his hands and twisted, causing the man to lose his balance and fall off on his side.

Like a raging panther, Liam was up and kicking the man in the side, over and over.

One of the man's friends didn't like the turn of events and picked up a rock and threw it at Liam, hitting him in the side of the head, knocking him backward.

The crowd of natives were now cheering for the big man to get up and end the fight. He came to his feet and ran toward Liam with both fists swinging at his opponent's jaw.

Liam stepped under the blow and swung around to the side, driving three quick blows into the man's kidney area.

The big man grunted, then swung his fist backward, catching Liam on the shoulder.

Liam grimaced from the pain as he was knocked backwards.

The big man continued coming around and with his other hand, he hit Liam alongside his head, sending him staggering backward.

Liam, trying his best to stay on his feet, shook his head and motioned for the man to come to him, again.

By now, both men were panting and needing a rest, but there were no rest periods in this fight.

For fifteen more minutes, the two warriors battled, each holding his own. Liam could see he was wearing the man down, but he also knew his own energy was beginning to wane.

Liam saw an opportunity to hopefully end the fight and took it. He slipped under the man's swing and stepped in closer, driving his fist into the man's throat., then darting away.

The man stopped in mid-stride and grabbed his throat.

At this point, the chief had seen enough and stepped in, declaring the fight a draw. Liam was no longer a prospect for supper, and welcomed into the tribe.

Both Liam and Emmelor declined staying for supper, suspecting it to be Mellor's remains.

Bruised and battered, Liam limped along with Emmelor, back to their small ship. As they boarded their ship, they heard the natives, shout, Liam! Liam! Liam! And then some gobbly-goosh Liam couldn't understand.

Once they were back aboard the home ship, Lucita was angry about Emmelor allowing Liam to go along with him, putting him in harm's way.

Emmelor had now changed his mind about Liam's ability and told Lucita, "He did well against the best they had. At first, I wasn't sure he would survive, but the man is a warrior and acquitted himself against a powerful opponent. He will serve us well."

Chapter 24

CURSES, FOILED AGAIN

The sound of heavy rain pounded against Thornton Howell's office window as Thornton slammed down the receiver on his desk phone. He'd been trying to get information about the President's condition, but his request was denied by some grumpy old nurse at the ward desk. Thornton had even threatened to have her fired, and the old biddy laughed at him. "Go ahead. I'm well past due for retirement, anyway," the woman had said before hanging up on him!

He turned and stared out of the window. He hated the wind and the rain. He hated Washington. He hated anyone and everyone who opposed him. A gust of heavy wind drove the rain against the window pane so hard it made Thornton jump.

He turned and pressed the intercom button on his desk phone and said, "Have my car ready, I'll be down in the garage within ten minutes," and released the button, not waiting for an answer.

Luella Barnes had been Thornton's secretary for a number of years and was used to his nasty moods. She lifted the receiver and touched a button on the phone, and when a man answered, she said, "The Bloodsucker is on the move in ten."

There was a chuckle on the other end and the man said, "In ten. Got it."

-

President Collier was sitting propped up on his hospital bed, watching the news on television. The curtains on his window were closed and he couldn't see the violent rain storm, but he could hear it.

He turned his head and smiled as his nurse; Viola Wilkerson came walking into his room. She was in her late forties, but looked much younger. She had a figure that made men's heads turn and a smile that made the pits of their stomachs do flip-flops. "Good morning, Mister President. How are you feeling?"

Sterling looked at her and said, "If we are to become friends, you need to call me, Sterling, which is my first name."

Viola blushed and said, "I would love to be your friend and one of these days I might even have the courage to call you by your first name, but for now, I will stick with Mister President."

"So, are you seeing anyone?" Sterling asked.

"Mister President!" she said, pretending to be shocked, then said, "No."

"That's hard to believe. You are a very attractive woman. I would think men would be lined up trying to get a date with you. You don't have leprosy or anything like that, do you?"

Viola looked at the floor and said, "No. My husband passed away a year ago and since his passing, I've... well, I've kept myself busy with my work."

"I'm sorry. I didn't know," Sterling said, feeling a bit of a fool.

"It's all right. There's no reason you should have known." Changing the subject, she said, "Let's have a look at your wound."

Sterling smiled and said, "It's still pretty tender. How bad was it? No one has said anything."

As she inspected the gunshot wound, she said, "You were very lucky. The bullet went through the muscle just below your armpit and grazed three of your ribs, but no vital organs were hit. It will take some time to heal and it will be sore for several weeks, but in the end, you'll be good as new. With only two small scars."

Just then, one of the President's guards stepped into the room and said, "Thornton Howell is downstairs, insisting on coming up to see you. Should I shoot him?"

Sterling chuckled and said, "No. But I don't want to see him."

Viola looked at Sterling and said, "Let me take care of this," waving the guard back out of the room. She then turned and pressed the button that lowered the bed down to a position where he could be comfortable, but still look as though he was on death's door.

She covered him up to the chin and told him to close his eyes because he was still in a coma. She then dimmed the lights and waited for Thornton to arrive.

The nasty ole nurse Thornton had spoken to on the phone had gone home for the day and the younger nurse was much easier to threaten. After the first threat, she gave up Sterling's room number.

As Thornton stepped off the elevator, one of the guards leaned in the room and whispered, "He's coming down the hall."

"Tap the door with your foot when he gets close," Viola whispered back.

Thornton was less than ten feet from the President's room when Viola heard the tap on the door. With her chart in her hand, she exited the room just in time to come face to face with the Speaker of the House of Representatives.

"Can I help you?" Viola asked.

"If you don't recognize me, my name is Thornton Howell and I am the Speaker of the House of Representatives and I'm here to see the President," he said, trying to step around the nurse.

Viola stepped over in front of him and said, "I'm sorry but he can't have visitors at this time."

"Young woman, did you not hear who I am?" Thornton hissed.

Viola smiled and said, "Yes-sir, I heard you and I'm well aware of who you are but even if you were the King of Siam, you still couldn't get in to see him."

"Why you impertinent..." was as far as Thornton got when the nurse beckoned him over to the window looking into Sterling's room, and when he followed her, he stared at the President who looked to be asleep.

Viola kept a straight face and said, "As you can see, the President is still in a coma and we have no idea when or if he will regain consciousness."

"So, the gunshot was that serious? Thornton asked.

"I'm afraid so," Viola said, looking down at the floor and shaking her head.

Both the security guards were grinding their teeth, trying not to burst out laughing.

Before leaving, Thornton handed Viola a card with his number on it and said, "I want you to call me the minute he wakes up, or I will…" he left the rest, hanging.

"Yes-sir, I surely will. And the moment he wakes up, I'll tell him you stopped by."

When the elevator doors closed, both security guards burst into laughter. "You deserve an Oscar for that performance."

Viola went back into the President's room and raised the lights back up.

Sterling opened his eyes and asked, "Can I assume he is gone?"

Viola grinned and said, "I just explained that you were in a coma and couldn't have any visitors."

"And he bought it?" Sterling asked.

"Hook, line and sinker," Viola said.

Just then, a doctor, not the President's doctor, walked into the room and asked, "What's everyone laughing about?".

When Viola told him what had happened, the doctor frowned and said, "Come. I want to speak to you in the hallway."

"Whoa. Hold up, doc," Sterling said. "What she did, she did under my orders."

The doctor, a staunch Thornton Howell follower, looked back at the President and said, "You may be the President, but you do not run this hospital. Miss Wilkerson was in violation of hospital rules and she will be punished, whether you like it or not." And with that, he dragged Viola out of the room.

"Stop him," Sterling yelled and before the doctor could go any further, he was slammed, face first up against the wall.

"I'll see you fired for this," the doctor yelled.

"Bring him back in here," Sterling ordered.

When the doctor was standing next to Sterling's bed, Sterling asked, "Who are you? And why did you come into my room? You're not my doctor."

The doctor turned and tried to leave, but the security guards grabbed him and spun him back around.

"I asked you a question, doctor, if you really are a doctor?" Sterling said.

"I am a registered doctor of this hospital, and I have every right to check on you," he said indignantly.

"Wrong answer," Sterling said, nodding at one of the guards, who immediately twisted one of the doctor's arms.

"Stop that. That hurts!" the doctor shouted.

"You tell me the truth and I won't have him break your arm," Sterling said, knowing he would never give that order, but the doctor didn't.

"I'm a friend of Speaker Howell. He called and asked me to come and make sure you really were in a coma or not. If I don't call him, soon, he'll know something is up."

Thornton Howell was in the backseat of his car, heading back to his office when his phone rang.

"Hello?" he said, not recognizing the number.

"Hello, Thornton. This is Sterling. I've just awakened from my coma and was told you had come by. So sorry I missed you. And for your information, I am not dead and have no intentions of dying. I will be conducting an investigation into my shooting, and if I find you are behind this, which I believe you are, there will be no place for you to hide."

Thornton sat there, his mouth hanging open, listening to a dead phone. The President had said his piece and hung up, not waiting for a rebuttal.

Instead of going back to his office, he instructed his driver to take him to the place he stayed at when he was in Washington. His real home was in Cleveland, Ohio.

Not waiting for the driver to open the door with an umbrella, Thornton rushed from the car as soon as it stopped, and was soaked by the time he reached the front door.

His soaking wet clothes lay on the floor as Thornton stood under the steaming hot shower with a bottle of bourbon in his hand. His mind was whirling with anger. He hated the President and all he stood for. Someday, somehow, he would see him thrown out of office. The bottle of bourbon was half empty and he was beginning to feel calm and relaxed when his cell phone rang.

He stepped out of the shower and picked up his phone. "Hello," he said, drowsily.

"For a hundred thousand dollars, I will make your enemy go away." The voice was female.

Chapter 25

A NEW ENEMY

Lucita helped Liam to the sick bay where she ordered him to take his clothes off so she could examine his wounds.

At first, he resisted, but Lucita convinced him this was strictly professional. Even so, Liam felt a bit embarrassed, standing in front of her in only his underwear.

Lucita gasped when she saw the extensiveness of his wounds. He was black and blue from his face to his feet. After placing her hands on his head and his body, she declared he had a mild concussion, both eyes were swollen almost closed, he had a broken nose, several broken or bruised ribs, his left shoulder was dislocated, and he had extensive bruises on his arms and legs – plus, two of his toes on his right foot were badly damaged.

"My God, Liam, how are you still able to walk or not cry out in pain?" Lucita asked, looking at him with tears in her eyes.

Through puffed lips and a sore jaw, Liam said, "Back when I was training to be a Navy Seal, they told us we weren't allowed to have pain. We were told if they wanted us to have pain, they would have issued it with our seabag."

"That is barbaric," Lucita said. "Here, let me help you lie down on the table so I can try to make you feel well again."

Lucita had been born with the power to heal. Her mother hadn't been a healer, nor had her grandmother, but she was told her great grandmother was. They said they never knew which generation would have the power of healing and they were surprised the first time Lucita did it.

She had been climbing in a tree to look at some bird eggs in a nest, and on the way back down to the ground, a limb broke and she fell a good fifteen feet or more. She hit the ground hard and broke her left arm.

When her mother heard Lucita cry out, she ran out into the yard and saw her daughter lying on the ground and her arm hanging at a funny angle.

"You've broken your arm! We need to get you to the hospital right away," her mother said.

But Lucita had smiled and said, "It's all right, mother. I can fix it myself." And with that, she had laid her hand on the broken bone and within seconds, the arm was healed as good as before it had been broken.

Her mother had smiled and said, "I see you were born with the gift. Let's hope when you grow up, you will do good things with your power."

And she had. She was now known throughout the entire planet as a great healer. She was also the only one with the powers to heal.

As Liam lay on the table, feeling Lucita's hands gently touching his wounds, the many pains began to subside. Within ten minutes, he was feeling like his old self again.

"That was amazing," he told her.

"It's a gift I was born with, passed down from my great grandmother, who also was a healer."

"Well, wherever you got it, I'm glad you did," Liam told her.

"Me too," she said, blushing slightly. "I'll bet now that you're feeling better, you'd like to have something to eat."

Liam grinned and said, "As long as it's not human."

Lucita made a grimace and said, "Ugh... I don't even like to think about something like that."

They joined Emmelor in the dining room where he was sitting at a table in deep thought. "May we join you?" Lucita asked.

"I was hoping you would. That's why I got us a table," Emmelor said with a smile as he looked Liam over from head to foot, then turned to Lucita. "You are truly a blessing, my dear. Indeed, truly a blessing."

Emmelor turned and looked at Liam and asked, "Have I ever told you how Lucita and I met?"

Liam smiled and said, "No, but I'll bet it's an interesting story."

"It is," Emmelor said, as Lucita butted in. "I'm sure Liam isn't interested in all of that."

"But I am," Liam said.

Emmelor continued as though neither of them had said anything. "In my youth, I was quite a warrior and I was selected to fight for this very planet in a battle with the Ufraidas against their mightiest warrior, who turned out to be a man-beast. We fought for nearly sixteen hours straight, before I finally bested him with a throw that broke his neck and back. I could barely stand on my feet and the doctors said I was too broken up to be helped. I was expected to die within a few hours. But in walked this young snip of a woman who declared, "I can save him." And, as you can see, she did."

Liam sat there with his mouth hanging open. This, mild mannered man had once been a warrior of great notoriety?"

"You were a warrior?" he asked.

"The best on the planet, and on the other planets, also," Lucita said. "In fact, I think he chose you because you remind him of himself back in his day."

Liam was both honored and confused. "If you are a great warrior, why aren't you fighting your own battles?"

Lucita grinned and said, "While I can heal wounds and broken bones, I can't restore a person's youth. Emmelor is nearly a hundred years old."

"And that makes you…?" Liam was asking of Lucita but got cut off.

"Rule number one. You don't ask a woman her age," Lucita said, smiling and batting her eyelashes.

As the three friends sat, talking about Emmelor's younger days and how he rose to prominence, a man entered the dining room and stood looking around. When he spotted Emmelor, he walked over and bent over and spoke into his ear. "You need to come to the bridge, Sir."

"Is it something serious?" Emmelor asked.

The man nodded his head and said, "Yes-sir."

Emmelor knew he wouldn't have come if it hadn't been of extreme importance. "Very well, lead the way," he told him as he stood up.

Without being asked, Lucita and Liam trailed along, and when they got to the bridge, the giant screen showed a picture of the capital building with a bank of microphones sitting on the upper part of the front steps. The camera panned the lower area to show several thousand of the planet's people standing around waiting for someone to speak to them.

"What's going on?" Emmelor asked.

The helmsman looked up and said, "We're not sure, Sir. We received a message saying vital information would be coming soon – information that every head of state on the planet needed to hear. I sent the Lieutenant to bring you here.

Just then, a very tall man in a general's uniform, flanked by six men armed with rifles, walked out of the building. The guards stopped just shy of the bank of microphones, while the man in the general's uniform continued up to the podium and stopped. He stared out at the crowd of people for what seemed, a very long time.

"People of, X-162, my name is Brigadier General Ziman. I am now in charge of this planet and everyone on it will bend to my instructions. You may have done away with General Mellor, but you will not do away with me. From this minute on, Planet X-162 will cease to exist. This planet will now be known as, X-165 – 1, and if you follow my orders, you may be allowed to go on with your life as you did before our arrival. But, if you choose to become a renegade, you will be tracked down and either made a slave for life or burned alive in your town square as an example of what we do to traitors."

"What about our war agreement?" someone from the crowd shouted.

General Ziman turned to one of his guards and said, "Shoot whoever said that."

The guard ran down the steps and stopped just in front of the speaker, then he pulled his pistol and shot the man through the heart.

As the guard returned to his position with the other guards, General Ziman said, "As you can see, I care nothing for your agreement. I am a soldier and soldiers fight, not hide behind some agreement where two men decide the fate of a planet."

He started to turn away, then turned back. "This goes out to Emmelor, the so-called leader of this planet. Turn yourself in or you and all with you will be destroyed. You have twenty-four hours."

And with that General Ziman walked back into the capital building as spy drones hovered over the heads of the people.

Emmelor sat down in a chair and stared at the screen as a news reporter came on and said, "Emmelor, are you out there, somewhere, watching? If you are, what are you going to do about this? We need…"

The screen went blank and a technician said, "All communication with that channel has been cut off."

Emmelor looked around the room and saw everyone was staring at him. He stood up and said, "That was a bit unexpected. I don't know who this General Ziman is, nor do I know anything about him. But from the sound of things, we have another Mellor on our hands or maybe worse."

He walked down the row of seats and stopped in front of a middle-aged man who smiled up at Emmelor and said, "You want me to find information on this General Ziman right?"

"As soon as possible," Emmelor told him. "I will be somewhere on the ship, awaiting whatever information you come up with."

Emmelor left the bridge and headed for the ship's library, with Lucita and Liam right on his heels.

Chapter 26

A NEW THREAT

The newscaster looked into the teleprompter and smiled. "This just in. President Collier is awake and recovering from his wound by an attempted murderer. The assassin was killed in a shootout with the President's guards, but he had nothing on him to identify him or who he might have been working with. But the good news is, the President will be resuming his duties today from his hospital room, and said he hopes to be back in the Oval Office within a few days."

Marcy Helens, staff writer for the Times, sat at her computer and wrote her headline – FROM HIS HOSPITAL BED, PRESIDENT COLLIER BRAGS ABOUT DODGING ANOTHER BULLET.

Marcy Helens was without a doubt in league with Thornton Howell and she was one of his biggest supporters. She went on to write more of the slanderous accusations put out by Thornton, along with stating IT'S TOO BAD THE MAN'S AIM WASN'T TRUER. IF IT HAD BEEN, WOULDN'T THIS COUNTRY BE BETTER OFF?

To make things worse, the editor of the newspaper congratulated her on the article.

When Sterling read the headline, like most everything else about this impeachment, he took it in stride and laughed.

"That's nothing to laugh about," his nurse, Viola Wilkerson, said as she examined his wound.

"What should I do? Rant and rave, or pout like a small child? I've had to deal with people like her even before I got into politics. As a lawyer, if I won a case, as far as certain news people were concerned, it was because I did something shady or under handed. But never because I was a good lawyer. And it's not just me. Some people do nothing more than look for ways to find fault. It's sort of like a writer who gets a page full of good ratings, but out of a hundred five-star ratings, there are two or three who think his or her writing is a piece of trash, or that the writer has plagiarized the piece. No, I won't allow them to drag me down to their level."

Viola looked at the man she had admired from the day he first ran for President and knew she had been right. He may not be perfect, but he had a lot of integrity and only wanted what was good for the people of this country. "So, are you just going to let her get away with her lies?" Viola asked.

Sterling thought for a moment, then said, "I'm pulled in several directions. One part of me wants to sue her and her paper for vicious slander. Another part of me says I should pay no attention and wait for it to go away. While a third part of me, tells me to stay calm and speak with my advisor, Daniel Glazer."

"You talking about me behind my back, again?" Daniel Glazer said as he entered the room with two cups of coffee.

"Always," Sterling said, taking the cup and taking a sip, then giving his friend a questioning look.

"Added a little zip to it. I figured you might need a little something after that slamming the newspaper did to you," Daniel said with a grin.

Viola raised her hands up, palms forward, saying, "I see nothing, I hear nothing and I believe I have duties elsewhere."

"Now, that's one smart woman," Daniel said as he watched her leave the room. "Beauty and intelligence – what a great combination."

Sterling grinned, knowing his friend was just jesting. He knew for a fact that Daniel was neither, a racist or a womanizer. "Yeah, lucky us," Sterling said. "I'm glad you're here. I want to discuss the article in today's paper."

Thornton Howell had also read the paper and smiled. When he'd finished, he reached for his phone and called the editor in charge of the paper – touting the young lady's abilities as a reporter.

Next, he called Marcy Helens directly and asked if she would join him for supper that evening, which she readily agreed to do.

Thornton had seen pictures of her and had given thought to what it would be like to spend the night with her. Now, if he played his cards right..."

He was about leave his office to go home and get ready for this evening's activities. He'd already called the pilot of his yacht and set up a moonlight dinner cruise. Plus, he'd arranged for his limo driver to pick her up and bring her to the harbor. Things were going perfectly, until...

"Excuse me, but I think you should turn on your television," Thornton's secretary, Luella Barnes told him.

He walked over to his desk and picked up the remote and pressed the on button.

The screen was filled with the President sitting upright on his bed. He was wearing a shirt and jacket that covered his wound. He looked a bit haggard, but all in all, not bad for a man who'd recently been shot.

He heard someone in the background, say, "You're on in, three, two, one."

Sterling smiled at the camera and said, "Hello America. I'm speaking to you this evening from my hospital room because of all the false rumors that have been filling the news. I know I could sit here and deny all the accusations, but that wouldn't satisfy you any more than the statements about me. So, I'll get right to the point. I am challenging both Speaker of the House Thornton Howell and the newspaper reporter, Marcy Helens, to a televised debate three days from now, where I hope to clear things up for all of you. I will be entrusting the debate and the questions to a woman whom I consider to be impartial and neutral, Maggie Smythe. Many of you know her, and for those of you who don't, Maggie is the widely respected Attorney General of these United States. I hope you'll all tune in and watch. Thank you, and God Bless America."

Thornton switched off the television and leaned back in his chair, stunned. He hadn't thought it would come to this. But now that it had, he would crush Sterling Collier in front of the entire nation. Maggie Smythe would be a tough person to deal with. She would run a tight debate, not allowing any interruptions, which was one of his strong points, but, no matter. He would anticipate any questions she might throw at him and have counter attacks that would convince the American people that Sterling really was a traitor and that the world would soon be under attack and that only he, could stave off the attack and save the planet.

His ego was soaring as he left the office, hoping for an exciting evening.

-

The camera people had gone and the President was enjoying a chocolate milkshake when his bedside phone rang.

"Hello, Maggie," he said into the phone. "I've been expecting your call."

"How did you know it was me?" she asked.

"Caller ID. It's great. You can see who's calling before you answer. And I want to say thank you for accepting the role of moderator for my upcoming debate."

"But I haven't agreed to do it…" she said.

"But I know you're chewing at the bit to do it, and in all honesty, I couldn't think of a more perfect person to fill the job. For sure, I didn't want some commentator who could be manipulated by Thornton or me. I chose you because I know you'll be fair. Now, say yes – please!"

Maggie had already given it a lot of thought before making the call. Of course, she wanted to do it. Even though, in her heart of hearts, she didn't believe a word Thornton had been saying – she would do her best to present an impartial debate to the world, for this debate would not be confined to the United States. Not by a long shot. This debate would be broadcast throughout the entire world.

"All right," she finally said. "But on one condition. I run the show on an unbiased platform and no arguments from either of you."

"Done," Sterling said, with a smile. "I would shake your hand to seal the deal, but it's a bit hard to do over the phone."

"Where?" Maggie asked.

"I'll leave that to you," Sterling told her. "I'm confident it will be somewhere neutral."

"I'll be in touch with both of you, tomorrow," Maggie said, then hung up.

Sterling leaned back on his pillow and sipped his milkshake. An episode of Gunsmoke was just coming on.

300 Trillion Miles From Home

Chapter 27

IT'S WHAT FRIENDS DO

Emmelor's spaceship sat high above the planet with its shields up. A panel on the side opened up and a smaller version of the orb, exited the mother ship, heading for the ground, far below. Inside the small craft were a pilot, a navigator, a radioman, Lucita, Liam, and Emmelor.

"Do you think he will accept the challenge?" Liam asked as the small craft made its way down toward the planet's capital city.

"I really can't say," Emmelor said as he paced back and forth, with his hands clasped behind his back. "All I can do is publicly make the challenge and wait for his response."

Lucita looked at Liam and asked, "Are you ready? Mentally, I mean. I know you are in top physical condition, but who knows what kind of adversary you might have to face?"

Liam looked through the front window at the city below, that was getting closer by the minute. Was he ready mentally? He was on an alien planet, possibly about to face an unknown warrior in a battle to the death. How could he be mentally prepared for that? As he thought back, not once had he been asked if this was something he wanted to do. No. He'd been abducted and told he was to be X-162's champion.

The truth was, he had come to like and respect these people, and people they were – pretty much like the ones on his own planet. It was puzzling how two planets so far from each other could be so much alike.

Liam?" Lucita said.

He was brought back by her voice and said, "Yes, I've given that a lot of thought and I guess all I can say is, I'll face that problem when it comes."

"Take your seats," the pilot said. "We're about to sit down."

The large crowd of people standing in front of the capitol building parted as the orb sat down. When it was settled just in front of the steps, a panel opened and Emmelor stepped out.

At seeing him, a loud cheer and clapping filled the air.

Emmelor walked up onto the top step and waited for the cheering to quiet down, and when it did, he said, "I am here under our agreement to do single combat and I won't agree to anything different.

To this there was more cheering.

Emmelor turned to face the building and shouted, "General Ziman! I am here! Come and face me if you are not afraid!"

Shortly, the front doors opened and several armed guards rushed out and made two lines. Ziman walked down between them and stopped a few feet in front of Emmelor.

"As you can see," he shouted to the people below, "I stand before the would-be great Emmelor; unafraid and ready for combat."

He was willing to commit to this one-on-one combat because he felt confident that his chosen warrior would defeat Emmelor in short order. Emmelor was old and would be no match for the creature waiting just inside the capitol building. There would be no neutral ground. The fight would be, here and now, on the front area of the capitol building, where the television cameras could capture his demise.

Ziman looked at Emmelor and said, "Do you think you are up to fighting my warrior, old man?"

Emmelor shook his head and said, "Just as I figured, you are all mouth, but when it comes down to it, you use someone else to fight your battles."

Ziman stared at Emmelor for a moment before saying, "Are you challenging me to a duel to the death, old man?"

Emmelor looked at Ziman and saw a man less than half his age. He had the build of a warrior and from the look in his eyes, the mind of a killer. It would not be an easy battle, but he had been training in secret, in case something like this happened. He was as ready as he would ever be.

Lucita and Liam had been standing inside the small space craft, watching and listening from the hatchway. Lucita clutched Liam's arm and said, "You're not going to let him fight Ziman, are you? The man is half Emmelor's age. Emmelor won't stand a chance!"

Liam stood for a moment, watching before he finally said, "Sometimes age isn't as important as experience and I suspect Emmelor wouldn't be saying the things he's saying if he had any doubts about the outcome. Remember, he was once the mightiest warrior on this planet."

"But what if he gets in trouble?" Lucita asked.

"I'll deal with that, if it comes. But I won't butt in unless it's absolutely necessary to do so. If I were in his shoes, I would not want someone butting in and making me look like a coward that needs someone else to fight for me," Liam said, in almost a whisper.

"But you are the warrior he chose to fight for this planet," Lucita told him.

"Yes, and I will go if I am called, but as you recall, I was told to stay here until I was called for," Liam told her.

"I know, but…"

Liam cut her off. "No but's. I need to concentrate on what's going on out there."

Ziman stared at the man more than twice his age and grinned. Fighting Emmelor and killing him in front of his followers would be a major coup. Since he was the one being challenged, he would get the choice of weapons. For weeks now, he had been practicing with the ancient art of fighting with a broadsword and felt he had become a master swordsman. Emmelor would be no match for his skill.

What Ziman's ego hadn't taken notice of was each of his opponents had been far more skilled than he was, but their fear of his anger far out shadowed their desire to win. So, each of them had allowed Ziman to win every mock battle, making him believe he was much better than he actually was.

Ziman looked out over the crowd and shouted, "You heard him. He challenged me to a duel to the death and the winner becomes the ruler of this planet – your rules, not mine."

Turning to Emmelor, he said, "I accept your challenge and since you challenged me, I will choose the weapons. I choose broadswords."

Emmelor groaned and Ziman saw the reaction and mistook the reaction as Emmelor's inability to use the broadsword. When in reality, he was quite adept with the weapon. His groan came from the fact that broadswords were big and heavy – along with sapping your strength should the fight go on for any length of time. At his age, the longer the fight went, the quicker his strength and endurance would disappear.

"As you wish," Emmelor told him. "Do you have broadswords at hand, or do I have to wait for them to arrive?"

"Perchance, there happens to be a pair inside the capital building, along with shields, because you see, I happen to be an expert with the broadsword," Ziman said with a wide grin. "You've played right into my hands, old man."

Ziman turned to one of the guards and said, "Bring the broadswords and shields."

Turning back to the crowd, he raised his hands and said, "Soon, you will all be bowing down to me, so maybe we should practice once or twice before the duel begins."

As one, the entire crowd turned their backs to him, forcing a scowl on Ziman's face. "You can do this for the time being, but once I've slain your precious, Emmelor, you will no longer have that choice.

Emmelor saw what his people had done and smiled, then glanced toward the small spacecraft and saw Liam and Lucita standing in the hatchway. He smiled and gave them a wink.

Liam glanced at Lucita and asked, "Is he any good with a broadsword? They take a lot of strength to handle for a prolonged fight."

For the first time since they'd landed, Lucita, smiled. "At one time he was the master on this planet in broadsword dueling and taught many of the later masters. As far as knowledge and ability, there is none better. My biggest concern is time. At his age he can't let it go on for any length of time. He has to finish it quickly."

Liam nodded his head and said, "I'm sure he's well aware of what his short comings may be."

He looked Emmelor in the eyes and pointed to himself.

Emmelor mouthed, "Thank you, no. I have this."

Liam relaxed a little, but only a little. He would keep himself ready should there be a turn for the worse.

The guard returned with the broadswords and Emmelor saw they had blade protectors on them and knew what they'd been used for. However, for this contest, the blade covers would be removed.

Ziman looked at Emmelor and pointed, saying, "I allow you the first choice."

Like it would make any difference, Emmelor thought to himself. They were equal, so he picked the sword and shield closest to him and backed away.

Ziman picked up the other sword and made a big to-do about swinging the sword in several killing slashes, then stepped back and bowed.

Emmelor just stood and watched and when Ziman finished showing off, Emmelor said, "I'm ready whenever you are."

With the speed of youth, Ziman jumped toward Emmelor with a killing slash, hoping to take him by surprise and end the fight in one swoop.

Emmelor parried the blow, and brought his sword in a backward swing that cut a long, thin, gash in Ziman's breast cover.

Ziman jumped back, astonished at not only the quickness of Emmelor, but that he had thwarted his attack so easily.

They circled each other warily, looking for an opening. Emmelor knew that he had to do something soon or lose the battle to a young, stronger, but lessor of a warrior. Just then he remembered a tactic he devised, all those many days during his own youth.

He lowered his sword in such a manner to make it look like the sword was becoming too heavy for him.

Ziman saw the sword drop and assumed exactly what Emmelor wanted him to think. Then Ziman did exactly as Emmelor expected him to do. He charged with a forward thrust, aimed at Emmelor's heart.

At the last moment, Emmelor shoved his opponent's sword aside with his shield, stepped to the side and lifted the blade in an upward swoop, cutting Ziman's hand off at the wrist. The hand and the sword fell to the floor as

Ziman screamed to his guards, "Kill him!" as he grabbed his wrist to stop the flow of blood.

Emmelor looked at the armed guards and knew his sword would be no match for their guns. Then, like a lightning bolt, Liam jumped onto the porch with a double-bladed spear in his hands, screaming like a wounded banshee Indian.

The startled guards reacted slowly and found their weapons knocked from their hands and their throats slashed from side to side. They fell down, grabbing their throats, to no avail.

As Liam turned and attacked the next two guards, he heard the others scream and with a quick glance, he saw Emmelor eliminate them with his broadsword.

In less than a minute, the guards had been taken from the fight. Emmelor and Liam both looked around for Ziman and found he had disappeared.

"He ran into the capital building," someone from the crowd shouted.

Emmelor, Liam and Lucita searched the building from top to bottom but found no trace of Ziman.

They walked back to the front steps of the capital building and when they exited the front doors, loud cheering filled the air.

Emmelor stepped forward and raised his hands for quiet, and when the cheering subsided, he said, "Thank you my friends, but it isn't over, yet. Ziman has escaped and I'm sure we haven't heard the last of him. But do not be disheartened. One day soon, I hope, we will restore peace and unity to our beloved planet.

Once more, the cheers filled the air and continued until Emmelor, Lucita, and Liam boarded the small spacecraft and lifted into the air.

Once Emmelor strapped himself into his chair for the ride into space, he looked at Liam and said, "Thank you. That was a brave thing you did."

Liam had, over the time since being abducted, grown fond of Emmelor and his people. They were a lot like the people of Earth – just more advanced. He smiled at Emmelor and said, "That's what friends do."

Chapter 28

THE DEBATE

The morning of the debate between the President of the United States and the Speaker of the House was overcast, with a cold wind. But even bad weather could not dampen Sterling's feelings.

He had just returned from his morning breakfast, down in the kitchen, even though he knew someone would bring him whatever he wanted. Since his wife's death, he enjoyed having his meals and snacks in the kitchen where he could pick his friend and chef's brain. "He may not be a scholar with a bunch of degrees attached to his name, but he has more common sense than any of them I know, and he won't try to schmooze me by telling me what he thinks I want to hear," he told his chief advisor and others who questioned his eating habits.

During his breakfast of waffles, ham and eggs, with lots of butter and thick maple syrup, he and Archie had discussed the upcoming debate.

"Just stay honest with your answers and don't hesitate like you're trying to come up with an answer that will pacify them," Archie told him. "They're going to be watching every eye movement, every lip twitch, every hesitation you make. Don't let them see any fear or indecisiveness. Hey, you called for this debate. You're in charge of how it ends," Archie said with a wide grin. "Now, go forth and smite thine enemy!"

Maggie Smythe awoke, feeling anxious to get on with the day. She had given a lot of thought to this debate and had decided that the debate should not be shot in a studio where only the director, cameraman and other technicians would be standing around. They needed an actual live audience. So, instead of shooting the debate in a television studio, she had contacted the owner of the Lexus Theater and asked him if the debate could be shot there. Of course, he'd said yes. It would be great advertising for him.

Maggie wanted the Lexus Theater because it held eleven-hundred people. She had put an ad in the newspaper, stating tickets would be free. She arrived early to make sure everything was in order. The television truck was sitting out front, with cables running inside. She was overwhelmed by the long line of people waiting to get in. The owner of the theater told her there would be a full house. "People from all walks of life from the rich to the poorest of the poor, were out there, waiting to get in.

To say Maggie was happy would be stating it lightly. The audience would be among the people who did the voting, not just the people who legislate.

After making sure everything was ready, she ordered the doors to be opened and the people flooded in like a giant tidal wave, the corporate executive wound up sitting next to a ditch digger, or a plumber, and in some cases, people from the underworld. There were people of all races – voters who wanted… no, *needed* to see this debate, live.

When Thornton Howell and Marcy Helens walked out onto the stage, they were surprised to see the President already there, sitting at his table just past center stage.

Their table sat on their side of center stage.

"I didn't know there would be so many people," Marcy whispered to Thornton.

"It's Maggie Smythe's way of grandstanding this whole production. I protested, but she is in charge and told me if I was too scared, I didn't have to show up. Her way of making sure I did," Thornton whispered, back. "Just relax and answer your questions as you see fit, and don't be surprised if she tries to toss in some trick questions, so pay attention to each and every word she utters."

They sat down in their chairs, not acknowledging the President, who grinned. He was relaxed and had waved to several people in the front rows.

"Are we ready?" she asked the participants from the side of the stage where she sat.

All three debaters nodded in her direction. She then looked at the director and asked the same question.

"In two and a half minutes," he said. "I'll cue you at ten seconds."

Maggie arranged the papers that held her questions and watched the clock.

"On my count, ten, nine… and after the count of one, he pointed at Maggie and said, "You're on…"

Maggie made her greetings to the viewing public and also to the live audience, thanking them for coming. Turning to look directly at the camera, Maggie said, "We are here this morning at the request of Sterling Collier, the President of the United States of America. He wants to clear up, if he can, once and for all, what he calls the slanderous and untrue remarks being said about him and reassure the people of this country that he has only their best interest at heart."

There was boisterous cheering from the audience, and when they'd been quieted down, she continued. My name is Maggie Smythe. I am the Attorney General of the United States, and I have the great honor to run this debate. As I have previously instructed each of the participants, this debate will be run by my rules. I will ask each of them a question and they will be allowed thirty seconds to answer. There will be no interruptions and no one will speak unless I ask them to. Anyone of them who disrespects my authority will immediately be asked to leave."

She looked at the three debaters and asked, "Are there any questions about my authority in this matter?"

All three of them shook their heads and said, "No."

"Then, let us begin," she said. "Before getting into the actual debate, I would like to clear something up, with a question for our news correspondent, Marcy Helens. Miss Helens, from who and where did you get the information you printed in your newspaper?"

Marcy took a moment, then said, "It is my opinion taken from what the President said during his speech from his hospital bed."

"And can it be assumed that some of what you said, also came from things the Speaker, Mister Howell, had previously said about the President?" Maggie asked.

Marcy didn't like the way things were going, but had been advised by her boss to tell the truth as much as possible. "Yes. I suppose some of my opinions could have come from his statements."

"Just one more question, for now," Maggie said, in a gentle voice.

Marcy sighed. Just one more question and she could relax a little while the others were grilled. She hoped the President would get it worse than she had, so far.

"Miss Helens, are you aware of the penalty for threatening the life of the President of the United States?" Maggie asked.

Marcy was taken aback and stared at Maggie for a long time.

"Did you not understand my question?" Maggie asked, knowing she had put the young reporter in a bad place. The audience had gone deadly quiet, waiting for her answer.

Finally, Marcy said, "I don't have the slightest idea what you're talking about."

"Very well, let me ask you this way, and I quote from your article," Maggie said. "'It's too bad the man's aim wasn't truer. If it had been, wouldn't this country be better off?' That is what you wrote, isn't it?"

Thornton Howell looked down at the table, knowing where this was going and he didn't like it.

Marcy looked across the stage and said, "Yes, that is what I wrote. And I stand behind it, but it is just my opinion."

"Oh, I think it's much more than just your opinion, young lady," Maggie said. Again, I go back to my original question. Do you know the penalty for threatening the life of the President?"

"But, I…" Maggie held up her hand and said, "Please, if you will. Just answer the question, yes or no."

Marcy swallowed and said, "No."

"Well then, let me enlighten you," Maggie said. "Threatening the life of the President is a felony, for which a person can receive five years in a federal prison, and or, a two-hundred and fifty thousand dollar fine. Had the President been killed, you would have paid the ultimate penalty, dying in the electric chair, or other means of doing away with your life. And right now, your future is in the hands of the President."

Marcy sat there, her mouth hanging open and her heart beating like a kettle drum. Why hadn't she been informed of this, or had she, she wondered? Maybe she should have read the stack of rules and regulations she'd been given when she was hired, rather just signing the paper saying she had.

Maggie turned to the President and asked, "Mister President, will you be filing charges against Marcy Helens for threatening your life?"

Sterling looked across the stage and could see the fear in the young woman's eyes. He turned to Maggie and said, "If the young woman will apologize and promise to publicly retract her statement, then I will not press charges. However, if she elects not to, then, yes, I will press charges against her."

Marcy stood up and said, "Mister President. Please accept my apology. I would never actually wish to see you or anyone else dead. My only excuse is that I am young and got overzealous. I promise to write a retraction, along with an apology for my hasty judgement and lack of information in such matters."

"You do that, and I won't prosecute," Sterling said.

Maggie looked at Marcy and said, "Thank you for being here. You are excused."

Like a cat who had just sat down on a hot stove, she jumped to her feet and made a quick exit. Thornton Howell watched her go and felt disgusted. This wasn't how he pictured the debate going.

"Mister Howell," he heard Maggie say. Are we to understand, you have signed impeachment papers against Sterling Collier, the President of the United States? Is that correct?"

Thornton sighed and said, "Yes, but I…"

"Thank you, Mister Howell. Now, for my next question. "After having time to dwell on the matter, do you wish to continue with this line of attack? You have thirty seconds."

Thornton sat up straight and squared his shoulders. He would not allow this woman to put him under the bus as she had the young reporter. He was the Speaker of The House and a powerful man. "It is my stated opinion that

Sterling Collier is in league with the aliens to take over this planet and needs to be held accountable for his actions. Yes, I stand by my opinion that he needs to be punished to the full extent of the law, which is impeachment and possibly time in prison."

A hush fell over the audience as they awaited what was coming next.

"Do you have anything to say about that, Mister President? You have thirty seconds."

Sterling smiled and looked at the live audience and said, "First, I would like to thank our most gracious Attorney General, Maggie Smythe for officiating over this very needed debate. Thank you, Miss, Smythe. Now, to address the question. I have never, nor will I ever do anything to overthrow this country, or this planet. I am not in league with any aliens from space or persons on this planet. I think it ludicrous to even think I would be."

Maggie looked at Thornton and asked, "What do you say to that, Mister Howell?"

"Ludicrous, you say? Then explain why they communicated with you and no one else on this planet?" Thornton asked with a sneer on his lips.

"To be perfectly clear," Sterling said. "I did not exactly speak to a real person. Why they chose to appear in the Oval Office, I do not know. I only know they did. And as I have previously said, the man who called himself Emmelor appeared as a hologram and told me they were not here to harm anyone. He said they were looking at us to see if in the future they might contact us as allies."

This brought an audible gasp from the audience.

Sterling went on to say, "he said we have a lot in common in many ways except they are far in advance in their thinking about war and technology. And, that we need to be less warlike before they will make contact."

Thornton was raising his hand to be acknowledged, and Maggie nodded her head and asked, "You have something to say, Mister Howell?"

"More to the point, I have a question, Miss Smythe."

"Then ask it," Maggie said.

"Mister President, you say they were here spying on us only to see if we are worthy of being contacted. If that is true, why did they kidnap your bodyguard, Liam Biggers?"

Maggie turned and looked at Sterling. "Mister President, what have you to say about that?"

"Spying is a strong word, Mister Howell, but I won't argue over semantics." Here, Sterling saw no problem with stretching things just a little if it would help dissolve this impeachment proceeding. "Mister Biggers was not kidnapped. He was as interested in the possibility of becoming friends and allies with a foreign entity as I am. To the best of my knowledge, Liam volunteered to go visit their planet to see what kind of world they live in. How long this will take, I have no idea. But I eagerly await his return to find out what he has learned. And, I have total confidence that he will be returned, safe and sound."

Thornton could see the audience was leaning toward believing the President and he had to somehow get them back on his side. He had no doubt about Sterling telling the truth. It had nothing to do with that. It was about getting rid of the man and being replaced with himself.

"Mister Howell," Maggie was saying. "After what you've just heard, will you continue with your quest of impeachment?"

Thornton Howell looked at the audience and then at Maggie. "I say this to you and the people of America. I would not believe a word Sterling Collier says, even if his hand was on a stack of bibles. I will continue with the impeachment proceedings and in the end, the people will cheer me for doing the right thing for America!"

Only, maybe, fifty percent of the audience clapped or cheered, but it was enough to make Thornton feel he had redeemed himself.

"And that, ladies and gentlemen," Maggie said, looking straight at the cameras, "will end the debate. It will now be up to you to decide whom you want to believe. Please give each man's response your full attention, as I will be doing. Thank you and good night."

Thornton didn't wait around for any more questions. He got out of his chair, even before the director called a halt to the production. He needed to get away and plan his rebuttal. He knew he had not one shred of evidence to back his statements, but with the help of his friends and colleagues, they would pose new questions that would make Sterling look like he was hiding the truth.

As the people left the theater, at the reluctance of his bodyguards, Sterling stood at the entrance and shook hands with the people as they left – thanking them for being there.

It was almost two hours later before he and Maggie Smythe were able to speak to each other.

"Thank you, Maggie," Sterling said, taking her hand in his. "As I expected, you did a great job! I owe you dinner."

"Thank you. I think it went well. And I accept your offer for dinner. And just so you know ahead of time, it will be at a very expensive restaurant," she said, smiling.

Chapter 29

THE HIDDEN ROOMS

In both the large orb and the small spacecraft, they scoured the planet, searching for Ziman's whereabouts, but found no trace of him. What they did see was thousands of his military patrols, still lording it over the people.

"What are you going to do about this?" Lucita wanted to know as she stood in front of Emmelor. "It seems our planet is still under X-165's control."

Emmelor slouched down in his chair and stared at the images on the large screen and asked, "Not only have we not been able to find, Ziman, but have you noticed that there are still thousands of alien military personnel, but not one soldier from our planet. Nor have I seen any of our military equipment." He let the room go silent for a moment, then said, "With none of my military to aid me, how am I expected to find Ziman and bring him to justice, along with driving the foreign soldiers away? I'm open to suggestions."

Lucita felt embarrassed by her question and said, "I have some unfinished business to attend to," as she almost raced for another part of the ship.

Emmelor watched her go, but said nothing. Everyone had the same question. The problem was he had no answer, and wouldn't have until he could find and apprehend Ziman and find his own military personnel.

Liam had also been watching the screen and had seen something that reminded him of a military scheme he'd once concocted. "Emmelor, would it be possible to turn around and do another flyover of that big, open space behind us?"

"You mean the Kolo desert?" Emmelor asked, rising from his chair. "Did you see something?"

Liam shook his head. "Not so much that I saw something, but it reminded me of a military coup I did a few years back when hiding from my enemy."

Emmelor ordered the turnaround and as they neared the wide desert, all they could see was blowing sand.

Liam edged Emmelor closer to the screen and said, "Without slowing down, keep an eye out for two things - one - small, almost undiscernible pipes protruding up from the sand. And second, small antennas that could have cameras on them. The pipes supply air to submerged rooms below, and the antennas carry cameras to detect anyone coming near."

As the orb flew across the fifteen-hundred-mile-wide desert, they spotted several of the pipes and antennas.

"Don't slow down or they'll know they've been spotted. Just continue on and, if we can, come to a stop just beyond the desert."

The pilot nodded his head and continued on until they were beyond the desert and then brought the orb into a halt, hovering over the land just as they had on earth.

"Do you think that's where they're hiding my military people?" Emmelor asked.

"I do, and in a much more elaborate system than I had. I just used tarpaulins and poles in my concealment. I believe there are huge rooms the size of airplane hangars down there. And I further believe they have your people, along with their soldiers and guns to defend the rooms. Getting in there will be very difficult."

I have an idea," Emmelor told him. We will try it out tonight. For now, we both need to get some rest."

Darkness had covered this part of the planet for several hours when the small space- craft flew out of the orb's hatch and dropped down toward the desert, coming to a halt about a hundred yards above a road leading into the miles of sand.

Liam had a puzzled look on his face. "Aren't you afraid of being spotted by someone if they come down the road?"

Emmelor grinned, "I highly doubt it since this ship has been using its cloaking device ever since we left the mothership."

"You mean we're invisible?" Liam asked, in awe.

"To the naked eye, yes. We haven't yet found a way to stay hidden from sonar or radar, yet. But we're working on it," Emmelor said with a grin.

Liam was about to launch a dozen questions when the pilot said, "We have visitors."

They watched in darkness as a line of vehicles came down the road and the small spacecraft fell in behind them.

They went into the desert nearly twenty miles before slowing down to nearly a stop. There were ten passenger carriers, with the capacity to carry forty people each.

The desert opened up and the people carriers disappeared into a well-lit maw.

"Shall I follow them?" the pilot asked.

Emmelor thought for a moment and as the giant door began to close, he said, "No. Not this time. We need to make a plan."

Over dinner on the mothership, Liam said, "I have an idea how we can get information on what's going on down there."

Liam told Emmelor and Lucita his plan, which was immediately rejected. "I can't let you do that. It's far too dangerous."

"So," Liam said, "I'd like to hear your plan."

Sadly, Emmelor had no plan.

"I say that's your best option. And isn't that why I'm here?" Liam asked.

"You, my friend," Emmelor said, "were brought here to do battle in a one against one fight, not take on who knows how many are down there where you will have no help."

"But if I'm successful, I won't be alone, will I?" Liam asked.

Emmelor frowned. "You are not a man to be argued with."

"Then, I'm going with you," Lucita said matter-of-factly.

"Not this time," Liam told her, leaving no room for discussion.

The following day around the same time as the people carriers had come, Liam was lying in the ditch next to the road, with magnets attached to his hands. He was just outside the limits of the cameras and sensor detectors.

This time, there were six people carriers with X-162 soldiers in them. Liam was hidden by the darkness, crouched, ready to spring onto the road.

When the last people carrier passed him and began to slow down, Liam leaped out of the ditch and jumped onto the back bumper of the vehicle, while slamming the magnets against the back of the vehicle, only to fall off and land on his back in the middle of the road. Thinking quickly, he rolled over and over until he was back in the ditch and hidden from sight.

Later, when Liam was once again back in the small spacecraft, Emmelor, with eyes filled with mirth, asked, "What happened. Were the magnets not strong enough?"

Liam didn't mind being the brunt of the joke, and said, "That was definitely a trick on me. Haha."

"What are you talking about?" Lucita asked, confused.

Emmelor smiled and said, "He's talking about the fact that magnets would do no good. The vehicles are made out of molon, not metal."

"Then why did you let him go down there? He could have been hurt, or spotted," Lucita said.

"He was insistent on using magnets," Emmelor told her, then looked at Liam, saying, "If you decide to try again, I suggest, this time, use suction cups."

Liam had to grin. He had been insistent that he knew what he was doing. Maybe listening to a little advice from someone who lives on the planet might not be a bad thing.

"Please, I'd like to hear more about those suction cups," Liam said with a smile.

The following evening, Liam was once again lying in the ditch, anxiously waiting for the people carriers. This time there were only three, but as expected, they were filled with captured soldiers from X-162.

Liam leaped onto the back bumper of the last people carrier and to his surprise, the suction cups held.

Just inside the entrance, the vehicles were stopping. Liam peaked around the side of the vehicle and saw the drivers' showing credentials to a guard, with three armed guards standing next to him.

"Aww, crap," Liam said, knowing that when the back of the vehicle passed, he would be exposed, and more than likely be shot.

Thinking quickly, Liam moved the suction cups as fast as he could and made his way to the far side of the vehicle where, hopefully, he wouldn't be seen. He found himself under the back window, staring into the face of a young lieutenant. The young man's eyes went wide and Liam shook his head from side to side, hoping the young man wouldn't expose him.

The lieutenant turned his head forward and stared straight ahead.

The opening closed and Liam knew he was now totally on his own. After traveling only a short distance, the three passenger carriers made a left turn, allowing Liam to leap off and make his way between two single story buildings. The last thing he saw was the young lieutenant's fist with his thumb pointed upward.

At the back of the buildings there was an alleyway of sorts – more like a gravel path that led between the backs of the buildings. He gave a low growl. The path was lit up as bright as the street out front. After a moment's thought, he decided not to use the path, but made his way along the backs of the buildings on his side of the path, giving him less chance of being seen, or so he thought.

At the end of the row of buildings, Liam was faced with a new dilemma, he was facing another wide, well-lit street. On the other side were more buildings. He was about to make a dash across the street when he heard the sound of vehicles coming from both his left and right, then the crunch of rock under the wheels of a vehicle behind him.

Liam was trapped on all sides as the vehicles pulled to a stop, shining bright lights on him. Soldiers were leaping from the vehicles with weapons pointed at him. Liam raised his hands in the sign of surrender.

Another vehicle pulled to a stop and Liam watched as a man with a bandaged hand and wrist got out.

Ziman, followed by two soldiers with weapons, walked up and stopped in front of Liam. Ziman looked at Liam and said to his soldiers, "Take him to the interrogation room."

Liam was placed in one of the vehicles and whisked away, deeper into the underground hideaway.

He was taken to a room with only one chair, where he was shoved down onto the chair and strapped to it, then left alone, in total darkness.

Hours later, a bright light was turned on that shone directly into his face. He couldn't see anyone, but Liam recognized the voice of Ziman. "You thought us such fools that you could come into my compound without being noticed. It is you, whoever you are, that is the fool. You were spotted the instant you entered the opening."

Liam sat quietly, listening, trying to anticipate what would come next – a long, grueling interrogation, physical abuse, maybe even electrical shock treatment.

"Who are you and where are you from? It is obvious by your size and abilities; you are not from here."

Liam listened carefully to determine exactly where the voice was coming from before saying, "My name is Liam Biggers and where I'm from is of little matter. What is of great importance, is that I am here to take you and your people into custody."

Ziman gave out with a huge, belly shaking laughter. "And just, how, may I ask, since it is you who are secured to the chair, with two armed guards with weapons pointed at you, that you plan to do that?"

With the bright light shining in his face, Liam could only guess that the two guards were standing on each side of Ziman and would need him to come closer if his plan was to work.

They had underestimated him when they brought him to the room and had not searched him. Strapped to his right and left wrists were knives that could be released into the palm of his hand. He had, sometime ago, released the knife to his right hand and cut the bonds that held him in the chair. He had tucked the ends behind his back to make it look like he was still bound to the chair and waited.

"I'll tell you, but you need to come closer. My throat is dry and it hurts to talk," Liam said.

Thinking Liam was still securely bound to the chair, Ziman walked over and bent down to hear what the man had to say.

Unexpectedly, Liam threw off his bonds and grabbed Ziman and twisted him around, using him as a shield, he yelled, "Drop your weapons or Ziman dies!"

The guards could see the knife stuck against their leader's throat and did as they were told.

Circling around with Ziman still in his grasp, Liam said, "Move over into the light and lay face down in front of the chair."

When they hesitated, Liam yelled, "Now!"

With great reluctancy, the two guards did as they were told.

Once he and his prisoner were in the dark, Liam grabbed Ziman in a chokehold that rendered him unconscious. He then picked up the two weapons and examined them. They were very similar to the automatic weapons that were used back on Earth and he quickly learned how to use them by sending a burst of fire over the guard's heads. "Stay put or the next burst will give you some added weight."

Hanging a weapon over each shoulder, Liam pulled Ziman to his feet and slapped him across the face, reviving him.

With a knife at Ziman's throat, they moved out into the hallway. "You'll never get away with this," Ziman hissed. "I have over a thousand military personnel down here."

"Maybe not," Liam told him. "But if I die, so do you. Think on that."

With Ziman as a shield, Liam moved down the hallway in the direction of where the prisoners were kept, and when they reached the prison section, Liam saw it looked much like a prison back on Earth. He told the man in charge of the cells to open them and release the prisoners.

The prison guard looked at Liam and said, "I can't do that."

"And just why can't you do that?" Liam asked. And before he got an answer, he felt a sharp prick in his neck and everything went black.

Liam felt hands grasping his arms, but for some reason, he didn't seem to mind. He was floating on air and was feeling very pleasant until the snakes started coming toward him, hissing and spitting venom at him.

There were hundreds of them and their fangs were all long and dripping with deadly poison. As one of them sank his fangs into Liam's leg, he screamed from the pain.

Chapter 30

THE BOMB

Sterling was sitting in the White House kitchen eating a BLT sandwich, and drinking a bottle of Dr. Pepper when the vice President came rushing in. "Your polls are gaining by the hour! If they keep going, they'll be even higher than when you were elected!"

"That sounds good," Sterling said, then turned to his chef, and asked, "What did you think of the debate?"

Archie was sharping a large knife and he tested the sharp edge with this thumbnail, then said, "You owe Maggie, big time. She did a great job and I believe you reinstalled yourself as the President. As for Thornton Howell, well, he'll always have a few of his followers who will continue to support him, but as far as the House of Representatives and the Senate are concerned, I'm guessing they've already dumped him, along with most of the voters."

"Let's hope so," Sterling said, taking a long pull on his drink. His mind told him one thing, and his gut said something different.

Had Sterling known what was going on right then, he might have done things differently but it's like the old saying, "You don't know what you don't know."

As the President and his followers reveled in what they considered a victory of the debate in a small town in the mid-west, Brandon Shots reached over and turned off the television, then reached for his bottle of whiskey and took a long drink straight from the bottle.

"Don't you be worrying, Mister Howell, we'll see that, that lying Sterling Collier tells no more lies or sides with aliens to take over our planet."

He sagged down on the couch, took another long drink of whiskey, then sat the bottle on the floor and closed his eyes. In seconds, he was oblivious to the world around him.

Brandon Shots had been a civilian for less than a year, having been drummed out of the Army for trying to blow up his captain's house. He had been successful. The house and all its contents had been turned into a pile of rubbish. His only problem was that the captain had not been home at the time of the explosion.

Brandon was unruly and disliked taking orders. He thought he was smarter than the men over him. He was very good at his job, and had risen to the rank of sergeant, three times. He'd also being busted back to private three times and had spent a year and a half in the brig. Based on his past behavior, this last incident had been the straw that broke the camel's back, as they say. He had been dishonorably discharged and because of his military record, no one would hire him – for which he blamed the Army, the government and the President. When he saw a chance to get even with the President, his spirits soared.

-

Maggie Smythe finished her makeup and looked into the mirror. She didn't use much, just a little here and there. She was, after all, fifty-three and time wasn't always nice to a woman. As the Attorney General for the United States of America, she had had plenty of stress to deal with.

She felt a bit giddy as she slipped into a light blue cocktail dress that matched her eyes, then adorned her neck with a pearl necklace and matching ear studs. She'd tried bangle earrings but didn't like it when the slapped against her neck, or got caught in her hair.

Standing in front of the full-length mirror, she ran her fingers through her hair to give it a more full look and said, "Maggie Smythe, you look adorable, even if I do say so, myself."

Within a little over an hour or so, she would be sitting across the table from the most eligible bachelor in the entire United States. Of course, she'd had a crush on Sterling for a number of years, but she had also been friends with his wife, Ellen. They had met at a party during Sterling's first term, and had become instant friends. Since her passing, Maggie had stayed in the shadows out of respect for Ellen. But now, Sterling had asked her on a date. Well, not a date per se. He was taking her out to dinner in return for the job she'd done running the debate. "Well," she said as she donned her coat and headed for the front door of her condominium, "he may not consider it a date, but…"

Brandon Shots eased out the back door of the restaurant and ran down the alley, then dashed across the street where he could watch the action when it happened.

He'd found out through an unlawful app he had on his computer that the President and the attorney general would be dining at a particular restaurant that evening. Their reservation was for eight o'clock.

At seven-thirty, he slipped in the back door of the restaurant, dressed as one of the people who cleaned off the table, then made his way to the table where the President would be dining. The security guard standing just a few feet from the table, stepped in front of Brandon as he approached.

Brandon held up some fancy silverware and said, "Our regular silverware won't do for the President."

The guard looked at the fancy silverware in Brandon's hand, then over to the silverware on the table, and grunted, making an arm motion for Brandon to change out the silverware.

Prior to leaving the kitchen area, Brandon had left a small surprise on the far edge of the stove that was activated by heat, and just as he was changing out the silverware, the small bomb blew up, causing a major hullaballoo.

The guard said, "What the?" as he raced toward the explosion, giving Brandon time to attach a second bomb under the table – one more highly explosive than the one in the kitchen.

He finished his job and left, saying as he met the guard returning. "All done. They will dine in style with our best silverware."

The guard just grunted and went back to the table to make sure no one could bother the President or his date while they dined.

As the President stepped out of his limo, he told his driver, Sam, "I'm a bit nervous. I haven't had a private dinner with anyone but my wife since the day we were married. Do I look ok?"

Sterling was dressed in tan slacks with a light blue, open neck shirt and a dark blue blazer. He wanted to look good, but not businesslike.

"You look perfect, Mister President," Sam told him with a smile. "Now, go enjoy yourself. Miss Smythe is a handsome woman and from what I've seen, I think you could be dressed in rags and she wouldn't care."

"Sam!" Sterling said in mock surprise. He too had noticed how she acted when she was around him, and to be honest, he kind of liked being around her, too.

He was seated at the table when she entered the restaurant, right on time. Sterling had to swallow. She looked gorgeous. He stood up as the waiter pulled out her chair for her and seated her. And when he'd gone, Sterling said, "Wow!" as he sat back down. "You have the attention of every male in this room, and I'm sure, some of the women also."

"I'm glad you approve," Maggie said, lifting up the martini sitting in front of her. "You remembered," she said, holding the glass toward him in a toast. "To better times ahead."

They clinked glasses and each took a sip. The way Sterling was suddenly feeling, he wanted to down the entire glass and ask for another one.

The waiter took their order and after he left, they sat there, making small talk and enjoying themselves. "There are a lot of people staring at us," Maggie said, knowing the pictures being taken would be on the front page of every newspaper in the country, come tomorrow morning.

From across the street, standing in the alley, with binoculars held to his eyes, Brandon said, "Five, four, three, two, one - Bingo!"

The explosion blew up the table, sending debris in all directions, smashing into people's bodies, injuring Maggie, plus killing three others. The large front window disintegrated into a thousand pieces, scattering glass all across the sidewalk. Six people had to be taken to the nearest hospital to get glass splinters removed.

How Sterling survived, he wasn't sure, even though he had several cuts on his body from flying debris, and the explosion had burned both legs, along with breaking his left leg when one of the broken table legs smashed into it, knocking him unconscious.

With his binoculars, Brandon trained them on the President and, as best as he could tell, the man looked dead. Satisfied, he turned and walked to the opposite end of the alley and got into his car and drove off, smiling. He had just made amends for the wrong he felt had been done to him.

As soon as Sterling's wounds had been treated and a cast put on his leg by the emergency room doctor, he insisted they take him to see Maggie.

The room was semi-dark and when his wheelchair was parked next to her bed, he motioned for the man to leave them alone.

She looked pale and Sterling felt the anger well up inside of him. Who had done this terrible thing? He hoped they caught whoever it was soon. He would personally pull the switch or press the button – whatever it took to punish him.

He reached out and took Maggie's hand in his and when he did, she opened her eyes and tried to smile as best she could, with swollen lips and face.

"I'm sorry," he whispered.

"Yeah, like it was your fault," Maggie said in a low tone.

"It kind of, is," Sterling said. "I'm the President and someone has a beef with me and tried to kill me. And you became part of the fall-out."

"Have they found who did it?" Maggie asked.

"Not to my knowledge, but I've been assured they will find him or her," Sterling said.

Again, Maggie tried to smile when she said, "You know, you still owe me dinner."

Sterling squeezed her hand and said, "And this time it will be in the kitchen at the White House where I know we'll be safe."

Maggie grimaced as she tried to smile, saying, "It sounds romantic."

Sterling wasn't quite sure of what to make of that, so he kept quiet.

Chapter 31

ESCAPE AND EVASION

Liam opened his eyes and looked around. He was in a cell with three other men – one of them being the young lieutenant he'd seen through the window of the passenger carrier.

"Welcome back," the lieutenant said.

"Guess I didn't do so well," Liam said, rubbing the stinging sensation in his neck.

"But you sure raised a stir," the lieutenant said with a grin.

By now his other cellmates had noticed Liam was awake and crowded around his bunk. They were intrigued by this newcomer who had almost bested Ziman.

"Who are you and where are you from?" one of the men asked. He had on sergeant's stripes.

Over the next half an hour, Liam held court and explained where he was from and why he was here. "But I don't plan to be in here, long," he said with authority. "Now, with your help, I think we can somehow come up with a plan to not only get out of this cell, but release all the others as well."

They looked at each other as though the shot to Liam's neck had caused him to have mental problems.

"Getting out of here is impossible," one of the men said.

"Why?" Liam asked. "Because that's what you were told?"

All four men nodded their head affirmatively.

"We have a saying back where I come from. Don't believe everything you hear, and only half of what you see," Liam said. "Now, with you or without you, I'm getting out of here. I would much prefer you come with me, but…"

"I'm with you," the young lieutenant said, sticking out his hand.

The two men shook on it and within less than a minute, the other men had each shook Liam's hand, promising to do whatever it took to escape. "Even if I die, it will be better than the torture I've heard about," the sergeant told them.

How long have you been in here?" Liam asked.

"Just under six moons," the sergeant said. "And almost every night, we hear the screams – blood curdling screams that I know one day will be coming from me."

"Anyone know where they keep their weapons?" Liam asked.

"I do," said a female voice from the cell on their left.

"Can we get to them from here?" Liam asked.

"Not without killing a few of them, first," she said.

"Such are the perils of war," Liam told her.

"We don't know what that means," one of the men in Liam's cell, said. "We don't actually do war on any of the planets in our solar system. At least not until Ziman showed up with his military personnel and began shooting us. And as you can see, we weren't prepared."

"What if it comes to us or them?" Liam asked.

"Put a weapon in my hands, and I won't hesitate to fight," the young lieutenant told Liam. "Before setting her on fire, the things they did to my fiancé was unspeakable. I want to see every last one of them, dead!"

With so much anger in him, Liam wasn't sure he wanted a weapon in the man's hands. He was too high-strung. He looked the man in the face and said, "You come with me - you take orders from me, which means no killing unless I say so. You understand me?"

The lieutenant swallowed and got an angry look on his face before relinquishing and saying, "I understand. I am a military man and will take orders – like them or not."

"All this talk is fine, but to make any of it work we need to be on the other side of these bars. Any suggestions on how we go about doing that?" the sergeant asked.

All eyes turned to Liam, who smiled and said, "Glad you asked."

With that said, Liam sat down on a bunk and commenced to take off his left boot. As they watched, he twisted the heel of the boot and it swiveled to the side, revealing several small articles; one being a small vial of liquid.

Liam stood up and walked over to the door and put two drops onto the door lock. Immediately, it ate through the lock mechanism and the door swung open.

"What is that stuff? Did you bring it with you? Where did you get boots with hollow heels?" one of the men asked.

"Let's just say, I try to be like a motto we have back home, 'be prepared'," Liam said, putting the vial back in the boot heel and then, put his boot on. He then lifted his other boot up over his knee and twisted the heel of his right boot. This time, he took out a garrote and laid it on the bunk.

"What is that?" the lieutenant asked.

"It's called a garrote, and it has several purposes. It's number one purpose is to strangle someone in a silent kill. And, number two, the wire is called a diamond wire loop. With just a few pulls back and forth, it can cut through one of those prison bars in just a few seconds. And third, it is strong enough to hold my weight, if need be," Liam told them.

Looking both ways, Liam eased from his cell and went to the one next to him and slipped the garrote wire across the locks bar and with just a few sawing motions, the door swung open. Inside were four women.

Liam looked down the row of cells and saw a closed door and asked, "Where does that lead to?"

Again, the woman spoke up, "That's where the door opener and closer room is. There is one man there."

Liam gathered them all together and laid out his plan.

The woman ran up to the door and looked through the window at a surprised guard. "Please, you must help me. My friends are dying!" she screamed and turned and ran back toward her cell.

Not only did the soldier wonder how she got out of her cell, but he wondered what could be happening as he jumped from his chair and ran out into the run area.

Liam was standing to the side and as the guard ran past him, he ran up behind him and dropped the garrote wire over his head and around his throat and jerked.

The man died almost instantly.

Liam then ran into the room and looked at the board containing buttons for each cell. As fast as he could, he opened each cell and watched as the men inside walked out, slowly wondering what was going on. There were close to a hundred and fifty of them.

The men and women from the two cells Liam had opened were making their way amongst them, explaining what was happening and pointing in Liam's direction.

Liam approached the woman from the cell next to his that he had spoken with and asked her if she would guide him to where the weapons were kept.

"Yes, but be prepared to run into more guards," she said. "And they will have weapons."

Liam reached into the cuffs on his jacket and removed several throwing disks. "Maybe these will even the odds, a bit."

So, with over a hundred men and women following him, they headed for where the weapons were kept.

They rounded a corner and came face to face with three armed guards. Before they could react, they felt the stab of the metal throwing disks and dropped to the floor.

Liam retrieved the discs and wiped them clean on the guard's uniforms. He then picked up their weapons and started to hand them to the men he'd shared a cell with.

All three men looked at him like he had a third eye. "What do you want us to do with these?" the sergeant asked.

"You are soldiers, aren't you?" Liam asked.

"Yes, but on this planet, soldiers aren't trained for physical combat." The sergeant said.

"Then what are you trained for?" Liam asked, flabbergasted by the sergeant's statement.

The sergeant looked at the floor and said, "As I think you know, we do war in a civilized manner – two men in an arena. As soldiers, we patrol the streets, giving out parking tickets, and helping the elderly to cross the streets, safely. Things like that, unlike the soldiers from planet X-165, who seem to enjoy killing."

"Aw, jeez," Liam said under his breath. He looked at the crowd of people behind him and asked, "Is there any among you ready to fight for your freedom?"

There was an agonizing moment where Liam wondered if he was alone in this fight. Then one hand went up in the air, followed by another and another until ninety-five percent of the hands were in the air, including the men from his cell.

Liam instructed the three men from his cell on the use of the weapons they were holding. "We don't have time for target practice, so, wait for my command, then point your weapon at the enemy and squeeze the trigger. When your opponent falls, turn your weapon on another, and so on. Any questions?"

No one seemed to have any questions, so he turned to the woman leading them, who Liam found out was called Meega and said. "Lead on."

Meega stopped them short of making another turn and said in a very low voice, "The room where the weapons are stored is just around this next corner. The door is kept locked and is guarded by two men."

Liam thought for a moment, then said, "Stay here until I call for you. It shouldn't take long."

He removed two throwing discs – one in each hand and walked around the corner in the direction of the two guards – whistling a song from earth – Yankee Doodle Dandy.

The two guards were startled to see the man coming and seemingly so relaxed. "Halt!" one of them called out as Liam got close.

"Gentlemen, and I use the term loosely, what are you guarding?"

Both guards seemed distracted by Liam's size and easy-going attitude, which was their mistake and demise. Both of Liam's hands flashed out and within the blink of an eye, the two men dropped to the floor, dead.

Once again, Liam retrieved his discs and cleaned them on the men's jackets, then gave a whistle and watched as the other prisoners came toward him.

"The door is locked and neither of the guards have the key," the lieutenant said, standing up.

Once again, Liam removed the vial from the heel of his boot, and with only one drop of the acid, the door swung open. The room was filled with weapons of several kinds, along with plenty of ammunition.

Each man and woman had been given a weapon and ammunition, and had been instructed on its use when they heard Ziman's voice calling out to them. "Mister Biggers, once again you have underestimated me! Throw down your weapons and come out."

Everyone in the room looked at Liam to see what his response would be. Liam stepped up close to the open door and yelled, "Don't think so. It's you who should lay down your weapons and we promise not to shoot you!"

The laughter that filled the air was like it was coming from something evil. Ziman quelled his laughter long enough to say, "How are you going to get out of that room. I have weapons trained on the doorway, and it is the only way out. Plus, just one of my armor piercing grenades is powerful enough to blow the entire room into nothing but small pieces, along with killing all of you."

Liam thought for a moment, then walked over and took a rifle from one of the prisoners and stepped far enough into the room to where he couldn't be seen by Ziman or his soldiers and lifted the rifle to his shoulder and took aim.

"I'm waiting for an answer, and my patience is wearing thin!" Ziman called out just before a bullet was driven into his right eye and out the back of his head, also killing the soldier standing behind him.

Before the stunned soldiers could react, the prisoners bore down on them. Within less than a minute, it was over. While Liam and his fellow prisoners were taking control of the underground prison, Lucita was pacing back and forth across the floor of the pilot room of the orb.

"Relax," Emmelor told her. "I'm sure Liam is doing what he was sent in to do."

Just then, the pilot said, "The portal is opening."

Emmelor and Lucita ran to the screen and saw Liam standing in the front floorboard of a vehicle with no top. He was leading a long procession of people carriers out from the underground prison. He was looking up in the direction of the orb and waving his hand.

Lucita broke into tears as she watched Liam – a man from a far distant planet she had grown far too fond of.

Chapter 32

ANOTHER ATTEMPT

The young reporter, Marcy Helens, was still filled with anger as she dropped the newspaper on her desk after learning the President had once again survived a threat to his life. "So, someone else had tried to kill him and failed," she mumbled to herself. She still hadn't had a reply from Thornton Howell on the throwaway phone number she'd given him. She'd laid a piece of cloth over the mouthpiece to disguise her voice when she called him and offered to kill the President for a hundred-thousand dollars.

"If Thornton comes through with the hundred grand, I won't fail," she hissed, looking around to make sure no one was looking at her. Ever since the debate, her colleagues had been giving her weird looks. Her editor told her he had no choice but to assign her to weddings and birthdays – at least until things calmed down.

A hundred thousand dollars would get her out of the country; maybe to some resort country where she could find a rich sugar daddy, and never have to worry about anything ever again.

She jumped when the throwaway phone in her purse, began ringing. She quickly pulled it from her purse and put it to her ear, placing her handkerchief over the mouthpiece.

"Hello," she said with a deep, gruff sounding voice.

There was a brief hesitation before a male voice said, "you said I should call this number. How do I know this isn't some kind of trick?"

Marcy thought quickly and said, "Because someone we both know and hate has offered me money to do you and I'm giving you a heads-up and offering to do him, instead – your choice."

"Half now and the other half when the job is finished," Thornton said.

"Done," Marcy replied. "Send it to this account number," she told him, giving him the number of a new account, she'd opened under an alias name. "As soon as I see the money has been transferred, Sterling Collier will be dead within a few hours."

"Don't mention names!" Thornton reprimanded. "The money will be in the account within the hour. I want this done today."

Marcy heard the click as Thornton hung up.

Less than an hour later, the money was in the new account and she smiled. Everything was going as planned. Now to do her part.

She saw on the news that the President was to speak at a Women for America meeting later that very day. She looked at her watch and saw she had time to get herself in position.

From the top of the building next to where the President would be speaking, Marcy positioned herself, making sure the rifle she'd purchased from a man who sold firearms from the trunk of his car, was loaded.

She didn't have long to wait until she saw the President's car coming. She put the butt of the rifle to her shoulder and tracked the car. She had decided to shoot him the moment he stepped out of his car.

What she didn't know was, with all the attempts on the President's life lately, the Secret Service had men arriving in advance of wherever the President would be going and had set up surveillance. In this case, there were four of them and one of them thought he saw the sun glimmering off of metal on the building across the street from him, just as the President's car was pulling up.

He put the scope of his rifle to his eye and saw a young woman, pointing a rifle down in the direction of the President's car. He'd never shot a woman before, but it was his job to protect the President and as he saw her sight down the barrel of her rifle, he squeezed the trigger of his rifle and saw the bullet reach its target. As she was knocked back onto the roof, her rifle fell to the pavement below.

Sterling heard the rifle shot and ducked back into his car as Sam burned rubber getting them away from the area. A block away, Sam got a call, giving the all clear, and he turned the car around and went back so the President could give his speech.

Later that evening one of the secret servicemen, a Mike Langley, entered the Oval Office and stopped and said, "Mister President."

"We needn't stand on ceremony, Mike. Please, have a seat and bring me up to date. I'm going to have a drink. Will you join me?" Sterling asked.

"Whiskey over some ice, if you have it," Mike said with a grin. He'd always heard the President was a cool guy but until now hadn't quite believed it. This was the first time they'd actually met, face to face.

Sterling raised his glass and said, "To you, my new friend. I'm sorry we had to meet under such circumstances, but thank you for saving my life."

After they took a drink, Sterling said, "Now, tell me, do we know the shooter?

Mike sat his glass on the coaster sitting on the table next to him and said, "We do, and I think you're going to be surprised. It was that young reporter that was on the debate – the one who had written about you."

"Are you serious?" Sterling asked, flabbergasted. "And you shot her?"

"As serious as a heart attack, and yes, I shot her. I had no other choice, Sir," Mike said. "And not only that, we also found out who paid her to do it."

Sterling's heart began to beat faster as he said, "Go on."

Mike took a long pull from his drink, then said, "She had one of those throw away phones on her when we searched the body. And with that, we were able to listen to a conversation she had with the man who paid her. We traced the call and you'll never guess who that person is.

"Thornton Howell," Sterling said, lifting his glass to his lips and taking a long drink.

Shocked, the secret serviceman said, "How do you know that?"

"Just a calculated guess," Sterling told him. "Has he been arrested?"

Mike swallowed and said, "As of when I came into your office, no sir. He seems to have disappeared."

"He's gone underground," Sterling said, swirling the bourbon around in his glass before taking another swallow.

"We'll find him, Sir. And in the meantime, until he is apprehended, you will be under our surveillance twenty-four-seven," Mike said, standing up. "Thank you for the drink, and don't worry about a thing. We'll get him."

After the secret service man had gone, Sterling fixed himself another drink and as he sat at his desk, sipping his bourbon, a thought came to him and he sat the glass on the desk and opened the right hand, bottom desk drawer.

He took out a military forty-five caliber pistol and laid it on the desk. After staring at it for a few moments, he picked it up, unloaded the shells and broke it down – giving it a good cleaning before replacing the shells. He hoped he would never have to use it, but it was best to be prepared. He had no idea how far Thornton Howell would go.

At that very moment, Thornton Howell was wondering the same thing as he drove down the coastal highway, heading south. His final destination would be an island off the coast from Charleston, South Carolina. A person he'd done what might be called shady business with a few years back had a hideaway home there and said he could use it. He'd called the man and was told the place was empty and for him to feel free to go there. He had no connection with the place and felt he would be safe there until he could figure things out. In the end, he just might have to do the job himself.

He was dead tired as he drove onto the ferry that would take him out to the island. He hadn't slept a wink during the entire trip. Coffee and no-doze pills had helped, but before the ferry pulled away from the dock, Thornton was sitting in his vehicle, sound asleep.

Sometime later, the honking of car horns woke him up. He started his car and drove onto the island, rubbing the sleep from his eyes.

The house sat on the far end of the island, away from prying eyes.

Chapter 33

LEAVING FOR HOME

Emmelor's home was a huge mansion-like affair with ten bedrooms. He had both upstairs and downstairs maids, along with two gardeners. The property sat on the bank of a huge lake, and a long pier jutted out into the lake, where a powerboat and sailboat were tied up.

The war was over and peace once again trying to settle over the planet.

Emmelor was sitting in a comfortable chair, sipping his favorite drink and looking out at the people on their sailboats, enjoying the afternoon. His only concern was Liam. The man was pacing back and forth across the veranda like a caged animal.

"Come and sit with me. Have a drink," Emmelor called out.

Liam stopped and looked at Emmelor. The man seemed to be at peace with the world, but not him. He'd been gone from earth far too long and was worried about his friend, the President.

"Please, at least come and tell me what's troubling you," Emmelor said.

Liam stopped his pacing and looked out across the lake at the sailboats, realizing that was what had set him to thinking of home. He had a thirty-four-foot sloop tied up at the dock back home on Crystal Lake, where he spent his time off, sailing and relaxing with whoever he was dating at the time.

Giving a sigh, he turned back and walked over to where Emmelor was sitting and sat down in a chair opposite him. "I believe I've done what you've asked of me. Your planet is back in your hands again, and things are going back to normal – right?"

Emmelor nodded his head and said, "You have done more than I ever expected you to do. You have saved this planet and I've been sitting here trying to think how I might reward you."

"You really want to know?" Liam asked.

"I do," Emmelor said.

"Take me home. I've done what I was brought here to do, and now I want to go home," Liam said. "There are people back there who need me."

"What's that?" Lucita asked as she walked out onto the veranda.

"He says he wants to go home," Emmelor told her.

Lucita got a sad look on her face. She'd come to have feelings for this earthman and she wasn't sure how she would deal with him leaving. She even knew it was wrong of her, but she couldn't help herself, and if the truth were known, she felt he had feelings for her, too. She also knew it was all ridiculous but she couldn't help herself.

"You don't like it here?" Lucita asked, pouting her lips.

Liam looked around and said, "This planet is almost a twin sister of Earth, and under different circumstances, I might feel differently, but Earth is my home. I have roots there. Plus, I have an obligation to my friend and the President of my country, Sterling Collier. I really need to get back."

He could see the pain in Lucita's face. They had gotten close and he had feelings for her, but it would never work. A relationship with them being trillions of miles apart was out of the question. He didn't like hurting her, but what choice did he have? Staying here was out of the question. He had obligations back on Earth.

She looked heartbroken and he desperately wanted to take her in his arms and tell her everything was going to be all right – but it wasn't. He wanted to go home and Emmelor had promised to take him back as soon as the job he was brought here to do, was done. Well, the way he saw it, he'd done far more than what he'd been expected to do.

Emmelor stood up and walked to the railing at the edge of the veranda and looked out across the lake. "I can't deny, you've done far more than was expected of you. And you are right in requesting we take you back. You have completed your mission."

He turned and walked back, stopping next to Liam and looked him in the face. "I guess I have hesitated because I was hoping you would like it here and want to stay. I know a certain someone we know, would also like that," he said, rolling his eyes in the direction of Lucita. "You could live the life of a hero. I could offer you the position of the head of our military or almost any other position you would like, other than mine. Don't you think you could be happy, here?"

Liam slumped down in the chair next to him. "You know I could, and believe me, I've turned it all over and over in my mind," he said, letting his gaze turn to Lucita who was still standing where she'd stopped. "But the bottom line is, I have obligations back on my planet – obligations I don't take lightly. I thank you for your very generous offer, but I do need to get back. And after all, it's only three hundred trillion miles," he said with a grin.

"Very well," Emmelor said. "I will make the arrangements. You will leave on the morning of the second sun from tomorrow."

Lucita filled Emmelor's sailboat with food and drink and she and Liam spent what time he had left of planet X-162 together, on the lake, enjoying each other's company. They sailed to the end of the lake and back and lay on the deck, looking at the two moons and her telling Liam of the star patterns that surrounded her planet.

On the morning he was to leave, Liam was almost tempted to stay. He could have a wonderful life here, and Lucita… She was all a man could want and more. But in the end, he tied up the sailboat and went ashore.

At the teleport, Emmelor introduced Liam to the pilot that was to take him back to Earth. His name was Eem. He was about Liam's age and anxious to make the trip.

"I'm sorry, neither I, nor, Lucita can accompany you. We have obligations here," Emmelor said, handing Liam a small box. "Inside is a communicator. Should you ever need our help, you can reach me. Just remember, being so far apart, it will take some time for your message to get to me and my answer back to you."

They shook hands and Emmelor left, leaving Lucita and Liam time for their parting.

For Lucita, there wasn't much to say. He was leaving and that was that. She embraced him, holding him tightly, whispering in his ear, "I'll never forget you, Liam Biggers," then released him and ran from the teleport, with tears streaming down her cheeks.

The ship he would be returning to Earth in was much smaller than the one Emmelor had traveled in, but still big enough to be comfortable.

Liam watched through the portal as the ship lifted off the pad and hurled itself into space and when he could no longer see the planet, he went in and sat down next to the pilot.

Eem grinned and said, "Once I've set the coordinates, we'll get into the sleep pods, and when we wake up, you'll be able to see your planet."

Liam nodded, remembering the sleep pod he was in on the way out. But he was still a little nervous about getting into the sleep pod. What would happen if something went wrong and there was no one there to take control? He stepped into the sleep pod and closed the door, feeling the mist begin to rise from his feet. He took a deep breath and felt his body begin to relax.

-

Some distance behind, a ship similar in size followed along. Zicor, Ziman's twin brother looked at the panel on the control board and when he was satisfied, he pushed a button and immediately a panel lit up. The panel read, 'Locked onto target. Tracking target.'

Zicor grinned and said, "You may have outwitted my brother but you will not outwit me."

Zicor and Ziman were identical twins in every way except for Zicor being far more power hungry and evil than his brother. Technically, Ziman was the older by nearly thirty minutes, which, on their planet, made him the older brother and the one with the final say about things. Zicor had always been envious, but now that Ziman was dead, he was free to do as he pleased – and his first mission was to kill the man who had killed his brother. He wasn't doing it out of honor, or love for his twin. If the truth were known, he hated Ziman. He was going to do it just because he wanted to prove to himself that he was the better man.

Once Zicor felt secure that the tracking device was working, he made his way to the sleep pod, and just before he closed the door, he said, "Maybe, after I kill this earthling, I just may take over his planet as its new ruler."

The two ships raced across the distance between planet X-162 and the planet Earth, at a speed unheard of back on Earth. Each ship had protective rays seeking out clear paths around other planets, and dodging any and all other debris floating around out there.

Chapter 34

OUT OF HIDING

Sterling went down to Camp David, where he hoped it would be safe.

During his stay at Camp David, he held meetings with representatives from all over the world, assuring them, the planet was not in danger from aliens, but from people who were trying to upset not only America but their countries as well.

"And just what do you mean by that?" the man from Zambezia asked.

They were having coffee in the living room and the President sat his cup on the end table next to the chair he was sitting in. "Their first agenda is to get me out of office by any means possible. As you know, there has already been several attempts on my life."

The man from Zambezia nodded his head and waited for Sterling to continue.

"Once I'm out of the way, they will make sure my successors will also be eliminated until the Speaker of the House, Thornton Howell, can step into the White House as President. And if that happens, America will be on a downhill rollercoaster, along with your country and any other country who has ties with America.

The man from Zambezia stared at the President of the United States for a long time before saying anything. He may have been born and raised in Zambezia, but he'd come to America for his college education – Yale law school, to be exact. He had watched Sterling's rise to the presidency and had followed him through the years until now and had liked what he saw. As far as he was concerned, Sterling Collier was the best President to come along in a good while.

"I agree," he finally said. "I do not believe the accusations against you and it is of great importance to the entire world that you stay alive and in the President's chair. So, with that in mind, I have taken it upon myself to see that special forces from not only Zambezia but also five other countries will take turns assisting your Secret Service in keeping you safe.

Sterling was stunned and all he could say was, "Thank you. I'm not sure that will be needed, but I appreciate the gesture."

"It has already been cleared with General Watson and the head of the Secret Service," the man from Zambezia told him. "Now, I must take my leave."

-

Thornton Howell paced the floor of the house just off the coast of South Carolina. He not only had business to attend to with Congress and the Senate, he had to bring this thing with Sterling Collier to a close. He'd decided it would be up to him to see it finished and done with. Just how he would accomplish it, he wasn't sure, but he would think of something.

Having made his decision, Thornton packed his bag and got into his car and left. He would have just enough time to catch the ferry going back to the mainland.

Literally, hundreds of ideas for killing Sterling had come and gone in Thornton's brain, but nothing had stood out as the perfect crime. Even during his ferry ride to the mainland, at least ten ways crept into his thoughts, but again, he dismissed each one.

Somewhere along the drive, the thinking had given Thornton a splitting headache and he pulled into a motel along the road in Virginia Beach, Virginia. After checking in, he unloaded his bag into the room, took a long, hot shower and went to a restaurant across the highway that sat on the beach.

Thornton sat outside on the veranda and sipped a drink as he listened to the waves lapping onto the shore. When his plate of Seafood Special arrived, the aroma smelled so good he could hardly wait to begin. He hadn't realized how hungry he was. There was lobster, breaded clams, deep fried shrimp, oysters on the half shell and a bowl of clam chowder on the side. He decided to eat the clam chowder first before it got cold. He disliked tepid or cold soup.

He'd finished the clam chowder and was delving into the rest of his meal when a thought crept into his brain, causing him to stop eating and look up at the moon that was sending sparkles off the ocean. "Why hadn't I thought of that, before?" he said to himself, going back to eating his meal.

With two more drinks under his belt, Thornton went back to his room, happy about finally coming up with a foolproof plan to kill the President of the United States of America.

Thornton awoke the following morning, pleased with himself, and before getting back on the road, he had a leisurely breakfast, turning the idea over in his mind from several angles, but could find no fault with it.

Later that day, he drove past his DC residence to make sure no one was waiting for him. When he saw no one, he pulled into the garage and closed the door, never realizing he'd been observed from the house across the street. Five hundred dollars a day can get you a lot of window gazing, which is what the government paid the people across from where Thornton resided.

-

Sterling answered his phone and heard a man on the other end, say, "He just pulled into his garage and closed the door. Do you want us to arrest him, now?"

Sterling thought for a moment before saying, "Yes. Bring the charges against him to the White House and I'll sign them."

Thornton was not surprised when the Secret Service men showed up at his front door with an arrest warrant and he was prepared for it. Being who he was, he was allowed to make a phone call before they took him away. He called his lawyer to meet him at the police department with bail money and was alarmed when he heard his voice message, "Hi, sorry I'm not available to take your call. I'm giving myself a weekend of fishing – no phones, just trying to land the big one. I'll be back in a couple of days. Ciao."

"Italian lawyers didn't go on weekend fishing trips, did they?" he said, turning off his phone.

"You say something?" one of the secret service men asked.

Thornton's mind was racing a mile a minute. What was he to do, now? "I'm sorry but the person I was trying to call isn't answering. I need to make another call. It won't take but a moment."

"Sorry, Mister Howell, but we gave you one call that we didn't have to," one of the secret service men said, taking the phone from Thornton's hand and putting it in his pocket. "This phone is now officially evidence."

"But, but…" Thornton protested as he was put in the back seat of the car used to spy on his house.

The truth was that Thornton's attorney, Lorenzo Esposito, had never been fishing and had no desire to ever go fishing. For several weeks now, he had been meeting with a certain senator's wife on the sly and this was the first time they could slip away. He'd rented a cabin in Aspen, Colorado, far away from anyone who might recognize him or her.

Thornton was safely hidden in South Carolina and Lorenzo had no cases pending. It was the perfect time for him to get away and as he stepped off the plane in Denver, he saw her standing there, waiting for him.

On the way to the station, while Thornton was fuming in the back seat, wondering what his attorney was really up to, the secret service man sitting in the passenger seat, made a phone call.

When Sterling picked up his private phone, he said, "Yes?"

The voice on the other end was good news. "Mister President, this is Secret Service man Frank Davis. Just thought you'd like to know; we have Thornton Howell in custody. We're taking him to precinct forty-nine, as we speak."

"Thank you, Agent Davis," Sterling said with a sigh of relief. "Thank you very much."

Sterling hung up the phone and for the first time in weeks, felt a calmness in his chest. But, along with the calmness came another feeling – one of curiosity and fear. What if he had an accomplice who was still out there, or another freelancer, waiting his chance?

Chapter 35

A SURPRISE HOMECOMING

Liam felt himself coming awake and was anxious for the process to be completed. He wanted to see Mother Earth, again. Even before taking a shower to get the chemicals off his body, Liam rushed to the pilot room and stared through the window. His anxiousness changed to confusion. All he could see was a lot of space.

"Looking for your planet, are you?" came the voice of Eem, from behind him.

Liam turned and looked at the pilot and said, "Yes. I was hoping to see Earth. You did say I would be able to see it when I woke up."

"Indeed, I did, and indeed, you shall," Eem said with a big grin. But first things first. We both need a shower, clean clothes and food in our stomachs."

Liam gave a sigh of disappointment. "I guess you're right. It's just that..."

"That you can hardly wait to get back." Eem finished his sentence for him. "I understand, perfectly," Eem told him. "I was the same way when I went on my first mission away from X-162. I couldn't get back fast enough."

Liam shook his head and grinned, feeling a bit foolish. What had he expected, for the ship to be hovering over the White House? An hour later, Liam and the pilot walked back into the main room of the ship and sat down in seats in front of the large screen. The pilot touched some buttons and said, "I'm now, once again, in control of the ship." He looked at Liam and said, "As I recall, you are anxious to see your planet – Earth, is it?"

Liam felt his face redden just a little. "Yes. That is the name of my planet, which happens to be very much like X-162."

"Then I too, will be excited to see it. Do you suppose I can come down with you?"

Liam thought for a moment, knowing they would have to do it under the sly because of the fear his people had of anything they didn't understand. Finally, he said, "Yes, but you will have to put us exactly where I tell you. Can you do that?"

"Of course," Eem said with a grin. When we get close, just point and it shall be done."

Suddenly, the screen was filled with the image of the planet Earth, and Liam's heart began to pound. He was actually going home!

Eem motioned for Liam to buckle himself into the seat. "Entering your atmosphere doesn't seem to be much different than my planet, so hang on."

Liam did as he was told and felt the jolt when the ship entered Earth's atmosphere. It lasted only a few minutes, then it was over and Liam could see Washington DC below him.

"I wonder what's happened while I was gone?" Liam whispered to himself.

"What's that, you say?" Eem, asked.

Liam sighed and said, "I was just wondering what has happened during my absence?"

Suddenly, the ship came to a halt, directly over the White House and Eem leaned back and said, "Now, just where do you want me to teleport us?"

Liam was astounded at how close the ship was to the White House. He was sure they could see the ship and the military would have planes and troopers coming any minute.

"Do you have your protective shield up? The military on this planet might think you are here to do harm and will be ready to fight," Liam said as a warning.

Eem smiled and said, "Have no fear, Liam. First, we are cloaked, so no one can see us, nor can your radar detect us."

Liam chuckled. "I should have known."

"I presume you want us to be inside that big white building?" Eem asked, pointing at the White House.

Liam looked at his watch and realized it was seven-thirty in the morning. Sterling would be in the kitchen, eating his breakfast. Won't he be surprised! "Can you put us into any room I want?" he asked.

Eem punched some buttons and the floor plans of the White House filled the screen. "Just point to the room where we are to go."

Once again, Liam was amazed by how much more advanced these people were to the technology here on Earth. He walked over to the screen and pointed to the kitchen.

Eem again touched some buttons and stood up saying, "Hurry, we have only ten seconds."

He pulled Liam to a spot in the center of the room, where Liam felt a warm light engulf him.

Sterling Collier and the White House chef, Archie Brooks, were sitting at the counter across from each other, enjoying their breakfast and talking about the arrest of Thornton Howell.

"I'm thinking trying to kill the President of the United States made him exempt from bail," Archie said as he picked up the coffee pot to refill both cups.

Just as he did, Liam and Eem suddenly appeared. "I'm back!" Liam said, grinning from ear to ear.

Archie jumped up, tossing the coffee pot in the air, yelling, "Holy Mother of God!

Both Liam and Eem had to jump out of the way to keep from being hit by the coffee pot. With lightning speed, Eem grabbed the handle of the coffee pot and kept it from hitting him, or spilling much of the hot brew.

Archie was white as a ghost, his heart beating faster than a jack hammer, while Sterling had calmed himself and said, "It's about time," as he stood up and walked over and gave his friend a hug. "You must have quite a story to tell. Have you eaten?"

"Yes, we ate just before coming down. And, I do have a lot to say, but first, I would like to know what has been happening here? I wasn't sure you would still be in in the White House, let alone here having breakfast but here you are. Apparently, not much has happened during my absence."

"I guess we both need to be brought up to speed, but first, I would like to be introduced to your friend," Sterling said, turning to the man standing next to Liam. Sticking out his hand, he said, "Hello, my name is Sterling Collier, and I am the President of my country, The United States of America."

"We have heard much about you, Mister President," Eem said, shaking his hand. "I am proud to be here on your planet and most proud to meet you, Sir."

Sterling was impressed and said so. "This is a most auspicious occasion. I wish the whole world could witness it."

Eem looked at Sterling and nodded his head, then said, "Ambassador Emmelor sends his best regards and has asked me to tell you thank you for the loan of Liam. He not only performed far better that we expected, but he has also saved our planet."

Sterling turned and looked at Liam who just grinned and shrugged his shoulders.

Eem reached into his jacket pocket and retrieved a fist sized stone, then presented it to Sterling.

Sterling took it and measured its weight. It was much lighter than it looked. "It will have a special place on my desk," Sterling said, tossing it up into the air and then catching it.

Eem stepped closer to Sterling and said, "Mister President, may I have a word?"

They walked to the far end of the kitchen where they could talk in low tones without being heard. Eem took the stone from Sterling's hand and said, "This is just not a stone from our planet. It is something only you need to know about."

And with that, he touched the stone in three places at once with the fingers of his right hand and watched as the stone opened to reveal a transmitter. "With this and a little instruction from me, should you find yourself in need of his help, you can communicate directly with Ambassador Emmelor. It is far more sophisticated than the one he left when he was here, and much faster," Eem said in a whisper. He then touched it in two places at the same time and it became a stone again. "Yes, I guess, a stone from another planet will be a nice addition to your desk, but be careful for as you know, it will also be very valuable, along with being very dangerous in the wrong hands."

Sterling knew anything from a foreign planet would be worth any price he wanted to set, but a transmitter that could put a person in communication with someone from another planet was more than priceless. Heads of State would kill to get their hands on it. No – it would not sit on his desk as a temptation. It would go in his private safety box.

When they returned to the others, Sterling said while pointing at Eem, "Eem, here, was just explaining to me how valuable this stone will be."

Liam knew that was only partly true. There was so much more to it than that, but he said nothing.

"Can I touch it?" Archie asked. "It's not radioactive or anything, is it?"

Sterling laughed and tossed the stone to Archie, who deftly caught it in one hand, and hefted it. "It's much lighter than it looks," he said, chuckling.

When he handed it back to Sterling, Archie said, "It's such a shame. I am speaking with a man from a faraway distant planet, and have held a rock from his planet in my hands, and I can tell no one."

"Maybe one day soon," Sterling said, giving Archie a wink.

Sterling canceled his day's activities to spend time with Liam and Eem, so they could each bring the other up to speed on what had happened since they last saw each other. Sterling was also trying to figure out how to introduce him to the world.

Maggie Smythe had a dinner date with Sterling and walked into the Oval Office with a protesting security guard right behind her. "Sir, I told her you were in a meeting, but she…"

Sterling looked up and smiled, waving his hand to the guard. "It's all right, Tim. She's welcome."

As the guard turned and left, Sterling was glad she was there so he could prove to her he was not in league with aliens to overthrow their planet. Maggie was standing ramrod stiff as she stared at Liam, who grinned and walked over to her and said, "Maggie, it's so good to see you again. Come, I would like to introduce you to my friend from planet X-162."

Maggie's eyes were as wide as saucers as she stumbled along with Liam. It was true then; Sterling was in league with the aliens. Suddenly she felt both anger and fear.

When they got close to Eem, Liam said, "Eem, please meet our Attorney General, Maggie Smythe." He then turned to Maggie and said, "Maggie, please meet Eem, from Planet X-162."

Eem bowed and stuck out his hand. "It is my pleasure to make your acquaintance."

Maggie was dumbstruck by the fact that he looked just like any other man here on Earth, and spoke like any American. As they shook hands, she turned and looked at Sterling for the first time since entering the room.

Sterling walked up close to them and said, "You see, they're not monsters and I can assure you, he is here only to bring Liam back. They are very peaceful by nature."

Maggie felt her nerves calm down just a little. This was something beyond her wildest dreams. "Is this true? You are only here to bring Liam back?"

"That and to see your beautiful planet that looks so much like where I come from. Except for your people being more prone to war than we are, we are very much alike in many ways. I am convinced as our ambassador Emmelor is that you are our sister planet, and hopefully someday, some of your people can come visit our planet and vice-versa."

Archie stepped up and handed Maggie a cup of coffee, with a smidgen of whiskey laced in it. "This will help with the nerves," he told her.

Maggie took a sip and immediately felt the calming effect of the hot brew.

Sterling took a few minutes to explain what they were doing in the Oval Office and his dilemma over how to introduce Eem to the world.

By now, Maggie was convinced everything was on the up and up and Sterling wasn't trying to take over the planet with a bunch of aliens. She was sitting on the arm of Sterling's chair, and stood up. "I think I know a way," she said, smiling. "Why not call a meeting with the United Nations and introduce him there. The meeting will be televised throughout the entire world. If there's a better place, I don't know where it would be."

And just like that, Sterling's problem was solved. He walked over and kissed her on the forehead. "Thank you. I'm embarrassed I didn't think of it."

She smiled and said, "You would have, eventually."

Within the hour, Sterling had made it clear he wanted a meeting with the United Nations, but not giving them a reason why. When some objected and stated they might not be available, he just said, "It is of world importance and I expect to see every nation represented."

When all the nations were counted, all finally agreed they would be there.

Chapter 36

ZICOR

The morning Sterling was to introduce Eem to the United Nations was filled with nervous anticipation. How they would react to meeting someone from another planet was still up in the air. Thornton Howell was still in jail and the reporters were swarming the station, demanding an interview with the Speaker of The House.

And he was more than ready to tell them how he had been wrongly incarcerated by the standing President, Sterling Collier. He told them Sterling Collier had colluded with the police and the secret service to come up with a phony story of a telephone conversation between him and a person, with the intent to murder the President. "Not only is that, absurd, but ridiculous. He's just trying to divert the truth about him, by directing it in my direction."

At least fifty percent of the reporters fell for Thornton's lies, while the other half were not quite sure. But the judge, a long-time supporter of Thornton Howell, said he believed Thornton's story and released him from jail, stating a wrongful arrest.

Sterling was seated in the Oval Office with Eem, Liam and Maggie, going over some final details of Emmelor's reason for coming to Earth, and his reason for being here now, when the newscaster announced the release of the Speaker of The House.

Sterling was about take a sip of coffee when the news about Thornton arrived. He sat his cup back down on the saucer and said, "Well, that puts a wrinkle in things."

Liam shut off the television, then turned to his friend and the man he was sworn to protect, and said, "I doubt if we have much to worry about, just now. He wouldn't be stupid enough to try something, without a way to stay disconnected, which I'm guessing will take some time."

"I think Liam is right," Maggie said, hoping to take a little of the worry off Sterling's mind.

"I suppose you're right," Sterling said, "But… what if just maybe he already has plans set in motion and doesn't need to wait?"

Eem stood, silently, watching and listening to these people he'd been so eager to meet. The one thing he'd learned since being on their planet was that some of them, like these people, were decent, while others had evil minds and seemed to relish evil deeds. It was no wonder Emmelor had said we should watch and wait for a better time to try and make friends with them. He would go to this United Nations meeting and say what needed to be said, then he would leave, Eem thought to himself.

With Thornton Howell on the loose, the security around Sterling and his group had been quadrupled. They even had a helicopter flying overhead on the way to the United Nations building. When they arrived, they found a long line of United States Marines guarding both sides of the entryway.

Sterling, Eem, Maggie and Liam entered the building without an incident.

Standing in the wings, waiting to be introduced, Eem peeked through the curtain and turned to Sterling and said, "Is your world so complicated that it has so many different leaders?"

"I'm afraid so," Sterling said, apologetically.

When he was introduced, Sterling walked up to the podium and turned and invited Eem, Liam and Maggie to join him.

They walked up and stood behind him.

"Good morning, and thank you for being here on such short notice. I know some of you flew in just this morning. My apologies, but this meeting just may be the most important meeting ever held."

Sterling took a moment to let his words settle on their minds and watched as their faces grew curious.

"You all know about the accusations filed against me about being in league with aliens to overthrow this planet."

Again, he took a pause and watched as heads nodded in agreement.

"This morning, I will be presenting evidence to prove that none of those rumors are true."

There was an audible sigh among the representatives as if to say, "Here we go again with another tale to cover up the truth.

Sterling could see the disbelief in their faces and asked, "What if I could let you speak directly with a representative from another planet – the one I'm accused of being in league with?"

A voice from somewhere in the middle called out, "And just how do you propose to do that, take us magically to their planet?"

Sterling chuckled and said, "Now that would be something, wouldn't it?"

When the laughter settled down, he said, "No, but you're close."

That got their attention and the room went deadly silent.

Sterling turned and motioned for Eem to join him at the podium, and when he did, Sterling said, "Ladies and gentlemen, please allow me to introduce Eem, from the planet, X-162."

The room remained silent as they stared at a man who was not green, with big eyes and a bald head. He looked just like any other person here on earth. Skepticism floated around the room like a heavy cloud of doubt.

"What proof do you have that he is who you say he is?" the representative from Egypt asked.

Before Sterling could respond, Eem stepped up to the microphone and not only spoke to him in Egyptian, but called him by name.

He then turned and spoke to the large crowd in several of their languages.

Still skeptical, the representative from Spain said, "It is not uncommon for a man to learn to speak several languages. Myself, I speak three."

Eem stepped to the side of the podium and rose into the air, saying, "Can any of you from earth do this? He then landed back on the podium and became invisible.

There was an audible gasp from the room and as they waited for him to reappear, they heard him say as he walked down the middle aisle from the back of the room. "I only did this to assure you that I am who I say I am. And, I would like to further assure you, I am here on a friendly basis. We on planet X-162, have no intentions on doing any harm to anyone on this planet and we do not want to invade or take over your planet."

By this time, he was back on the stage and standing next to Sterling. "We do hope that, someday, when you are less aggressive against one another, that we might be friends. Our two planets may be trillions of miles apart, but somehow are sister planets in almost every way, except your war-like ways."

"Then why did you come here in the first place?" a voice cried out.

Eem thought for a moment, then said, "Because our wars are fought much differently than yours. Our wars are fought by two warriors, only. The winner of the duel wins the war. Each side tries to find the best warrior he can to represent them."

Turning to Liam, he pointed and said, "We searched several galaxies before finding a man here on your planet. This man, Liam Biggers not only won against insurmountable odds, he saved our planet and we will be forever grateful. He is truly a hero on our planet."

The room remained deadly quiet as they tried their best to absorb the information given to them.

Eem continued. "My ambassador, Emmelor, sent me to bring Liam back to his home here on Earth, and to give you our thanks for his service."

Suddenly, the room was filled with cheers and applause.

When the applause died down, Sterling was about to speak when a man walked down the middle aisle, clapping his hands slowly. "I applaud you, Eem, for your touching speech, but I am here to tell you that your ambassador, Emmelor, is dead and I am the new ruler of planet X-162, and soon to be the ruler of this miserable warmonger of a planet."

Liam stared at the man, not believing what he was seeing. Ziman was alive and here on Earth! How could that be?"

"Ah, Mister Biggers, I see a surprised look on your face," Zicor said, stopping just in front of the stage. You're wondering how that sniveling twin brother of mine, Ziman, could still be alive? Well, he isn't and good riddance. He didn't have the backbone to do what needs to be done – but rest assured, I do. My name is Zicor and in a very short time, I will be the new ruler of this planet."

Eem looked down at Zicor and said, "I don't believe you. Emmelor is still alive and well. If something would have happened to him, I would have been notified."

Zicor could see his lie had not worked on Eem, but no matter. He pulled a weapon from his belt and pointed it at Eem and squeezed the trigger. A blue and red flame shot from the barrel of the weapon and struck Eem in the chest.

Eem was immediately incinerated. A small pile of ashes lay on the spot where Eem had been standing.

"And now, you," Zicor said, swinging the weapon in the direction of Sterling. But before he could squeeze the trigger, Liam threw himself off the stage, driving his shoulder into Zicor, causing him to drop his weapon.

Zicor went down, but immediately came to his feet and stood up. "This is not over," he said as he touched a button on his belt and dematerialized right in front of the entire room.

"Come with me!" Sterling yelled, as he ran off the stage, with Liam and Maggie right behind him, leaving a stunned room full of United Nations representatives.

Within minutes the trio was back at the White House and Sterling was placing his fingers on the stone. When it opened, he sent a message to Emmelor, telling him what had happened and asked for help, then paced the floor, not knowing how long it would take to get an answer, if one ever came.

Maggie walked out onto the veranda and looked up at the sky., wondering what was going to happen next? "Mother of God, what are we going to do, now?"

"Figure out some way to fight back," Sterling's voice said, coming up behind her.

"Does Liam know how to get back up to that ship he came back in?" Maggie asked.

Liam had followed Sterling out onto the veranda and had heard Maggie's question. "No. I wish I could. We can only hope that Zicor guy doesn't have someone with him who can get aboard and fly it."

Chapter 37

EMMELOR

After a long day dealing with the captured soldiers from planet X-165 and trying to assure his people that they were no longer in danger, he was about to climb into bed for some much-needed rest, when the small box sitting on his dresser began to vibrate and he heard a high-pitched sound in his ears.

He rushed over and switched the box on and listened to Sterling's message. When it was finished, Emmelor switched off the box and looked out through his bedroom window at the star-studded sky. Sleep and rest would have to wait. He walked over and switched the box on and said, "Help is on the way," then turned it off, again.

Within two hours, six large orbs carrying weapons of war lifted off planet X-162 and headed at full speed out into the far-reaching space in front of them. Emmelor was in the lead orb, hoping he wouldn't be too late.

It was two o'clock in the morning when Sterling was awakened by the vibrating and loud screeching in his ears. He leaped from his bed and turned on a light, then ran to the dresser and picked up the stone. It was already open and when he touched the receive button, he gave a huge sigh. Emmelor was on his way. But would he get here in time to do any good? That was the question. Zicor had already shown his power by knocking out several electric power stations, leaving most of Washington DC without power.

He had also had the audacity to show up in the Oval Office in the form of a hologram, telling Sterling he would continue to destroy power stations around the world, which would leave not only businesses, manufacturing, and people without power – but hospitals and other places where people would die without electrical power.

He'd even laughed and said it didn't bother him that thousands, maybe millions would die. "This planet is overcrowded as it is," he told him.

Trying to buy some time, Sterling pleaded with Zicor to give him time enough to contact the countries around the world, asking them to surrender. "You have twenty-four of your hours," Zicor told him.

"But that's not nearly enough time," Sterling pleaded. "You saw how many foreign representatives there were at that meeting. They will all need to be contacted one at a time and pleaded with because they will each want to argue that we should fight."

Zicor was getting bored and his hologram asked, "How much time do you need?"

"At least thirty days," Sterling replied.

"You shall have ten of your sunrises," Zicor said. "And while I am waiting, I shall be traveling around your planet to find what I want to keep and what I want to destroy."

That had been one day ago.

He walked over and sat down on the edge of his bed. His head ached. He hadn't had enough sleep. Would Emmelor get here in time to help fight against this power crazed man from so far away? By receiving an answer from Emmelor, he knew the man had been lying when he said Emmelor was dead. What else was he lying about? Did he really have the power to destroy this planet without them being able to fight back? If only Liam could figure a way to get into Eem's ship? Just the thought of what had happened to Eem saddened him. The man had been killed needlessly.

Sterling got off the bed and plodded into the shower. There would be no more sleeping this night, he was to wound up. When Archie walked into his kitchen at five o'clock that same morning, he was surprised to see the President and Liam, sitting there, talking and drinking coffee. "What is so important that you feel the need to invade my kitchen this early in the morning?"

Sterling poured a cup of coffee for his chef and pointed to a chair next to Liam. "We're trying to figure a way to get Liam on board Eem's ship."

Archie took a sip of the hot brew and let it slide down his throat, warming his insides. After a couple of seconds, he said, "That may not be as hard as you think."

Both Sterling and Liam looked at the chef and waited for more information.

Archie looked at Liam and asked, "When that other fella, Emmelor, I think you called him, was here, we shot rockets at his ships but they were not able to get past his protection barriers? Right?"

"That's right," Liam said. "So, what's your point?"

Archie sat his cup on the counter and asked, "When the two of you arrived, did Eem put up a barrier shield like Emmelor had?"

Stunned that he hadn't thought of that, he said, "I don't know."

Sterling said, "With Zicor off exploring the world, now would be a good time to find out, wouldn't it?"

Within the hour, a single jet fighter flew toward the hovering orb, expecting to be turned away.

From inside the viewing room at the military base, a loud cheer erupted when they watched the fighter jet do a wing wobble to indicate he was successful in getting close to the foreign ship.

Sterling turned to the commanding officer and asked, "Now, how do we get Mister Biggers, aboard that ship?"

The commanding officer walked over to the console and picked up the microphone. "This is General McIntyre from command base to the pilot who just did a flyby of the orbiting space ship. What is your altitude?"

"Twenty-four-thousand, two-hundred and nineteen feet, Sir," came the reply.

"Thank you," the general said. "You are free to return to base," then set the microphone back down on the console.

He turned to Sterling and said, "We're in luck. The new ZF2X manned helicopter can reach an altitude of twenty-six thousand, five-hundred, feet. The alien ship is well within its range, Mister President."

Sterling turned to Liam and asked, "What do you think?"

Liam looked at General McIntyre and said, "I'm ready to go when you are. What do I need to do?"

The general told Liam that he would need to get the helicopter and a crew ready for flight, which would take, maybe an hour. "Plus, we will need to get you fitted for a spacesuit. Even though the helicopter is pressurized, the crew will be wearing them in case something goes wrong, and you will need one to go between the helicopter and the spaceship."

"Getting you up there is all well and good, but once you're up there, how will you get inside?" Sterling asked.

Liam smiled and said, "One thing about Eem, he was thorough. When we went aboard back on his planet, he showed me the code to open the door, and during our flight, he showed me how to fly the orb..., even let me try my hand at the controls. Also, the gun aboard this one is the same type as the one on Emmelor's ship, so that's not going to be a problem."

Following Liam's directions, the helicopter hovered over the section of the spaceship where he thought the opening should be. He looked through the window and studied the side of the ship until he saw the small code box. "That's it," he told the pilot.

In less than a minute, he had his helmet on and was put into a sealed room attached to side of the helicopter and hooked up to a special tether that would lower him down to the surface of the ship.

It would be tricky since the surface was not made of the same material as the ships on Earth were made of and magnetic soles on his shoes would not work.

After closing and sealing the interior door, the two crewmen gave Liam a thumbs up and opened the outer door. "We are ready when you are," Liam heard in his helmet.

He took a breath, then stepped out of the helicopter and felt his weight being held by the strap made of something stronger than steel.

Once Liam was close to the hatchway, the helicopter had to maneuver a little to Liam's left to allow him to reach out and press the numbers on the code pad – and when he did, a panel slid open.

Liam pulled himself inside the ship and released the strap, hoping he wouldn't be sucked out into space, because he wasn't wearing a parachute.

As soon as the strap-hook left the opening, Liam touched the close button and the hatchway closed.

Stepping a little further inside the ship, Liam reached up and twisted his helmet and lifted it off. Fans were whirling and he breathed in the manufactured air.

Taking a small box from the belt he was wearing, he pressed the call button and said, "So far, so good. I'll take it from here. Many thanks for your help."

After getting out of his spacesuit, Liam went to the control center and sat down in the pilot's seat, studying the console in front of him – forcing his brain to remember everything Eem had told him about flying the craft. He took his time, not wanting to do anything that would send him hurling off into space.

He was studying the console when out of his peripheral vision he saw something coming toward him and more instinct than anything, he hit the button that raised the shields around the ship just in time to see Zicor's ship shoot a beam at the descending helicopter.

Liam screamed, "No!" as he watched the helicopter explode before his eyes. Anger filled him like standing under Niagara Falls and he ran to the gun position and swung the gun to train on Zicor's ship, but before he could pull back on the trigger, Zicor pulled up his shield and vanished from sight. Liam fired anyway in the hopes the ship was still there, but apparently it had already moved. His shot went off into space. He hoped it would die before it hit anything.

With a little practicing, Liam was able to fly the orb and eventually, landed it on the White House lawn.

After giving Sterling and Maggie and of course, Archie, a tour of the ship, he said to Sterling, "have an idea I'd like to run past you.

That night, Liam contacted a Navy buddy who was an ace pilot and made arrangements for him to be on loan to the President as the pilot of the small orb, while Liam manned the gun.

They spent several hours that same night, flying around the world, practicing the controls, while at the same time searching for Zicor. The piloting went well, but not the search for Zicor. The man had disappeared.

"We need to find him soon. I want to give him the same thing he gave those poor men in the helicopter," Liam said, putting up the shields around the ship for the night.

In truth, Zicor was hidden high up in the Alpine Mountains, nestled in between two cliffs - hidden by the falling snow.

Chapter 38

THE CALVARY

Emmelor and his six ships were hurling through space at a speed unheard of on Earth. The ships were traveling at maximum speed, just shy of the redline indicator.

Emmelor paced back and forth. "How could I have not seen this?" he said to no one. "How did I not know Ziman had a twin brother? One even more vile than he was?"

Lucita had overheard Emmelor and approached him., placing her hand on his shoulder, saying, "There was no way you could have known. Ziman came out of the shadows while we were searching for a warrior. No one knew he existed until he showed up and began taking over. And as far as his twin brother, I doubt anyone knew of him. He was just waiting in the wings, hoping his brother would fail so he could take over."

"But he could do so much destruction to those people down there," Emmelor told her.

"He could," Lucita said, "but don't forget, Liam is there."

"But what can he do against this Zicor? I doubt Liam knows how to fly an orb, and I'm sure none of the earthlings do, either. If only Eem hadn't been killed." He sighed and said, "There will be no sleep mode on this trip. There is too much to discuss."

Lucita smiled, shaking her head. "It wouldn't surprise me if Liam could fly the orb every bit as good as Eem."

Emmelor looked her in the eyes and said, "But he can't be in two places at once. He can't fly the orb and man the laser gun at the same time."

Lucita led Emmelor over to a table where she sat him down and poured him his favorite drink, then sat down opposite him and said, "But... he did say our weapons are very similar to the ones they have on Earth. So, maybe he brought someone familiar with them to do the shooting while he flies the orb?"

Emmelor thought that analogy through and finally conceded it was possible. Still, he would much prefer to be there with his ships and weapons, which were bigger and more powerful than the ones on the smaller ships.

There was nothing he could do but wait and hope he would be in time to help.

While Emmelor and his ships were flying at top speed to reach Earth, Liam and his pilot friend, Milo Carnes, were searching the globe for Zicor, but always seemed to be one step behind.

Zicor had earlier made his notes on possible sites to destroy and he was in the process of doing so. So far, he had made six hit and run attacks on major power plants around the world before sneaking off to his hiding place in the Alpine Mountains under his cloak of invisibility.

"He's out there, right under our nose, but he seems to be one step ahead of us all the time," Liam said.

Milo, who was now very familiar with the controls of the orb, spun his seat around to face Liam and said, "We just have to figure out where he's going to strike next and be there to greet him."

Liam studied the world map on the screen for a long time, making note of the plants already taken out and stepped back and whistled. "If my calculations are correct, his next target will be the Russian Nuclear Power Plant, Chornobyl."

Milo studied the screen for a moment, then said, "If he does, that would cause a chain reaction of the other nearby nuclear plants. It would wipe out most of Russia, Turkey, The Ukraine, Romania, Poland, Germany, Austria, and with a little assist from the wind, France, Switzerland, The Netherlands, Belgium, Finland, Denmark, and Sweden – and God only knows where else. With high winds, and the chain reactions of other nuclear plants, it could wipe out the entire world."

Milo was trying to wrap his mind around the idea of what might happen any time now, when he spotted a small dot on one of the other screens and by instinct, rolled the orb back up and away, just as a bolt of energy tore through the sky.

Zicor cursed when his shot missed the orb. He watched as the ship moved away and disappeared above him. By the time he got from the laser gun to the pilot's seat, the orb was beyond his tracking range. "You may have learned to fly the orb, Mister Biggers, but you can't fly it and man your weapon any faster than I can." The statement made him wish he'd brought a gunner with him.

With Biggers flying the orb the way he was, made Zicor rethink his plan. The man was obviously an ace pilot, something he hadn't known. And what if he has a gunner with him, which would give him the advantage? He needed to rethink things.

After settling into his hiding place in the Alpines, Zicor sent a message back to his home planet, X-165, demanding six war orbs be sent to his precise coordinates, immediately.

He knew it would take some time for his message to get to his planet, then some more time to get the reply, along with the time to get the orbs here. In the meantime, he would study this planet and gather information. Maybe, if he decided to take over this planet, he could use these earthlings and the resources they could produce.

-

After making sure Zicor was not headed for Russia, or any other place they could determine, Milo had flown the orb back to a secluded place in the woods, near Camp David and set it down. Not only was it hidden by the trees, but they kept the cloaking device on for added safety. They could have easily sat down at any of the nearby air bases, but that would endanger many lives, should Zicor find them and attack.

After telling Sterling about what they believed Zicor's next targets might be, he got on the phone and after a lengthy discussion with the Premiere of Russia, they were reluctantly given permission to fly over all Russian territories to make sure Zicor didn't attack one of their nuclear power plants.

In truth, it was just a matter of courtesy because with the orb's shields up, none of their fighter planes, nor any of their rockets could do them any harm.

"Do you really think he will attack the nuclear power plants?" Sterling asked as they sat eating dinner at Camp David.

"If he wants to destroy this planet, yes," Liam said, still questioning his choice of places Zicor might attack."

Again, Sterling brought up the question of why. "Doesn't he realize or understand what he has to gain by just taking over the planet instead of leaving it a wasteland for the next thousand years? We have so much to offer."

"You sound like a man who is ready to surrender, Mister President," Milo said, setting his fork down on his plate.

"No, no, I didn't mean to sound like that. I'm never going to surrender. I want you and Liam to find him and blow him into a million pieces. It's just that the thought of this planet being destroyed when we have so much to offer…"

Day after day, Liam and Milo patrolled the entire world, searching for Zicor, but never got even a glimpse of him.

"He's gone into hiding," Sterling said on the night of the eleventh day of finding no trace of Zicor.

"But why?" Milo asked.

Sterling sat his drink down on the small table next to his stuffed chair and said, "I'm convinced he came here by himself, thinking it would be easy to take over our planet. When he killed Eem, he was convinced that all he had to do was destroy a few small targets and we would fold like a wet blanket, giving him control of us. But it didn't work out that way. You and Liam learned to fly the opposing orb and fought back. He doesn't have anyone helping him, so he can't fly the orb and fire the laser gun at the same time. I believe he went into hiding to call for help – and he's just biding his time until help arrives."

Neither Liam or Milo could find fault with the President's analogy. It was Milo who asked the question, "If that's the case, we need to be out searching for him, don't we?"

Liam stretched his legs, took a sip of his drink, then asked, "What good will that do if he's in hiding? First, he will have found a place where he believes he is well hidden, and I'm fairly sure he's bright enough to use his cloaking device, just like we do. So, how do we find him under those circumstances?"

Frustrated, Milo stood up and paced the floor. "We can't just sit here and do nothing. At least if we're out there, patrolling, he will know it and hopefully stay put. Plus, if we're out there, won't we stand a better chance of seeing the enemy orbs if and when they arrive?"

The following morning, Milo lifted the orb into the sky and was about to head for the Amazon area in search for Zicor. The Amazon was one of the several places where a person could hide his ship without anyone from the air being able to see it.

They had been crisscrossing the jungle for a little over three hours when seven giant orbs appeared in the sky above them.

The main screen on their ship lit up and they could see Emmelor standing before them. He spoke in a no-nonsense tone. "Zicor, or whoever you call yourself, surrender your ship immediately or you will be blown out of the sky."

Liam grabbed the microphone and pressed the talk button. "Hold on Emmelor, it's me, Liam Biggers. My friend, Milo and I, are in Eem's ship, out looking for Zicor. We believe he's gone into hiding!"

When Emmelor's screen lit up with Liam and Milo, he grinned and said, "I knew it all along. I was just having a bit of fun. Scared you, didn't I?"

"You nearly gave us a heart attack," Liam said back.

Emmelor said, "Liam, I will transfer you to my ship so you can fill me in without any other ships listening in on our conversation."

Before Liam could answer, he felt himself begin to dissolve, and in the next instant, he reappeared on Emmelor's ship. Once Liam realized he was put back together, again, he reached out and shook Emmelor's hand, telling him how good it was to see him.

"What about me?" a familiar voice on his left, said.

Liam spun around and saw Lucita standing there. Instead of a handshake, she got a hug that nearly squeezed the air out of her lungs. "I can't believe you came, too!" Liam said, grinning from ear to ear.

"What term is it you earthlings use? I believe it's, the calvary has arrived," she said.

"And we're glad you came," Liam said with a big smile.

Over drinks in Emmelor's quarters, Liam told him and Lucita everything, even about their speculation that Zicor had called for backup.

Emmelor nodded his head and said, "That is not only a reasonable assumption but you slammed the nail on the head."

"It's, hit the nail on the head," Liam corrected – laughingly. He then became sober and curious. "Why would you say that?"

Lucita laid her hand on Liam's arm and said, "Needing something to do, I was sitting at the console, searching the frequencies for… I don't know… anything unusual when I heard someone calling for help – demanding they send six war ships to Earth."

Emmelor butted in, saying, "She flew across the room, and dragged me back over to where she'd been sitting and replayed the message for me."

"So, when we detected you and your pilot crisscrossing that jungle down there, we guessed what you were doing and Emmelor decided to have a little fun with you, along with turning three of our warships around to wait for the incoming ships from X-165."

Liam shook his head and said, "I need to take you and Lucita back down with me so you can meet our President for real, this time. He will be most pleased to see you."

Emmelor put his pilot and second in command who was in charge while he was gone and they were beamed back to Liam's smaller craft.

They were introduced to Milo, who was wide-eyed and amazed, but still able to set the ship back down in the woods behind Camp David without incident.

When they approached the house where the President was staying, Marine guards stepped in front of them with their hands on their pistols, demanding to know who the man and woman were.

Liam wasn't sure how to answer him so he called the President on his private cell number. When Sterling came out of the house, the two Marines stood rock solid until he told them it was all right to stand down. When the President said the two strangers were all right, the two Marines stepped aside without questioning him.

Inside, Sterling called out to Archie, his chef, for food and drinks all around then stuck out his hand to Emmelor. "It is truly and honor to finally meet you in person."

Emmelor took the President's hand in his and felt the strength of the man. "I'm truly sorry it is under the circumstances it is, but I too, am very happy to meet the man Liam has spoken so highly of."

"I didn't tell him about the fun things we did," Liam said, shrugging his shoulders with a sheepish grin on his face.

Emmelor got a questioning look on his face and Liam explained. "Remember some of the shenanigans you told me you pulled as a young man? Well, the President and I have a few skeletons in our closets, as well."

"I see," Emmelor said, smiling. "I'm glad to find out you're not a… what do you call them… a stuffed shirt?"

Sterling turned his attention to Lucita, noticing how beautiful she was. "Hello, and welcome to my part of this planet. My name is Sterling and you are?"

Not knowing protocol, she bowed slightly at the waist and said, "I am called Lucita and I am thrilled to be here. On my planet, I am a healer and advisor to Ambassador Emmelor."

Her eyes twinkling when she looked at Liam, had not gone unnoticed by Sterling and it made him wonder what had gone on between them while he was gone. He wondered if she had come along just to see Liam again or if it was strictly business. He leaned forward and said, "If Liam vouches for you, then you must be someone I would like to be friends with."

They both turned to look at Liam whose face turned red as he said, "Yes, I will vouch for her, big time."

In that moment, Sterling got his answer. He just wondered how it would work out. This would be the biggest long-distance relationship ever. No, either she would have to move here, or he would have to go to her world. If it was his choice, it would be her moving here. He didn't want to lose Liam.

When Archie summoned them to the dining room, he was almost tongue-tied. He was actually meeting a man and a woman from another world. How incredible was that! Not to mention they were what he considered to be royalty, at that.

Sterling invited Archie to dine with them, which he quickly accepted – and soon found himself chatting with Emmelor like he was just a man from just down the street who had come to visit the President.

"Someday, if it is possible, I would like to visit your planet," Archie said.

"The way you cook, I would love to have you come back with me as the head chef of the palace," Emmelor told him.

"Sorry," Sterling said, raising his hands in the air. "He is welcome to go for a short visit, but I'm not giving Archie up to anyone here on this planet or any other."

They all got a good laugh, with Emmelor telling Archie he hoped in the future they could bring a lot of people to his planet and bring a lot of his people to visit earth.

After bringing Sterling up to date on all the information and Emmelor's reason for being there, Emmelor and Lucita went back to their ship, promising to let them know of any changes.

It was four o'clock in the morning when Liam tapped on Sterling's door, and when he called out "Come in," Liam walked into the room and said, "I've just heard from Emmelor. Zicor's ships are two days from here and he wants me to go up to the ship. He's planning on going out to meet them, so that any warfare they might have will not affect our planet."

Sterling leaped out of his bed and said, "Hold on cowboy. You're not going without me."

"But Sir," Liam protested.

"No, but sir's," I'm not about to miss this," Sterling said, climbing into a pair of jeans, some sneakers and a sweatshirt.

He grabbed a jacket and fell in behind Liam as he headed for the small orb sitting on the White House lawn.

Sterling hated to sneak off without letting anyone know where he was going and what he would be doing, but he couldn't resist the chance to go into space in a foreign space ship and possibly go to war with other space ships. The thought of them losing never crossed his mind, although it was causing Liam a lot of grief. How was he to protect him?

Chapter 39

THE PRESIDENT GOES INTO SPACE

They had to sneak out through a secret tunnel escape route that had been built many years ago. It now had six inches of standing water and the inside was covered with cobwebs. When they had made their way through and were once again breathing somewhat clean air, if one could consider that Washington DC actually had any clean air, Sterling wiped the cobwebs from his hair and said, "Well, that was fun."

Liam touched the talk button on the device Emmelor had given him and said, "Two to come aboard."

"Two?" came the answer.

Liam sighed and said, "Yes. Me and President Collier."

"Just a minute," came the reply.

Shortly, Emmelor's voice came through the device. "Are you sure about this?"

Sterling took the device from Liam, pushed the talk button and said, "Only with your permission, Ambassador, but I truly do want this experience."

"Stand close to Liam," was the reply.

When he materialized on board the orb, Sterling touched his chest, shoulders and head to make sure he was all there. "That was astonishing!" he said to the smiling Emmelor.

"Welcome aboard, Mister President," Emmelor told him.

"C'mon, we're friends. It's Sterling," he said back.

As soon as Liam and Sterling were aboard, the ship began to move. "We'll be traveling at better than a thousand miles an hour, Emmelor told Sterling but Sterling couldn't feel the movement. "Extraordinary," was the only thing he could think of saying.

"Actually, quite a bit faster than that," Lucita told him as she stepped up next to Liam and took his arm in hers.

While Lucita and Liam headed for the pilot room of the ship, Emmelor gave Sterling a quick tour of the ship.

It was difficult for Sterling to comprehend this kind of technology, but he did the best he could. When they got back, or if they got back, he would get rebuffed by the Secret Service for sneaking off like he did, but it would be worth it for the experience of going into space, and going to war, on an alien ship.

In the pilot room, that was filled with enough buttons, switches and gadgets to boggle the mind, Sterling watched through the front viewing screen as the orb raced through space at an unthinkable speed.

"We should be somewhere between your moon and the planet you call Mars when we make contact. Unless they begin firing at us, we will try to get them to surrender peacefully," Emmelor told Sterling.

"And if they refuse to surrender, or start shooting at us?" Sterling queried, hoping it wouldn't come to that. He wanted to get back down in one piece.

"Let's hope it doesn't come to that, but we will be making contact far enough in advance so we will know and be prepared if it comes to a fight," Emmelor said, trying to sound calm – which he wasn't.

Sterling knew about war first hand as a military man and as the leader of a nation and he could see right through Emmelor's calm exterior. "Back on Earth, I have been involved with war on more than one occasion and one thing I have learned is, your enemy is inclined to lie if he thinks it will give him the advantage of a surprise attack."

Emmelor smiled at his new friend and said, "Thank you for that piece of wisdom. And just for the record, just because I'm a peace-loving person, do not think that I will hesitate when it comes time to fight. Nor will I be easily fooled."

Sterling could see something in Emmelor's eyes that told him the man spoke the truth, and would not be easily fooled or taken without a fight.

-

Back down on Earth, Zicor was receiving a signal from the orbs still deep in space, telling him they could detect seven large orbs coming toward them, asking what they should do.

Zicor signaled back, "As soon as you are in range, fire on them and keep firing on them until you have blown them into pieces!"

After taking a couple of deep breaths, Zicor signaled them again, saying, "I will create a distraction down here so they will be forced to send at least one or more of their ships back down to Earth. We will talk again when this is all over. And remember my order - you are never to surrender!"

With that, Zicor signed off and lifted his ship up into the sky and then flew in the direction of Zurich, Switzerland. Emmelor, Sterling, Liam, Lucita and the pilot were staring at the screen, watching the tiny dots grow larger when the communications officer approached Emmelor and said, "Ambassador, I have just intercepted signals between a ship down on the planet and the ships coming toward us."

After hearing what the communications officer had to say and listening to the conversations, Emmelor gave the order for full battle alert, then turned to Liam and asked, "Would you be willing to go with one of my ships back down to your planet to deal with Zicor while we take care of things up here?"

"In what capacity?" Liam asked.

Emmelor didn't hesitate. "As the pilot and in command of the ship. My pilots are good, but they don't have combat experience and I believe you have the skills to outwit Zicor. I will teleport you to the ship now, with orders that you will be taking charge."

Sterling touched Emmelor on the shoulder and said, "With your permission, I will go with Liam as his gunner's mate. If they're like the ones you have on this ship, I can handle it very well. And to be honest, for what he's put me through, I believe I deserve a chance to get even."

Emmelor looked at Liam, who nodded his approval.

For the second time, Sterling had been teleported and when he was fully materialized, he touched his torso, marveling at what had taken place. "I don't know if I can ever get used to this," he told Liam, who had just materialized next to him.

"Yeah, it does take a bit of getting used to.

Captain Lonna was standing off to the side and said, "Welcome to my ship. I am Captain Lonna and I have been informed by the ambassador that you, Mister Biggers, will be piloting my ship during this search for the man you call Zicor."

They shook hands. Liam introduced the captain to Sterling and the captain looked back to Liam and said, "It is an honor to have you aboard my ship, Mister Biggers. You are a hero back on our planet." He then turned to Sterling and said, "As the President of your country, you will receive the same respect as our ambassador. It is a pleasure to meet you. I understand you will be manning one of our laser guns."

"That is correct, and Captain, if you will, please, it's just Sterling. Now with your permission, I would like to see the weapon I will be shooting."

Liam looked at the captain and said, "If you don't mind, I would like Sterling to man the turret on the front of the ship, just below where I will be sitting.

The captain smiled and said, "He can man any weapon you want."

-

Zicor left his hiding place in the Alpines and headed toward Zurich, Switzerland with the intent on destroying their power plant, but changed his mind. His hatred for Emmelor and what he had discovered – this planet being so much like his own, had crazed his mind to the point of wanting to destroy it and everyone on it. – especially the man called Liam Biggers. The man had not only killed his twin brother, but destroyed their plans for taking control of planet X-162.

But after seeing the resources and knowledge on Earth, he decided his best option would be to destroy the powerplants that provided power to run their industries and homes. At first, he had targeted big cities – ones that would make a big impact on them, but readily changed his mind. It was destroying too much of their industry that he could use to help his own planet, along with keeping this planet alive.

Then in a fit of anger, he was prepared to destroy several of their nuclear plants and start a chain reaction that would destroy the entire planet, but before he was able to implement such a radical plan, he came to his senses and called for help because Emmelor and his ships had shown up to spoil his plans. His mind was in a constant battle with itself.

With his ships arriving with battle hardened warriors aboard, he felt sure they would be victorious against Emmelor's non-combative military. The only thing standing in his way now would be Liam Biggers, who he was sure would come back to look for him.

Zicor flew high above the planet, sending out search impulses – hunting for one of Emmelor's ships, knowing it would be commanded by Biggers. If he could destroy Biggers, taking control of this planet would be easy. Then, after his men destroyed all of Emmelor's ships, X-162 would be his, too. He would be the greatest ruler in this and all of the other universes.

Zicor heard a ping and looked down at his screen, which showed an approaching ship. It was still a good way from him, but coming swiftly in his direction. He smiled and rose from his seat and sat down at his turret, swinging the laser gun around to face the oncoming ship.

"I think we've found him," one of the technicians said to Liam, who had also seen a blip on the screen.

"Yes, I see him," Liam said, as he studied the screen. He leaned back in his seat and thought to himself, 'He can't possibly think we are going to fly into his gunsights so he can shoot us out of the sky, can he?'

They were still several miles apart, but Liam gave the order to come to a stop and hover there.

When the ship was hanging in space at a standstill, Liam gave the order to be ready to move at great speed to the left on his order.

"What are you up to, Mister Biggers?" Zicor said to himself as he studied the hovering ship. He was puzzled by the tactic and unsure what to do next.

He was about to go back to his pilot seat when, without warning, the enemy ship moved to his right and in the blink of an eye, disappeared.

Fearing he would be attacked from behind, Zicor spun his ship around to face his rear, but could see nothing. Knowing the enemy ship was using their cloaking shield, Zicor ran to his turret and fired three quick shots in the direction he suspected the enemy ship would be.

He watched as the killing beams disappeared into space. In a panic, he ran back to the pilot's seat and changed directions again. This time, moving several miles one way, then several miles in a different direction – zig-zagging back and forth until he felt safe enough to stop.

Liam had moved his ship to the left, then upward to disappear inside a huge raincloud, which would hide the ship from Zicor's detection.

As he hovered inside the cloud, Liam tried to guess what Zicor's next move would be and as he did so, he felt the vibrations of Zicor's three shots as they went past, causing the ship to rock back and forth.

"That was a little too close for comfort," Captain Lonna said, shaking his head.

"He's scared and firing in panic," Liam said.

"Where is he now?" Sterling asked into his microphone.

"Probably a long way from here," Liam said. "We won't know for sure until we leave this raincloud so we can send out our tracker beams."

"Then I suggest we get a move on. We don't want him getting away, again," Sterling said. In truth, he was itching to get Zicor in his gunsights.

Liam agreed and eased the ship out of the rain cloud and immediately sent out tracker beams in all directions, but got nothing of importance.

Keeping the tracker beams active, Liam sped up the ship, moving faster across the sky. Then just like that, the tracker beam locked onto Zicor's ship again.

"We've got him!" the technician shouted.

This time, Liam turned in Zicor's direction, shut off the tracker beams and told Sterling, "As soon as you get him in your sights, begin firing."

Ten seconds later, Sterling was sending death beams at Zicor's ship, and saw it being knocked to the side.

Zicor felt the shot ricochet off the side of his ship and immediately hit the cloaking button and flew downward, then off to his right for a short distance, then dropped altitude again until he could turn and head for his hiding place where he could repair any damage made to his ship.

He was angry with himself for allowing his ship to be damaged. He would be more of a ghost in the future, using hit and run tactics until he could catch his enemy's ship off guard. Then, he would destroy Mister Biggers.

Chapter 40

EMMELOR'S FIRST REAL WAR

Zicor's ships were now getting close enough that, unless they surrendered, they would be going into battle.

Emmelor called one of his young pilots to the bridge and told him that he wanted him to man Eem's small ship, conducting hit and run tactics. He asked if he was up to the task and the young pilot replied, "I'll do my best, Sir."

"I know you will. I chose you because you tested the highest in your class. You will be on your own because I will be too busy here fighting against their ships. I want you to stay cloaked until you are ready to attack, then dash away and become cloaked again until you are ready for your next shot. Do you understand what I'm getting at?" Emmelor asked.

"I do, Sir!" the young pilot said, his eyes wide with excitement.

Emmelor took the young man by the shoulders and looked him in the face. "This could be a suicide mission. I want you to know that."

The young pilot's eyes went from excitement to serious and he said, "I will not let you down, Ambassador. And I will return."

"Well said," Emmelor told him. "Now, get to the teleporter room and may the Gods be with you."

The young pilot saluted, spun on his heels and left the bridge.

Milo Carnes walked up to Emmelor and said, "Ambassador, with your permission, I would like to take the laser gun in the front of your ship. I know you think of me as a pilot, but I can be very effective at shooting down enemy ships."

Emmelor smiled and said, "I was hoping you would say that. Permission granted."

As Milo hurried away to take his position in the front turret, Emmelor smiled. He would have the best chance of his ship surviving with Milo there. He picked up the microphone and began giving orders of the upcoming war.

Pelee had never actually been in a position of battle such as the one facing him, now, but he had no doubts he would be victorious. "The ships and men of X-162 have no battle experience. This should be an easy victory," he said to himself as they came close to being within firing range.

He lifted the microphone to his mouth and squeezed the button. "This is Pelee. We are nearing our firing position. I want all weapons ready to fire on my order!"

All gunners reported in that they were ready and waiting.

Pelee looked at the screen, then over to one of his technicians and said, "Tell me as soon as we are in range."

The technician, who was concentrating on his screen, raised his hand in the air to indicate he would.

Pelee stood watching the screen and the enemy ships in front of him, his nerves about to explode. He had to win this battle or he and his men would die here in a foreign universe, where they would be remembered in disgrace.

The ships were getting close and Pelee could feel his excitement rising. He looked at the technician and saw the man's hand beginning to rise.

Just as Pelee shouted into his microphone, "Fire!" he watched as all of the enemy ships, changed directions. Some going one way, while the others went a different direction. He watched as all the shots coming from his ships, missed their targets.

Off to his left, he saw one of his ships being struck with a beam that sent it flying off into space, tumbling out of control. "Where did that shot come from?" he yelled as his ship turned to face the direction the shot came from. The sky was empty.

The young pilot had circled high and above the enemy ships under his cloaking device and when the fighting began, he was able to uncloak, fire on one of their ships, then disappear again, with the cloaking device hiding him. He liked the idea of hit and run tactics. This just might be his calling as a fighter pilot.

The young pilot watched as Emmelor's ships moved in different directions, too, but had yet to fire. He didn't understand the ambassador's decisions, but right now, he had his own mission to take care of.

This time, he dropped down below the enemy ships, which had now formed into a straight line, ready to fire at the ambassador's ships again. Still under his cloaking device, he eased up as close as he dared, wanting to get a direct hit on one of the ships. Being a small ship, his laser wasn't as powerful as those on the ambassador's ships, so he needed to be close enough to hit something vital on the enemy ship.

Suddenly, one of the enemy ships turned and fired a beam at him. He moved his small ship to the side, but not fast enough to miss being hit. His ship was hit a glancing blow that sent the ship end over end, back out into space. Warning signals were blaring in the young pilot's ears and he could feel the air pressure inside begin to drop.

The young pilot grabbed for his air mask and put it on, then brought the ship back under control, and put it on hover – then ran to assess the damage.

It was slight – just a small crack in the hull – and within minutes, the young pilot had the crack repaired and the air quality back where it belonged. He took off his mask, then resumed his place in the pilot's seat.

He had just sat down and looked at the screen. What he saw caused his heart to race. The enemy ship was coming toward him at a slow pace. It was searching for him with the intent of destroying him.

Still far enough away to not be picked up by the enemy because of the cloaking device, the young pilot lifted his ship up upward, then flew in the direction of his enemy. When he had gone far enough, he dropped down behind the craft and took aim.

He fired, then lifted his ship out and away, wanting to be as far away as he could because he knew the repercussion would be strong enough to injure his ship with flying debris.

His shot had been true and slammed into the mechanism that propelled the ship.

The explosion was gigantic as the ship was blown into thousands of pieces, spreading debris in all directions. The sky lit up as bright as any sun in the sky.

The sound of the explosion would travel through space for thousands of miles before dying out.

Not only did Emmelor and Zicor's ships feel the concussion, they were hit with debris. Down on Earth, people looked at the sky and saw the bright light, then heard the explosion.

Liam spoke to Sterling and said, "I hope that was one of Zicor's ships."

By now, all of the ships on both sides had scattered all over the sky and it came down to a one against one battle, with the enemy being on the losing side of the fight.

For hours, they fired at each other, creating damage to each other without any of them getting a direct hit, except for Milo, who caught an enemy ship trying to get away from one of their ships and had fired on it, not realizing how close they were.

The explosion knocked Emmelor's ship backward in a spiraling motion, sending it tumbling over and over. The sound was deafening and Milo was sure he'd killed them, too. But that was not the case. The pilot of Emmelor's ship was quick to react and hit the button that sent them straight up and away from the blast, at least far enough that he could take control of the ship again. There was damage to the ship, but nothing that couldn't be repaired very quickly. There were also some personal injuries, but nothing deadly – just bruises and three broken limbs. Lucita had been slammed against the bulkhead and then thrown into the air where she collided with one of the men. They both fell to the floor and each grabbed onto the nearest thing they could and held on for dear life.

When the ship finally settled down, Lucita struggled but was able to get to her feet and hobbled over to check the man she'd collided with. He was unconscious, but breathing. Using power she didn't know she had, she hefted him onto her shoulder and made her way to the infirmary, where she left him with the attendants who were themselves, just getting to their feet. She would come back later if her services were needed.

The pilot's room, or bridge as it was called on Earth ships, was a mess. She saw Emmelor standing nearby, giving orders. He had blood running down his face from a cut on his forehead. The skin around his eyes was turning black and were swollen to the point where he could hardly see. His clothes were ripped and she could see blood seeping from several cuts. "We need to get you to the infirmary," she said as she stopped next to him.

"I'm fine," Emmelor told her, wiping blood from his swollen eyes. "There is too much to do right now. I will go, later," he told her as he moved over to look at the main screen. Picking up the microphone, he said, "This is Emmelor, all ships report to me as soon as you are able. Within minutes, all of his ships had reported damage, but nothing that couldn't be fixed.

A sound coming from the main speakers was filled with Milo's voice. "Sorry about that. I hope we're still all right."

Emmelor squeezed the button on the microphone and said, "A little bruised and a little worse for wear, but we're still able to go back into the fight."

In the distance, the fighting was still going on, with Emmelor's gunners, encouraged by Milo's hit, along with the small fighting craft, quickly destroyed the other enemy ships – and suddenly, the battle was over.

Down in his hiding place, Zicor had seen the explosions and expected to hear that his warriors had won the battle, but when nothing came, he tried to make contact with them, but got nothing but silence.

A feeling of dread enveloped him, knowing he had lost the war. What was he to do, now? He guessed he could attack them and take out as many as he could before he was blown out of the sky. The only problem with that was, he didn't want to die.

Maybe, if he was careful, he could destroy a few of their large cities. And while they were trying to repair the damage, he could sneak off and make it back to his planet where he would be safe. He hated running away, but what choice did he have? His only hope was to get a direct hit on Mister Biggers' ship before he left for home.

Fully cloaked, Zicor moved through the air at a snail's pace, hoping his movement would not be detected. His detectors were searching in all directions. He was keyed up and nervous. Should he continue to try and find Biggers' ship or just slip away and go home?

He knew in all reality, he should leave, but something inside him kept gnawing at him to find and destroy Biggers. It was called pride. He was not used to being in this position and it worried him like a dog chewing a bone. He knew Emmelor and his ships were still here, so there would be no chance for him to take over this planet, at least not at this time.

After several hours of searching and still not able to locate Biggers' ship, Zicor decided to do some more damage in the hopes it would attract Biggers.

Dropping down to just three thousand feet above the surface, he flew at a higher rate of speed, being careful not to find himself in the flight path of small engine airplanes.

Somewhere in the middle of this place called the United States, Zicor saw what he was looking for, a good size power plant, feeding a medium size city and a few surrounding towns.

Turning his ship to where he could point and fire his laser gun, Zicor got out of his pilot's seat and hurried over to the turret, sighted the laser gun on the target and squeezed the trigger.

The explosion was even greater than Zicor imagined and his ship was being tossed around by the time he got back in the pilot's seat and took control of his ship, speeding away to a safe distance.

Once he was safely away, he put his ship in the hover mode, cloaked it and waited.

A black cloud filled the sky and Wichita, Kansas and the towns surrounding it were without power, and would be for some time.

Liam's ship was also under its cloaking device and he saw in the far distance below him, the black smoke cloud rising into the sky, and a section of the country that was completely dark.

Sterling was sitting at the console of Liam's ship, talking to him about what to do next, when they saw the black cloud. "He's trying to draw you in close," Sterling said with a lot of conviction.

"I know," Liam said. "And I'm going to investigate – just not how he expects me to.

Sterling grinned. This was why Liam was his personal bodyguard. He was always one step ahead of his enemies. "So, what's the plan?" he asked.

Liam held up his hand and picked up the microphone and said, "Emmelor, I request a personal visit."

Chapter 41

SEARCHING FOR THE PRESIDENT

Every law enforcement in the country, including the FBI, the Secret Service, and every information seeking entity was searching for President Sterling Collier.

According to Archie Brooks, the President's chef, "The President came in as usual to eat his breakfast while he watched the news. He heard about the arrest of Thornton Howell and seemed pleased about it.

"When he finished eating, he thanked me, and left for the Oval Office. That's the last I saw of him." Archie said.

"You never saw or spoke to him again?" the television reporter asked.

"I have not seen nor spoke to him since he left my kitchen," Archie told the host of reporters standing next to their television cameras, sending his words out to the entire world.

"Do you know if his disappearance had anything to do with the explosions in the sky or the destruction of the powerplants around the world?" one of the reporters asked.

"If you're asking my opinion, I would say, no," Archie told him.

A female reporter made her way to the front of the crowded room and stuck a microphone in his direction. "Are you telling us, all this destruction has nothing to do with the President being in league with the aliens to destroy or take over this planet?"

Archie looked directly into the television camera pointed at her and said, "I have known the President for many years and you can take my word for it – President Collier is not now, nor has he ever been, in league with anyone, on this planet or off, to destroy or take over this planet. You can rest assured, wherever he is, he is doing his best to save this planet. And that's all I'm going to say about it. Now, please, leave. I have work to do. Go pester someone else."

And with that, he ushered them out of his kitchen.

When they finally retreated to wherever they go, Archie poured himself a cup of coffee and sat down at the kitchen table. He looked at the ceiling and said, "I did just as you told me to do, Mister President."

He lowered his head and stared at his coffee, wondering and hoping the President was all right. All the explosions in the sky had him worried too. There was a war going on up there and he had no idea about who was winning. The powerplants being destroyed was another concern. He looked at the ceiling again and said, "Be safe, my friend."

The world was baffled by the disappearance of the President of the United States, along with the bombing of the powerplants, which made him look all the more guilty. Thornton Howell was screaming his head off, saying, "I told you this would happen!"

Opinions were flying around like a flock of birds. Some said the President was doing just as he'd been accused of, while others were either denying his involvement, or straddling the fence.

The streets and highways were flooded with vehicles trying to leave the cities – searching for a safe place to be if the aliens attacked. Panic was spreading across the world like a tsunami tidal wave.

The entire world was out of control.

Chapter 42

THE CHASE

Emmelor appeared on the bridge of the ship Liam was commanding and asked, "Is this about the explosion down on your planet?"

"It is," Liam said. "He's expecting me to come for a look-see at the destruction he did, which would give him the opportunity to blow me out of the sky. I believe he is sitting not too far away, hidden by his cloaking device."

So, what do you plan to do?" Emmelor asked.

"What I want will involve your help," Liam told him.

-

Zicor was sitting, waiting for Liam to appear, but not patiently. "C'mon. C'mon, where are you?" he said to the empty screen.

Suddenly, Zicor began to see small dots appearing on his screen. He counted six of them and the hair on the back of his neck began to stand on end. Anger filled him and he said, "How could I be so stupid to believe the coward would come alone? Instead, he brought Emmelor's fleet with him to trap me."

Zicor began to move his ship down closer to the earth, then off to his left until he was out and away from Emmelor's ships. He watched his screen and saw they weren't moving. "The fools think they have me trapped," he said as he began to move his ship upward and farther away from his enemy.

When he thought he was far enough away he set his guidance control for home and hit the button, putting the ship in charge of his flight. He leaned back in his chair, laughing at how he had outsmarted them. He was about to stand up to go get something to eat and drink. It had been a good while since he'd had either. He was halfway out of his chair when a red light on his screen began to blink. He sat back down and enlarged the picture. There, blocking his path was Emmelor's ship.

Over his intercom, Emmelor's voice came at him, loud and clear. "Zicor, you are done for. Give up or be blown out of the sky."

Knowing his smaller ship could move in any direction faster than the larger ship, Zicor touched the button on his microphone and responded, saying, "All right. You have beaten me. What do you want me to do?"

As Emmelor's voice was coming to him with instructions, Zicor redirected his flight pattern and pushed the speed to full, and in the blink of an eye, he was gone from Emmelor's sight.

Zicor's plan was to circle behind Earth's moon, then speed off into space.

As he rounded behind the moon, he was laughing at how easily he'd outsmarted the famous ambassador, Emmelor.

Suddenly, another red light began blinking on his screen and he looked through his front window and saw Eem's ship hovering not far in front of him. "Biggers!" he shouted. There was no time for him to run to the turret and fire at the other ship, so he turned his ship toward outer space and pushed the control to hyperspace speed.

Liam watched as Zicor's ship disappeared. "Are you ready to see what is really out there?" he asked Sterling who was manning the small ship's laser gun.

"In for a penny, in for a pound," Sterling said, raising his thumb in the air.

"Then hang on!" Liam called out as he pushed his control lever to hyperspace speed.

In a short period of time, Liam saw Zicor's ship ahead of him. He couldn't actually see the ship. What he saw was the small blip on his screen.

Zicor zigged and zagged and made every evasive maneuver he'd learned to try and get away from Liam's ship, but the man followed him relentlessly, firing shots at him. He turned his ship again and headed toward the planet called Mars.

As Liam sped after Zicor, Sterling came up and sat next to Liam and stared through the large front window, marveling at the speed they were traveling. "Where do you think he's headed?" Sterling asked.

"Eventually, he hopes to get back to his own planet which is several trillion or so miles away but first, he has to get rid of us. And,, I'm sure blasting us out of the sky is his number one priority," Liam said, staring out through the same window. "But right now, it looks like he's headed for Mars."

"Several trillion miles, you say?" Sterling asked, shaking his head. "And this ship carries enough fuel to travel that far?"

Liam smiled. The ship doesn't carry fuel, per-se. It makes its own fuel as it needs it. Some invention they made on Emmelor's planet so they could travel the universes without fear of running out or getting stranded somewhere."

"And we're headed for Mars?" Sterling asked, still bewildered by it all.

"Looks like it," Liam told him.

On Mars, Zicor landed and tried to hide, but Liam located him and Zicor lifted back into the air and the chase was on again.

They dodged and shot at each other, leaving scars on the hulls of each ship – small wounds that each could repair and continue to fight. They fought around the planets of Jupiter, Saturn, Uranus, and Neptune, but it wasn't until they reached the small hunk of rock they called, Pluto, that Liam was able to catch up with Zicor.

Zicor knew he couldn't go any farther without possibly being blown up by Biggers, because by now he realized Biggers had someone aboard the ship who was manning the ship's weapon.

He came to a stop, turned his ship around and hovered there in space – sending out a message to the other ship. "Biggers! Just you and me, here – man to man in the space between our two ships."

"What's he talking about?" Sterling asked, not liking the pictures in his head.

Liam looked out through the large window and saw Zicor's ship, not more than two hundred feet away. "He wants us to don spacesuits and meet out there between our two ships and fight it out."

"Surely, you're not going out there?" Sterling asked.

"Well, I could swing the ship around so you could take a shot at him and hopefully destroy his ship. But from the look of his position, I'd say he's already sitting with his finger on the trigger, waiting for my answer. If I try to move my ship around, he'll know what I'm planning to do and fire on us before I could get you into position, which would more than likely be the end of us. No, I need to go out there and end this once and for all."

"Wait a minute!" Sterling yelled, his voice almost in a panic. "What happens if you go out there and God forbid, you lose the fight. How am I going to get back? I don't know how to fly this thing!"

"First," Liam said, "I don't plan on losing, but you're right, something could go wrong and if it did, I'm sure Zicor will have no qualms about blowing up this ship before he leaves."

Liam walked over to the control center and set the controls to return to Earth, at high speed, then stood up and pointed. "If I should happen to lose the fight out there then, before he can get back to his ship, I want you to press this button. This button will swing this ship around into firing position. I want you to destroy his ship, then sit down in this chair and press the green button and hang on. The ship is programmed to return to Earth at a high speed. When you get close enough, touch this yellow button and the ship will slow down. You should be able to see Emmelor's spaceships, and when you are close, touch the bronze button and you will stop. Then pick up the microphone and hail Emmelor. He'll do the rest."

Sterling was running the procedure through his mind over and over so he wouldn't forget. When he saw Liam dressed in his spacesuit and putting on the jet pack, he rushed over to him and said, "Forget everything I said about losing. You kill him and get back here, you hear?"

Liam put a gloved hand on his friend's shoulder and nodded his head, then stepped into the chamber leading to the outside door and closed the chamber door behind him.

When the outer door opened, Liam stood there, waiting to see Zicor leave his ship before he ventured out. Zicor was not someone you could trust.

He didn't have to wait long before he saw Zicor leave his ship. He squeezed the trigger on his jet pack and flew out to meet his enemy.

They were no more than twenty feet apart when Liam heard Zicor's voice in his helmet.

"Thank you for making it easy for me to kill you, but first, I have to know, who is manning the laser gun on your ship?" Zicor asked.

Liam wasn't about to tell him it was the President of the United States. Zicor would definitely want to see him dead, too. "It's one of the gunners from Emmelor's ship. Why do you ask?"

Zicor hovered there in space, looking at Liam. "Because I am not foolish, like you may think. I'm sure you left instructions for him to kill me after I kill you. So, I will need a little insurance to allow me to get far away before I destroy you."

Zicor's meaning came to Liam and he said, "So, your plan is to wound me and take me back to your ship as a hostage, and leave without being shot at. Then, somewhere between here and your planet, you dump me out into space where I will float around, forever. That that about the size of it?"

"You are a smart one," Zicor said as he raised his laser gun and took a shot at Liam, who squeezed his jet thruster and moved to the side just as the beam rushed past him.

Not to be denied his kill, Zicor swung his gun and sent another laser beam in Liam's direction, which also missed.

"Shoot back!" Sterling was screaming as he watched through the front window of the ship

Liam was moving in a zig-zag pattern, waiting his chance and after dodging the third beam shot at him, he got his chance. He raised his laser gun and fired.

Liam watched as the beam struck Zicor in the helmet as he tried to move away.

And just that quick, it was over. Zicor was dead. The war was over and there could be peace on both Earth and planet X-162.

When Liam told Sterling he would be flying Zicor's ship back to Earth, Sterling wasn't all that pleased about it.

"You'll be fine. We'll stay in contact the entire way," Liam said with a grin. "Besides, it will give you time to think about the story you'll have to tell."

Sterling nodded his head. He would have a story to tell, not only to the entire population of Earth, but his kids and grandkids if he ever had any.

Chapter 43

THE HOMECOMING

When Emmelor and Lucita heard Liam's voice hailing them, they jumped up and down, holding each other's arms – smiles spread across their faces.

They were in the dining room at the time and ran to the bridge and watched as two small orbs came to rest, hovering just beyond Emmelor's ship.

In short order, Liam and Sterling were teleported onto Emmelor's ship where he and Lucita were waiting.

Lucita's joy at seeing Liam couldn't be contained and she ran over to him and hugged him tightly, then to Liam's surprise, she kissed him on the mouth.

"I was so worried about you," she said, standing back and looking him over to make sure he wasn't hurt.

While Liam was being greeted back by Lucita, Emmelor shook Sterling's hand and asked, "I'm guessing you were successful?"

Sterling stood there, remembering the entire experience, then finally said, "Emmelor, as a man who has never traveled into space, it was an experience like none I've ever had. As far as Zicor goes, yes, he is no longer a threat. We brought his ship back."

Sterling went on to describe the chase around the planets, and finally the fight between Zicor and Liam. "It was like nothing I've ever seen except in science fiction movies, but this time it was for real."

Emmelor laid his hand on Sterling's shoulder and said, "I understand more than you realize, my friend," remembering his first time in space, all those many years ago.

In a room filled with computers, giant screens and technicians at each station, the vice President and an Airforce general stood, looking through the window at the sky above. Six giant orbs hovered just above Washington DC.

"What do you make of that?" the vice President asked.

General Grant Harden stared out of the window and said, "To be honest, I'm not sure, Mister Vice President. So far, they've just been sitting there. So, until they contact us or do something, all we can do is, wait."

"Do you think the President is in cahoots with them like Thornton Howell and the news people say? Do you think he up there with them, right now?"

General Harden had been a long-time fan of the President and it was hard for him to believe he would turn against his own people, but with everything that had happened, his belief in the President was beginning to wane. He took a deep breath and said, "If he is up there with them, I honestly believe it is not of his choosing. I believe he was taken against his will."

The vice President was about to say something when one of the technicians, a sergeant, said, "I think you need to see this, General."

General Harden and the vice President ran over to the sergeant's station and looked at the screen. A smaller orb was descending – coming straight for the tarmac outside their building.

By now everyone in the room was watching the screen and saw at least fifty armed military personnel run out onto the tarmac with their weapons pointed at the small orb as it settled down on the ground.

When the panel slid back, President Sterling Collier was the first to walk down the ramp, with his hands held out in front of him – palms forward. "Lower your weapons. There is no need for them. These people are not our enemy."

The men continued to point their weapons at Sterling, unsure whose side he was on. General Harden and the vice President came running onto the tarmac and came to a stop directly in front of Sterling.

The general looked into Sterling's eyes and asked, "Are you alright, Mister President?

He then looked over Sterling's shoulder and saw Liam and a man and a woman standing in the portal. Liam was smiling and had his arm around the woman's shoulders.

Sterling lowered his hands and said, "General, if you'll listen for a moment, I can explain."

The vice President said, "Don't listen to him, General. They have him under some kind of a spell!"

Secretly, the vice President didn't want Sterling to return. It would mean he wouldn't become President, and he desperately wanted to become President.

Liam could see what was happening and walked down the ramp, stopping next to Sterling. "General, you know me. I served under your command six years ago. And you know I do not lie. I'm telling you, these people are friendly. They could have attacked us on several occasions, but they did not. They even helped us destroy the one who was trying to take over this planet."

Liam looked at the vice President and said, "And you, little man, are not worthy to walk in Sterling's footprints. You just want him arrested so you can take his place."

"You... you... you're nothing but a warmonger," the vice President whimpered, knowing Liam was right.

Liam turned back to the general and said, "If you believe this man," pointing to the vice President, and Thornton Howell, who also wants the presidency, then you're not the man I've always believed you are."

Just then, Emmelor walked down the ramp and up to the general, then stuck out his hand and said, "My name is Emmelor. I am from the planet, X-162, several trillion miles from here. I come in peace. I believe we are enough alike that we can become sister planets someday, and we can share our technology with you."

General Harden looked into the eyes of the alien and saw truth in them. He then turned his head and looked at his President, who nodded his head in agreement.

Making his decision, General Harden reached out and shook the alien's hand, saying, "I am General Harden, United States Air Force. Welcome to Earth."

They were taken to the White House and as they stepped out of the limousine, they saw a man rush from the bushes, brandishing a pistol, and pointing it at Sterling.

Thornton Howell had lost all reasoning and knew the only way to get rid of Sterling was to shoot him himself. He raised the pistol and fired at the same time the secret service men pumped bullets into him.

Liam saw what was happening and was reacting, but an instant too late. Emmelor had already leaped in front of Sterling and took the bullet in his shoulder.

With his dying breath, Thornton Howell looked at Emmelor and asked, "Who are you people?"

The impact of the bullet knocked Emmelor to the ground and Sterling dropped down on one knee and took his friend in his arms.

"Hang in there, medical help is on the way," Sterling said, hoping they would not be too long.

"No need," Emmelor said. "Lucita is here."

Lucita bent down to Emmelor, took a small vial from the bag attached to her belt and put it under Emmelor's nose. He took a whiff and smiled, nodding his head. From the bag, she took a pair of tweezers and removed the bullet, as Emmelor watched, feeling no pain.

Next, she filled the hole with some salve and Sterling, the general, Liam and the secret service men watched as the hole closed over, leaving no scar. It was as if he'd never been shot.

Lucita put another vial up to Emmelor's nose and again, he took a sniff – and in less than a moment, he stood up, saying, "I'm fine now," then turned to the President and asked, "Sterling, were you hit?"

Sterling smiled and said, "No. Thanks to you. You saved my life."

What none of them realized, was, when they arrived, there were at least a dozen television trucks sitting there, awaiting their arrival and had televised the whole thing. Emmelor saving President Sterling's life was seen throughout the entire world.

Sterling wasted no time calling a meeting of the United Nations, for the following morning.

The room was packed to capacity, including news people, with still cameras and television cameras. There were even radio reporters, broadcasting live.

President Sterling Collier, stood at the podium and explained everything that had happened, then introduced Emmelor.

After thanking Sterling, he looked out across the room and spoke into the microphone. "We of planet X-162 are thrilled to know we have a sister planet and I can assure you, we come in peace, and will do all in our power to help you improve your way of life. I would also, like to extend my hope that one day in the near future, we can bring some of you to our planet for a visit, as well as bringing some of our people here, to visit you. I feel sure there are many things we can share with each other."

He raised his palms forward and said, "Let there be peace between your planet and mine."

Afterward Emmelor spent two hours shaking hands and talking with the various representatives in each one's language.

Sterling Collier's ratings went through the roof and congress passed a new law, allowing Sterling to run for a third term in office.

At a press conference, with Maggie standing next to him, Sterling announced he would be seeking a third term, but this time, not as a bachelor. He and Maggie Smythe were engaged and would be married in the spring.

The press ate it up as the news traveled around the world.

When Emmelor was ready to depart, the surrounding area was filled with thousands of well-wishers, all cheering and asking him to come back soon.

Sterling, Maggie, Liam and Archie stood next to the small orb, shaking hands and promising good things for the future.

Lucita looked at Liam and said, "Well?"

Liam looked at her and said, "Well, what?"

She put her arms around Liam's neck and said, "Are you coming with me, or am I staying here with you?"

THE END

ALSO BY JARED McVAY

Other works by Jared McVay

Jared McVay is an award-winning author who writes, Westerns: A western series: Historical Fiction: Action/Adventure: YA: Children's books: screenplays: teleplays: Short stories, and also does storytelling.

NOVELS:

Western: Clay Brentwood Series- 10 Books:

Historical Fiction: The Legend of Joe, Willy & Red – award winner

Historical Fiction: Silent Runner, Guardian Warrior

Western: Hacker's Raid – award winner

Historical Fiction: Legend of Jubal Courtney

Action/Contemporary - Not on My Mountain – double award winner

JUVENILE FICTION

Brody O'Shea – 3 Books

SCREENPLAYS

The Hobos

Jared & the Warden

Talltree

TELEVISION PILOT SCRIPTS

McClusky [6 episodes] - Drama/Comedy

ACT Acute Care Transport - Drama/Comedy

Melinda: Award winning short story

MEET THE AUTHOR

Jared McVay lives in Oregon where he writes his books, does storytelling, book signings, speaking engagements, and gets in a little fishing from time to time. Before becoming a novelist, Jared was a professional actor – stage, film and television, and a ghostwriter for screenplays.

As a young man he worked as a cowboy, a rodeo clown, a lumberjack, barker for a carnival and a truck driver. During the 1950's he rode the rails as a hobo and during the 80's, a blue water sailor. He spent his military time in the US Navy Sea Bees, where he learned his electrical trade as a power lineman, then spent ten years as a lineman for Kansas Gas & Electric. But it was his love of entertaining people that led him into acting and writing.

Jared has five children, eleven grandchildren, fifteen great grandchildren and four great, great grandchildren.

THANK YOU
FOR READING!

If you enjoyed this book, we would appreciate your customer review on your book seller's website or on Goodreads.

Also, we would like for you to know that you can find more great books like this one at
www.CreativeTexts.com